Coleen Moore-Hayes is a recently retired university professor who lives with her husband Allen on Cape Breton Island, Nova Scotia. After decades of writing for academic publications and technical journals, *A Picture Puzzle* is her inaugural foyer into fiction.

Coleen says that what started out as a retirement project has become an absolute passion, with characters who now feel more like family and friends.

An avid golfer who spends winters in Florida, Coleen hopes that you will enjoy traveling with her through *A Picture Puzzle*.

A PICTURE PUZZLE

Coleen Moore-Hayes

A PICTURE PUZZLE

Vanguard Press

A CIP catalogue record for this title is available from the British Library.

ISBN 978 1 784655 92 1

Vanguard Press is an imprint of
Pegasus Elliot MacKenzie Publishers Ltd.
www.pegasuspublishers.com

First Published in 2019

Vanguard Press
Sheraton House Castle Park
Cambridge England

Printed & Bound in Great Britain

Dedication

My first novel is for the boys: with love to Ken, Allen, Barry, Paul
and in Memory of Wayne.

"I have seen the Canadian and the American Rockies, the Andes, the Alps and the Highlands of Scotland, but for simple beauty, Cape Breton outrivals them all." - Alexander Graham Bell

Chapter 1

January is a cold month on Cape Breton Island. Of course, the old folks and lifelong residents would argue that spring can also take its bloody good time shaking off the remnants of winter—but at least by the time April comes, you know for certain that good weather is just around the corner. With each passing day after New Year, Molly O'Neil swore that she could feel and even smell the change in the air. And even though those glorious days sometimes took a little longer coming than she would like, as far as she was concerned, it is well worth the wait.

Now fortunately, most Cape Bretoners are born with a short and most forgiving memory as it relates to their weather. So, when daylight hours begin to diminish, and temperatures drop, the hardy islanders simply bask in fond, warm memories of having spent another magnificent summer on one of the world's most beautiful islands. Yep, according to *Travel and Tourism* magazine, Cape Breton ranks a mere fraction of a point behind the Greek island of Santorini, and Bali, as the best island destination in the world... not bad for a diminutive atoll perched on the edge of a continent. But even such a prestigious designation, along with its natural beauty, majestic coastline and pristine waters, cannot erase the reality that January is one damned cold month.

And so, it was on the frosty Feast of the Epiphany, while storing away or disposing of the trappings and memories of Christmas 2014, that Molly came upon the first picture. Molly always felt that the Feast of the Epiphany, also known as Old Christmas, was the best day to take down holiday decorations. Her rationale being that no one was really sure of the actual date upon which the feast fell. Apparently, the confusion dates to the 1700s with the switch from the Julian to the Gregorian calendar. Whereas most countries continue to recognise January 6th as the end of the Christmas season, Russians and Ukrainians elect to observe Old Christmas on January 7th. And as if that wasn't perplexing enough, for Austria, Columbia and Poland, the Feast of the Epiphany can be celebrated anywhere between the 2nd and the 8th of January.

As a consummate procrastinator, Molly was only too happy to have a full seven-day window from which to pick before tackling the arduous task of holiday un-decorating. One last check of her calendar confirmed that the date was indeed January 8th, leaving her officially out of options. With a sigh of resignation, Molly descended the stairs to the lower reaches of her home.

The spot in the O'Neil's' basement allocated for storage might best be compared to the kitchen junk drawer. Just when you thought you couldn't squeeze in one more useless cooking doodad; a broken potato masher, an impressive tangle of used twist ties and a dozen less-than-hygienic drinking straws would make the trip from the drawer to the garbage can, thus leaving room for more jumble. Today, however, as Molly stood knee deep in boxes while gazing at the chaos spread in front of her, she begrudgingly realised that the gig was up. Regardless of where she looked, it was crystal clear that every square inch of storage space was finally and fully utilised.

"Well, I guess it had to happen sooner or later," Molly said out loud. Her husband, Patrick, had warned her this day was coming. He often suggested that the basement in their home was possessed by some sort of evil force. His theory being grounded in experience from the countless times he himself had tried to find anything in that pitifully cramped little room. According to Patrick, no matter how many times they culled through the pile of boxes, rather than creating more room, the space somehow managed to decrease.

Stepping back to reassess the situation, Molly knew it was time to move on to Plan B. The only hope was a radical restructuring of the entire space. Fixing a look of determination on her face and tucking a stepladder under her arm, Molly gritted her teeth and marched bravely into the abyss that was her storage room.

Chapter 2

Molly Halloran-Connor became Molly O'Neil when she married the love of her life, Patrick O'Neil, in the spring of 1993. Born Molly Halloran, she was a descendant of her proud Irish grandfather and her fanatically Irish father, both of whom she loved dearly. The Connor surname was the result of a brief, tumultuous first marriage to Dr. Mark Connor, which had ended in tragedy nearly twenty-five years ago.

At twenty-four widowed, pregnant and jaded with the notion of ever marrying again, Molly had pledged she would remain single for the rest of her days… and for the first few years after Mark's death, she held to that plan. But like many of her expectations, the not getting married thing, along with everything else in her life, changed the moment when she met Patrick O'Neil.

For more than two decades now, she'd been proud to call Pat her husband, partner, lover, best friend and for the purpose of this discussion, Jack of all trades. And while she believed with the certainty of a woman in love that this wonderful man was hers and hers alone, Molly knew she would be deluding herself to even pretend she didn't share 'Patrick the handyman' with anyone in the community who owned a telephone to call him or a set of knuckles to knock on their door.

If lawn movers, snow blowers, appliances or home furnishings needed fixing, Patrick got the call. Even those neighbours who were quite handy themselves were quick to call her husband if they were missing a tool to complete a particular job. It also became clear that his reputation and prowess as the fixer of all things was passed along through the generations. For whenever a sad little face was pressed up against the patio door, you could be pretty sure that a broken bicycle or doll carriage was not far away. And but for the occasional jar of jam, bottle of homemade pickles or a freshly baked apple pie, Patrick received and expected no other remuneration for his assistance. Although he did joke from time to time that if he could ever find a bank that would exchange 'thank-yous' for hard cash, he would be a wealthy man.

Molly enjoyed thinking about her life with Patrick. It certainly helped pass the time today as she worked diligently, attempting to cram twenty boxes filled to the brim with memories of Christmases past into a space that on a good day might accommodate a dozen. First, she tried combining the contents of two boxes into one, but that proved futile, given that every carton was already stuffed to the gunnels. She even resorted to bracing her feet against the wall and pushing the boxes with her backside, hoping to gain another few inches of space. But all that got her was a sore butt and dirty pants. Having approached the task from every imaginable angle, without success, she knew it was time to ditch the current plan and move on to a new one

Imprisoned by the boxes that surrounded her, she called out to the man upstairs. "Pat!" she yelled. "Can you help me?"

"Sure," her husband answered. "I'll be right there." Translation: *I'll be there just as soon as I finish reading the paper or watching this story on the news or talking to one of or our children on the phone*. Yes, another bond that tied the couple together was their shared reluctance to get dragged into each other's projects. Not that Patrick would ever see this as a character flaw. A high school physical education teacher until his retirement, he saw himself as more of perfectionist, insisting he preferred to complete one job fully before beginning the next.

Molly learned early on that in times like these, patience was definitely a virtue. She knew Patrick would eventually come to her rescue and anyway, she was happy to embrace the opportunity to enjoy a little rest. As she sat among the maze of boxes, Molly let her mind wander to much more pleasant thoughts.

This coming May, Patrick and Molly would be married for twenty-two years. For their anniversary, the couple was going back to Hawaii where they spent their honeymoon and had made plans for their new life on the magnificent beaches of Kaua'i. Having successfully survived two decades (plus two years) of marriage, two kids and now retirement, they felt as though they had earned a special vacation. Both agreed that there was no better place on earth for them to reconnect and plan for their next exciting chapter than the spectacular jungle paradise of Kaua'i.

The Hawaii trip had been planned for the O'Neil's' twentieth anniversary and then again for their twenty-first but, as so often happens, life got in the way and both trips were postponed.

The first delay was for their son's wedding, two years ago. Cole was Patrick's son from a previous marriage, however, Molly was the only mother he'd ever known and nothing, not even blood, could not have made them closer. The following year, Cole and his wife Laurie blessed Patrick and Molly with their first grandchild; a beautiful baby girl. Patrick was willing to delay the trip until Miss Kelly Ann O'Neil made her safe arrival, but Molly had a different plan. "There isn't a chance in hell that I will be leaving town until I'm sure Laurie and Cole are ready to fly solo with the parenting of my precious grandchild," she proclaimed. And so, the date for their trip was changed again.

But once the baby was safely past her first birthday, Molly reluctantly admitted that Kelly Ann's health and wellbeing were clearly not in peril. Cole and Laurie were competent and loving parents. In fact, Laurie, who worked as a paralegal in Cole's office, decided that she would not be returning to work until the baby was at least two years old. Oh sure, they still asked for Nana's advice from time to time but Molly had the distinct feeling that they were doing so as a kindness to her rather than out of any real need. "OK, you win," Molly had told Patrick as they kissed their granddaughter goodnight after one of their frequent visits. "Happy very belated twentieth anniversary honey, I'm ready to go to Hawaii."

Thinking about her family always made her feel happy. With a contented sigh, Molly beamed back to reality and returned her attention to the task at hand. She was thankful for her children, her granddaughter and the life she and Patrick had made for themselves and she looked forward to the future. Except that right now, Molly's future looked very much like an undersized warehouse at the North Pole.

As luck would have it, that same cramped space that housed the holiday paraphernalia was also home for many long-forgotten photo albums, journals and all manner of memorabilia from the Patrick and Molly's life before and after they were married. With a happy heart and renewed vigour, Molly shifted her attention from Christmas storage to the upcoming anniversary vacation. "Hmm," she mused as she climbed out of her nest of boxes. "If only I could remember where the heck we put the travel information."

You would think that with limited storage space, there would not be too many places where one could have stowed away such treasures… well, you would have been wrong.

Undaunted, Molly once again pulled out the stepladder and began searching. With her iPad tuned to one of the many wonderful free music stations where you could still listen to the best of the 60s music, she tied back her hair into a ponytail and began to tackle a new load of boxes, storage bins, suitcases and duffel bags, which were precariously perched on both sides of the Christmas storage space.

As the first hour passed, the mission was going well, that is to say that lots of boxes were being moved from one location to another. Then, just when she was getting a good momentum going, the inevitable occurred. With so many containers and so little room in which to manoeuvre, Molly was making the final stretch to reach a carton that looked like it might be the one she was searching for, when she lost her footing.

In the blink of an eye, Molly found herself hurtling unceremoniously toward the floor, bringing with her three suitcases, two bent tent poles and a somewhat mouldy sleeping bag. In fact, the only object that didn't dislodge in the ensuing calamity was the damn carton she had been trying to reach. Now, the upside of this unfortunate event was that the resulting commotion brought Pat scrambling down the basement steps. "Molly Kathleen Sapphira Halloran-O'Neil!" he admonished. "Are you OK? Have you hurt yourself?"

Hearing "no" as her response, his diatribe continued. "What in the name of God were you doing? Where did all this crap come from? You've hardly been down here fifteen minutes and I can't even see the floor, much less the Christmas boxes. What grand idea popped into that head of yours and distracted you from your job this time? Honestly Mol, I never met a person who could make such a big mess in so short a time."

When it sounded like the barrage of questions and accusations was coming to an end, Molly jumped at the opportunity to get a word in. "Well, for starters, I have been down here for well over an hour. As for what I was doing, I was actually killing time until you got around to gracing me with your presence. And the *crap* you so elegantly refer to, is a montage of three lives well lived, yours, mine and ours. And finally, the idea that popped into my head, which by the way was a grand one, was to get started on the planning of our anniversary trip".

"Ah, Mol," Pat said, his demeanour instantly changing from annoyed and concerned, to contrite and loving. "That's a wonderful idea. I can't believe that we have been together for twenty-two years. We're done a lot of living in two decades, baby, and I know those early days were anything but easy. Yet looking at you sitting here among all this rubble with your ponytail askew and a smudge of dirt down your cheek, you look no different to me than you did the day we met."

Patrick loved Molly's rich auburn hair. He always said her hair was the exact colour of an evening sunset. "Here, let me help you up and we'll tackle the rest of this job together." With nothing but her pride hurt, Molly took Pat's extended hand, tucked a few rogue strands of hair behind her ear, wiped some of the dirt from her face and happily accepted the kiss her infuriatingly wonderful, sexy husband planted on her.

She did, however, make a mental note to remind him that it was not necessary to call her by every name she had ever been given just because he was angry or otherwise upset with her. First, it was way too dramatic and secondly, she spent most of her life trying to forget that her parents had chosen Sapphira as her baptismal name. Apparently, it was the religious name of some ancient relative of her father, who was a nun. But for now, with Patrick's kiss still lingering on her lips, Molly decided that the lecture could wait for another day. Instead, she cranked up the volume on her iPad a few more notches as they joined forces to liberate the stubborn box.

At six-foot two, Patrick was not so vertically challenged as Molly, and he was easily able to reach and dislodge the container in question. Once extracted, he carried it carefully to the only clear spot on the basement floor where he proceeded to open it. To the couple's surprise and delight, instead of the anticipated trip-planning information, they found themselves staring into the faces of two much loved but long forgotten teddy bears, namely Hector and Fonda. Accompanying the teddies was a picture of their children, each holding one of the stuffed toys.

Given that the bears had been sitting side by side—well actually, butt to face, for more than fifteen years, Molly and Patrick agreed that they had fared pretty well. Apart from one missing eye, three slightly tattered ears and an odour that could only be described as *eau de box-in-the-basement,* the beloved toys looked as though they were surviving their retirement and confinement quite well. And if ever two teddy bears deserved a peaceful retreat, these guys had certainly earned that privilege. So, with Hector in Molly's arms, Fonda sitting on Patrick's lap and the Beach Boys' *God Only Knows What I'd Be Without You* playing in the background, the storing of Christmas decorations quickly became a distant memory. Eventually they decided to finish storing Christmas decorations later... well, certainly before Valentine's Day.

Chapter 3

Second marriages, regardless of their origin or back-story, are often fraught with baggage that could only be attributed to, well... second marriages. And theirs was no different. At the ages of six and two respectively, Cole Patrick O'Neil and Ava Marie Halloran became stepbrother and sister as a result of Molly's marriage to Pat. By some miracle, within a year, the children had forged a bond so strong and so true that it was hard to imagine them as anything but loving big brother and adoring little sister.

That is not to say that their early months as a family was easy. For as long as they could remember, each child was used to having their one remaining parent all to themselves. Then, in what must have felt like the blink of an eye, both kids found themselves not only sharing their parent but also adjusting to a new one.

Enter the teddy bears. Hector was exactly two years younger than Cole. He arrived on Cole's second birthday along with a glut of other gifts from friends and relatives. Hector came from Aunt Michelle, his mother's younger sister.

Michelle was the spitting image of Pat's first wife, Pamela. And although Cole hardly remembered his mother, he always had a special affection for Michelle. Not surprisingly, on his second birthday when he opened Michelle's gift, he immediately forgot about all the other presents he had received. He even lost interest in opening the remaining gaily-decorated parcels. Two chubby hands reached into the box and lifted Hector the bear from his plastic and twist tie restraints. With a big kiss and a thank you to aunt "Achell", he toddled off to his room to begin a friendship that would last for six more years.

It immediately became clear to all who knew the family that Hector came into Cole's life at a very important time. In short order, Hector took on the role of nightmare chaser, thunder and lightning protector, monster buster and trusted confidante.

Over drinks one evening, Sam explained to Molly that in the early days after Pam left, he would stand outside of Cole's bedroom and listen to the conversations that leaked from under his door. Sometimes, Cole would talk to Hector about what Santa might bring him for Christmas. Other times, they discussed and even argued about the best climbing trees in the neighbourhood. But the most heart-wrenching conversation Patrick recalled was when he heard Cole ask Hector if he ever thought about what it would be like to have a mommy who lived in the same house as them.

To their great joy, only a few months after merging their respective families, Pat and Molly stood together outside of Cole's door after tucking him in for the night. This time, they heard Cole's sweet voice telling Hector he was pretty sure there wouldn't be as many monsters in his new house. He also informed the understanding teddy bear that for Christmas this year, instead of asking for toys, he was going to ask Santa if he could keep Molly as his forever mommy. Pat held Molly's hand as they walked silently away from their son's bedroom. No words were needed to describe what they were feeling, which worked out well because neither could speak for the lump in their throat.

Now, Fonda bear came into the O'Neil household under very different circumstances. Fonda was actually a gift from Hector.

For as much as Cole flourished and thrived in his new family, Ava did her level best to disrupt any semblance of harmony that dared to surface. She was openly hostile toward Patrick, especially when he displayed affection to Molly. Further, she would yell in her two-year-old shriek whenever Cole was within her sights. Meals became a scene from *The Exorcist* with Pat and Cole ducking and running for cover while Ava flung fistfuls of food with the precision of a trained sniper from her command centre, which doubled as her high chair.

Patrick and Molly tried separately and together to comfort and appease the unhappy Ava, certain that her behaviour would improve as soon as she settled into her new surroundings. But progress seemed painfully slow.

Even though their patience was sorely tried by Ava's antics, Patrick and Molly always showered her with love and affection. They set aside time for her and they reminded her daily that she was their special girl. They even tried ignoring her more extreme behaviour, hoping for some kind of reaction, but it was all to no avail. It appeared as if this sweet, golden-haired toddler had made it her life's work to disrupt any hope for peace and harmony in her new family... and she was hell-bent on fulfilling her mission. When the struggling parents were down to their last tactics and their last nerve, salvation arrived. It came in the form of a six-and-a-half-year-old big brother.

While Patrick, Molly and Cole were trying, unsuccessfully, to engage Ava in a rousing game of who has the button, Cole quietly left the kitchen. He ran upstairs to his room and returned with a stuffed toy, a small teddy bear that had been long since banished to the bottom of his toy chest. Cole had tied coloured ribbons around the bear's neck, arms, legs and ears. After stuffing the bedecked teddy, along with Hector, into a clear garbage bag, he marched out to the kitchen where Ava was sitting on the floor, giving Patrick yet another stink-eye. In an unprecedented move, Cole hurled the parcel at Ava, toppling her over where she sat. Perched in front of her with hands firmly planted on his hips, Cole proclaimed, "Ava, the ribbon bear is Hector's sister, he is giving her to you... and by the way, her name is Fonda".

Whether it was the shock of getting bowled over by a bag full of bears, or maybe it was the attraction of the rainbow of ribbons, Ava rolled herself back to an upright position, reached into the bag and pulled Fonda out by her pink-ribboned ear. After conducting a thorough examination of her unexpected gift, she tucked Fonda under her arm and proceeded to make the rounds of the kitchen, insisting that all those present acknowledge and welcome the newest addition to the clan.

Once the ceremony was complete, Ava returned Hector to Cole, rewarding him with a sloppy wet kiss. And with that simple, beautiful gesture, the O'Neil family's life, as one mother, one father, a sister and brother and two teddy bears were off to the races.

Still touched by the memory, Molly rhetorically asked Patrick, "Wow, where did the time go?" Thinking back to those early days, it was hard to imagine that their spirited little girl had already completed one degree and would soon be graduating as a Nurse Practitioner.

"No more stinky box for you two," said Pat as he carried the toys upstairs to a spare bedroom. In recognition of their homecoming, Molly planned to ship them off to the local Toy Hospital where Hector and Fonda would be professionally cleaned, repaired and preserved, with the intention of handing them over to little Kelly Ann and hopefully another a grandchild or two in the future.

With the teddy bear's future settled, Molly moved on to the second item they found in the box, the picture of Cole and Ava with their teddy bears. Upon closer examination, Molly was thrilled to see how well preserved the photograph was, given the time it had spent in a cardboard box in their crowded basement.

Although she didn't share her older sister June's talent for photography, Molly remembered the many lectures she received from June when she would catch Molly throwing a picture in a drawer, vowing to "one day" put it in an album. As a result of June's tutelage, Molly knew exactly what to do to preserve the print and protect it from further damage. Holding it up for Patrick to see, Molly promised, "There'll be no procrastinating on this job. I have everything I need to protect this memory."

Happy to have found the picture of Ava and Cole with their teddy bears and buoyed by the memories of their early days together, Patrick and Molly returned to the basement where they once again searched for the box of travel information. While Molly continued to look in the room where she found the teddy bears,

Patrick moved on to check the rafters in the furnace room. "I hit pay dirt, Mol," yelled Patrick. Hearing his excitement, she climbed carefully over the chaos on the floor and joined him in the furnace room.

"Well, where was it hiding?" Molly asked without admitting she had already thoroughly combed through that room without success. Patrick pointed to a section of the open ceiling, partially hidden behind the water softener.

"Up and to your far left," he said. "Smack in the middle of all that sports equipment that we were going to dispose of the last time we attempted to clean down here".

Sure enough, high up in the rafters, lodged between what appeared to be a badminton racket and a black wooden block, sat a box that they both recognised at once. But like all things that had been put away for safe keeping, the box in question was being held captive and needed help escaping, before the sought-after prize could be claimed.

With Pat perched precariously, one foot on a stool and the other on the side of the oil tank while Molly held his foot to stop it from slipping off the tank, he was able to dislodge the storage box and its captors without incident. As it turned out, the first barricade was indeed a badminton racket. It had no strings, the rubber handle was mostly rotted off and neither Pat, Molly, nor their children, had ever played the sport...so it was a mystery as to how it had landed up there. The square black object, which blocked the other side, was a wooden picture cube.

Whereas the origin of the badminton racket remained a mystery, Molly absolutely knew the source of the picture cube. Her eyes misted when she rubbed a smudge of dust off one glass frame and looked into the smiling eyes of her beautiful sister, June.

As Molly lovingly cradled the picture cube, Patrick suggested they call it a day. Pausing only to wash the surface grime from their hands and put on a pot of tea, they placed the cube on the kitchen table where they could have a better look at another lost treasure.

Chapter 4

Bridget June Halloran was four days shy of her thirty-sixth birthday when the world lost one of its most beautiful souls. On that day, Molly lost her best friend and only sibling. Eleven years her senior, June lived larger in those thirty-six years than most people would if they lived to be a hundred. Those who know her best said that even if June had lived that long, she still would have left the earth without seeing or doing half of what she had planned.

The things about which June was passionate were infinite. She was dedicated to her family. She believed herself to be truly blessed, having been born in Cape Breton. She loved photography, music, and painting. But above all else, her greatest passion was travel.

As a very young child, June read atlases and maps the way other children read nursery rhymes and picture books. She never grew bored with hearing stories about faraway places and she never stopped asking questions about what the people who lived in these places were like. Did they speak the same language as her? Was the weather warmer, colder or the same as it was in Cape Breton? And every piece of information she received made her all the more interested in learning even more.

Molly's mom loved to tell the story about when the pre-school-aged June learned there were towns and villages in Cape Breton Island that had the same name as places in Ireland and Scotland. Whenever it was June's turn to choose where the family should go for their Sunday afternoon drive, she insisted they visit one of the shared-named towns. Young June believed that the very act of going to Iona, Loch Lomond, Inverness, Barrahead or Dundee would surely help her to better imagine what it would be like to live in one of those wonderful countries across the ocean that she longed to visit.

Whereas other children dreamed of a family trip to Disney World, June would trade that opportunity in a heartbeat for the chance to visit her ancestral home in Ireland.

Of course, their father was delighted that his elder daughter shared his love of this part of the world. Much to their mother's chagrin, Dad – who was one generation removed from those of his family who were born on Irish soil – repeatedly proclaimed to anyone who would listen that there were only two types of people in the world, the Irish and those that wished they were Irish. He regaled family and friends with tails of the beauty and splendour of the 'emerald isle'. And although he had never actually set foot on Irish soil, their dad could reel off the names of presidents, royalty, sport heroes and movie stars who shared his Irish heritage... sometimes claiming them as relatives. Such comments often caused their mother to ask him why he never spoke of the less savoury segment of his family tree who also journeyed to Nova Scotia from Ireland. Such admonishments would stop him for a while... but not for very long.

June didn't care if the stories were true or make believe and she never tired of hearing them. She was always happy to sit at her father's feet and listen intently.

Another fact about June Halloran was that she was possibly the greatest ambassador of her time, for Cape Breton, and she never failed to take full advantage of all it had to offer. But as much as she loved her island home, her desire to experience the rest of the world never left her.

As a teenager, June would secretly tuck her copy of *National Geographic* or *Travel Weekly* inside the cover of a *Teen Beat* magazine. She said it made her feel more normal around her friends. And because no one asked her questions about her choice of reading material, June was able to escape into her own fantasy world in the same way her friends did in theirs.

Once, in the seventh grade, while sitting through a seemingly endless Math class, June let out a loud shriek, causing the teacher to drop her book and the children to take cover under their desks. Apologising while running from the classroom, June declared that she had been stung by a bee and was going to see the school nurse. Safely out of the teacher's line of vision, June headed for the nearest washroom where she recovered the magazine she had been reading during class. She wasted no time finding and rereading the article that caused her to lie to her teacher and bolt out of the room. And there it was in black and white. National Geographic was offering summer travel camps for students in grades nine to twelve.

The themes of the camps included expeditions, conservation-in-action trips, photography workshops, community service programmes, and even an opportunity to explore global issues alongside top experts in the field. In short, a veritable dream come true for June.

From the moment she heard about the programme, June dedicated herself to doing whatever was necessary to ensure she would be able to take part in this experience as soon as she met the age requirement, and within two years, June had saved $2,500.00, one half of the registration fee. She excelled in her schoolwork and won the provincial geography award, which covered the rest of her expenses. All she needed now was for her parents to sign the permission slip and for grading day to arrive, bringing with it the requisite completion of grade eight.

Done and done. The first camp June attended was a two-week expedition to Belize. She was fourteen years old and three weeks past middle school graduation. While June's parents were understandably concerned about letting their teenage daughter travel to a foreign country on her own, they were confident June would be fine. She had always been a responsible child and the National Geographic Explorers camps were extremely well supervised. Also, her parents knew that she would drive them crazy if they refused to let her go.

Molly was happy for her big sister but when the time came for June to leave, she hid her concerns, just as her parents did.

When Molly's big sister returned home safely in the last week of July, it was clear she had found her calling. As soon as she caught up on some sleep and enjoyed a few days of their mom's cooking, she was ready to hold court. Friends from school were also excited to hear all about her adventure.

The focus of June's trip was for the students to learn about how they could play a role in preserving the ocean habitats for future generations. June told everyone amazing stories about snorkelling in the clear blue waters of the Turneffe Atoll where she got to monitor the health of the reef and record its data for posterity. She talked about the sea life she encountered, the people she met and the sights she saw. But mostly, June came home from her first trip with a blueprint for what she wanted to do with the rest of her life.

Still holding the newly found frame a little closer to her heart, Molly thought, as she had so many times before, how much she missed her sister. Apparently twenty-three years was not long enough to erase her pain and grief. Taking a deep breath, Molly shifted her attention back to the five pictures in the wooden cube.

The first picture was of June with her arms wrapped around the neck of a dolphin as they played in the waters of Belize. In the photo it looked as though both June and the dolphin were mugging for the camera. Perched atop his back, June held a large sign that read, 'I named this dolphin Molly'.

"Pat, I just miss her so much," Molly whispered as she stared at the photograph. "Who else but our June would take the time to think about her kid sister when she was on the adventure of a lifetime?"

By her senior year June had once again raised enough money to register for a second Explorer's camp. This being her graduating year and, therefore, her last year of eligibility for the National Geographic expedition, there was no question as to where June would apply to go. Since the age of four she had dreamed about visiting Ireland, the home of her ancestors and the country so inextricably linked to her beloved Cape Breton Island in its geographical features, climate and culture.

Molly remembered vividly how June climbed into her bed the night before she left for university and regaled Molly with stories of her most recent adventure. She talked about the Dublin Castle in such vivid terms that Molly could easily imagine herself dancing at one of the festive balls that lead up to St. Patrick's Day.

Then with a gentle brogue that June could switch to so naturally, she told her little sister about the *Gaeltacht*, in Galway where Ireland's traditional ways of life hold strong and Irish Gaelic is still the language of the land.

She reminded Molly that the very first sign a visitor saw when they left the mainland of Nova Scotia and drove over the Canso Causeway onto Cape Breton Island, was the Gaelic greeting, *Céad Míle Fáilte* - A Hundred Thousand Welcomes. She even taught her how to imitate the guttural sounds of the language.

But her favourite leg of the trip through Ireland was the time she spent in the Aran Islands getting to meet and talk to the local fishermen and farmers, innkeepers and shopkeepers about their daily lives.

The photo from Ireland that June selected to include in the cube frame was taken during her Dublin trip. June and five other students were participating in a traditional Irish step-dancing class. The picture showed three boys and two girls diligently trying to master the steps while June, her head thrown back in laughter, danced as she always had, to her own music.

Over the next five years, as was her plan, June completed both a bachelor's and master's degree in Science. Each year, as part of her studies, she did an internship in an area related to environmental conservation and sustainability. By the time she graduated from university, June had already amassed an impressive resume that included research, grant acquisition, as well as the practical experience in the application of science to community sustainability.

It was, therefore, not at all surprising that following her graduation, June was actively recruited by numerous universities, government agencies and private companies. What was perhaps a bit unexpected was that she did not choose any of these impressive options. True to form, June chose to take an administrative position as director of a small environmental agency in Dongtan, in the south of China.

Working in Dongtan appealed to June because it was well known that the environmental regulations in in this area were extremely weak and for the most part unmonitored. Such lapses in supervision made it attractive for large industries to establish and operate businesses in the area and this meant they were free to do more harm to the environment at less cost to the company.

With no restrictions governing the dumping of toxins into the land or water supply, mining companies flourished in the area. Even when it became evident after medical records were examined, that unusually large numbers of children living in the vicinity of a lead refinery near Dongtan had been diagnosed with excessive lead in their blood, neither government nor company owners took steps to correct the problem.

As time went on, it became abundantly clear that China was not as concerned about the negative impact of lax environmental regulations as it was about boasting full employment. June, of course, had a very different opinion about what should be done, and she was not about to keep her opinion to herself.

Along with some colleagues, including several members of the medical profession, June organised a series of information sessions to let the good people of Dongtan know what was causing so many of their children to be sick. Infuriated by the negative publicity June and her associates were generating, government officials and CEOs tried very hard to stop their efforts, but to no avail. Knowledge of the devastating toll of toxic poisoning spread around the country making it impossible for the government to continue to ignore the situation.

Within months of the protests, scientists, environmentalists and public-health workers flooded into Dongtan to conduct tests and analysis of the soil and water; among them a lawyer named Sam Friedman.

Chapter 5

Samuel Friedman III was born in New York City and received his law degree from NYU. Graduating first in his class made his father Sam II – also an attorney – proud and hopeful that soon the younger Sam would take his place in the prestigious law firm that had been established by his own father: Samuel Friedman Senior, LLB. But family pride and optimism were short-lived and readily replaced by disappointment and even a bit of anger when Sam III announced he would be leaving New York to practice environmental law, wherever he felt he would be was most needed.

Their partnership was symbiotic from the moment he met June. Like her, Sam had given up a much easier and far more lucrative life to follow his dream and his conscience.

New York City, despite its progressiveness in so many areas was responsible for the Love Canal, complete with 22,000 tons of buried toxic waste. And then there was the acid rain, which by the mid-1980s, was responsible for the decline and indeed the loss of entire fish populations. No, Sam III had no desire to practice corporate law on Wall Street, he knew he belonged somewhere where he could contribute to positive change and that place turned out to be Dongtan.

Sam fell in love with the vivacious June Halloran the day he met her, although it would take him a long time to let her know his feelings. He joined the agency where June worked and for the next few years they toiled diligently, shoulder to shoulder. Fully dedicated to the task at hand, within five years they managed to open branch offices in offices in South Africa and Brazil where environmental regulations were also overlooked in favour of business interests.

While Sam managed all three operations, June continued her research and lobbying efforts. She worked tirelessly with her staff, especially the young interns, teaching them, encouraging them and instilling in them the love she felt for each project their company undertook.

It seemed as though there were never enough hours in the day for June to accomplish all that she had set out to do. Time and time again Sam reminded her that she was working too hard and far too many hours. He was sure that when he was away at one of the other sites, June would get so caught up in her work that she would forget to eat and sleep.

The students training under June told Sam she rarely got more than two or three hours of sleep each night and sometimes she didn't go home at all. Sam continued to remind her that she would be of no use to anyone, least of all herself, if she didn't start taking better care of herself. He became so worried about her that he began to manage the South African and Brazilian offices from China, not wanting to leave her alone.

And then quietly and without warning, on April 1st, just before her thirty-sixth birthday, June Friedman passed away in the arms of her husband. An autopsy performed at Sacred Heart Hospital revealed that the cause of death was complications from Addison's Disease, an adrenal-gland malfunction that prevents the body from making enough hormones to deal with extreme physical stress.

There was no way of knowing if June was aware of her illness. What the doctors did explain to Sam was that there was no evidence that June had received medical treatment for her condition. The symptoms, according to the doctor were extreme exhaustion, weakness, loss of appetite and light-headedness, all which June displayed. Sam listened to the doctor knowing he would never forgive himself for not taking better care of his beloved wife.

When Sam called June's family with the shocking news, it was obvious that a part of him had died that day as well. He brought June home to Cape Breton and apologised to her parents for not protecting their daughter, as he promised he would.

No funeral or interment arrangements had been made or discussed. And really, why would they have been since June was a vibrant young woman with her whole life ahead of her?

Molly and her family knew that June would never forgive them if they had confined her body to a coffin and buried her in the ground. Instead it was decided that June's ashes would be scattered in those places on Cape Breton Island she loved the best. So June's final resting place, or places as it were, included a wave out on the Atlantic Ocean that could only be reached if you were standing on top of Smokey Mountain on the Cabot Trail in the Highlands of Cape Breton. The next drop off was a secluded beach in Whale Cove on the western side of the island. This was a special spot June visited every time she came home. She would sit on the cliff overlooking Chimney Corners and watch the pods of pilot whales circling a school of fish at mealtime. She loved the idea that the whales worked together to find food for each other. Her greatest delight was watching each whale, in turn, peeling off from the circle to have their meal and then returning to the circle allowing the next beautiful mammal his or her turn to enjoy dinner. The final vial of ashes returned to China with Sam. It seemed only fitting and fair that part of June should remain with her family in Dongtan and with her husband who loved her dearly and missed her so much.

The service and committal ceremony did little to ease Molly's grief. Her own husband Mark didn't get home for the funeral and while Molly understood that he was unable to get away from work, it hurt her deeply that he didn't seem to realise or care how badly she needed him to be with her.

Molly was thankful that Sam had allowed the family the honour of dealing with June's memorial in the manner they believed she would have wanted. And while Molly took some solace in knowing that June's death came quickly and while doing something she loved, nothing would ever erase the sorrow she felt for not having had the chance to say goodbye to her sister.

The three remaining photographs in the cube were a picture of June and Sam proudly standing in front of their first office in

Dongtan; an old family photo of their mom and dad, June at age twelve holding the not-yet-one-year-old Molly in her arms and finally a picture of Molly, their mom and June at June's wedding.

Molly especially loved this picture, because she was pregnant with Ava at the time. Pulling herself, once again from her reminiscences, Molly's eyes sought out Patrick when she said, "Pat, this is the only picture I have of me with these three amazing women."

Exhausted from hard work and the beautiful, albeit painful memories, Patrick gently took the picture cube from his wife's hands and carried it and the box of travel information from their last Hawaiian vacation upstairs to what use to be Cole's bedroom. The room now served as a combination office/den/guestroom. In truth, it would take a considerable amount of clearing out to be able to accommodate a guest. Even Cole, on those rare occasions when he stayed in Cape Breton overnight, opted to sleep in Ava's room or on a sofa.

Following Patrick into the room, Molly quietly removed the cube from the box and brought it into their bedroom. She realised that after all these years it finally felt like the right time to bring a physical reminder of June back into her home. Filthy from its time in the basement rafters Molly nevertheless placed the cube on her vanity table with a promise to carefully clean each unit... someday.

Chapter 6

The weather bureau forecast another nor'easter for the upcoming weekend complete with high winds, heavy snow and freezing temperatures. Since they would, likely, be captives in their own home until the storm blew over, Molly and Patrick agreed it would be a fine time to treat themselves to a nice bottle of wine, light the fire and start some serious anniversary trip planning. "Who knows, we might even get around to packing away those Christmas decorations," Patrick added, knowing that was probably not likely to happen.

Right now, however, all Molly could think about was a hot bath, which she apparently said out loud.

"OK, that sounds like a terrific plan," Patrick answered with a hopeful grin when he heard where she was headed.

"Sorry," Molly replied, "this one is going to be a girl bath." As much as she enjoyed sharing a bath with Patrick… and God he *did* make it enjoyable, after today's chores, Molly just wanted to run the biggest, hottest bubble bath ever, turn on some music, lock herself in the bathroom and have a nice long soak. Patrick, understanding as always, told her to enjoy herself and even promised to drop off a glass of wine a little later.

With her preparations well underway, the bathroom already smelled exotically inviting. Even the random iTunes selections were cooperating. Right at that moment Paul Anka was encouraging Molly to put her head on his shoulder, as she prepared to step into the hot, scented water. When that song ended, and the room filled with John Lennon's melodious voice singing *In my Life*, she felt the first sting of tears spilling from her eyes. Molly wept while listening to the tender message. *There are places I remember all my life, though some have changed. Some forever not for better, some have gone, and some remain.*

Jumping out of the tub, Molly grabbed a towel and rushed to her bedroom to retrieve the picture cube. Returning with her newly re-found treasure Molly caressed the dusty wooden block, gently touching each photo. Although she probably looked at these old pictures hundreds of times in the past, the emotions she experienced today were as raw as the day she learned that June was forever gone from her life.

Forgetting about her waiting bath, Molly continued staring at the wooden cube. Without thinking she began to disassemble the frame, carefully setting aside each picture while she wiped and dried the five glass sides.

When the glass sparkled to her satisfaction, Molly turned her attention to the cube itself, which looked like it was also in need of a good cleaning and maybe even a paint job. Obviously, it would be so much easier to discard the original frame and buy a new one. Considering that option for a moment, Molly's mind once again drifted to the lyrics of *In My Life. All these places had their moments with lovers and friends I still can recall. Some are dead, and some are living, in my life I've loved them all.*

She knew that people all over the world suffered loss and disappointment every day and often there was very little anyone could do to change the sequence of these tragic and sad events. But this time, no matter how insignificant the gesture, Molly was hell bent and determined to take control. She would restore the frame, and the wonderful memories it held, to its original glory and she would display it in her home for all to see, enjoy and remember.

Still in her towel, Molly turned the frame upside down to get a better idea of where to begin. In the course of her examination, she realised that what she thought to be solid bottom was in fact a sliding panel. Stuck solidly in place with grime, age and God knows what else, Molly found a hair clip, bent it and dug at what appeared to be the opening. When enough of the gunk loosened, she used a nail file to rock the panel back and forth.

Not wanting to further damage the old frame, she was about to give up and ask Pat to come and help, when she noticed the edge of a piece of green paper barely sticking out from one corner. With renewed resolve, Molly began urging the panel from side to side until it spread apart just enough that she could grab the paper with a pair of eyebrow tweezers. "Who needs men or tools," she said to her reflection in the mirror, "when clearly every essential gizmo for the job could be found inside a woman's cosmetic bag."

Grasping the protruding paper with the skill and precision of a heart surgeon, Molly applied a gentle, even pressure to the paper with one hand while the other hand continued to worry the bottom of the cube until it was loosened. Working with purpose, she continued the procedure until two things happened: the door slid open with ease and Molly found herself in possession of the piece of green paper.

Pleased that the operation was successful, she put her instruments and the mysterious paper aside and began to examine and clean the now empty cube. She remarked to no one in particular that it was pretty amazing what a person could accomplish with a damp cloth and some elbow grease. In no time at all, the black wooden picture cube shone brightly from its makeshift workbench, aka, her bathroom vanity. Thankfully, the once musty odour that emanated from the frame had also vanished with the dirt.

With the photographs safely set aside, the glass shining from the paper towels upon which they rested, and the frame restored to its natural state, Molly turned her attention back to the much-anticipated bath. Not surprisingly, the water had lost some of its heat and most of its bubbles while Molly had been occupied with the frame. She remedied the situation by turning on the hot water tap and pouring in some more luxurious bath salts.

When the temperature was perfect, Molly slowly eased her tired body into the steaming, scented water. It occurred to her that drink of wine Patrick had offered would go down pretty smoothly right about now, but what the heck, she would enjoy her bath first and perhaps share a glass or two of wine with Patrick later. And anyway, she was far more interested in finding out what, if anything was on the paper she had so diligently dug out of the frame.

Lifting her arms to shoulder height, Molly was careful not to let the paper get damp. After gingerly unfolding the delicate parchment she was completely taken aback when she saw that it was in fact, a note written in June's hen-scratch handwriting. For such an accomplished artist, it always amazed Molly that June's handwriting could be so bad.

Closing her eyes, Molly smiled as she recalled the often-told story of June stomping down the hallway into the kitchen of their home two hours after classes were over, vowing to quit school in grade 4 if those mean nuns didn't get off her back about her 'unseemly penmanship', their words, not hers. "With all the exciting things to learn in school," June would protest, "how could anyone give a rat's ass about my sloppy writing. I can read it and if they can't, well, I'd be happy to read it to them."

These outbursts from the nine-year-old June usually resulted in a lecture on language and respect from Mom and a choked back chuckle from Dad who absolutely agreed with June's logic about the state of the education system and about the nuns that were teaching his daughter. In fact, the particular nun June was referring to in her tirade had also been his grade 4 teacher some thirty-five years earlier.

Holding the paper in her hand, Molly no longer felt like rushing to read what June had written. Knowing June, it could have been a reminder to pick up her laundry at the drycleaners. But it really didn't matter what was on the paper. In just a few minutes she would be sharing a connection with her sister in a way she hadn't been able to for over twenty years.

How lucky am I? thought Molly. She had often heard people who lost someone they loved lamenting that they would give anything to hear his or her voice just one more time. "Well" she declared, "This is my opportunity and I sure as hell don't want to rush it."

Chapter 7

When the bubbles, once again started to dissipate and the music on her iPad changed to a selection of Chuck Berry songs, Molly was ready for the verdict. She took a deep breath, dried her hands on a towel and finished unfolding the parchment. In that split second, Molly's focus shifted from reading June's message to staring bewilderedly at the small photograph of a child that was attached by paper clip to the top of the page. A closer examination confirmed that this was a child Molly did not know. Tossing the picture to the recently discarded towel on the floor for safekeeping, Molly's eyes dropped to the paper she was holding, frantically trying to read every word at the same time to solve this new mystery.

Dear Mol, the letter began. *I am sorry to be so clandestine in delivering this message to you. I hoped we would have had more time together, but as you recall, we only arrived home from Dongtan the night before our wedding and had to leave again the following day. I was torn between whether or not I should even make you aware of this, but I love you too much to risk letting anyone hurt you. Knowing how nostalgic you are about photographs, I have to believe that your penchant for reminiscence will lead you to this picture and my message. When you do, please show the photo to Mark and ask him to explain this to you.*

I am overjoyed that you are planning a trip to my beautiful Chongming Island in September. If you haven't found this note by the time you get here, I promise I will tell you what I know when we are together. I love you little Molly and I pray that I am doing the right thing by you. I am so happy with Sam and my joy will be complete when you come to our beautiful country to visit.

With all my love, June xxx

"*Mark,*" Molly said aloud. "What information could Mark possibly have about this?" During their brief marriage, Mark had been away frequently. Molly knew his work brought him to different parts of Asia on a number of occasions. She wondered if perhaps that's why June told her to ask Mark about the picture. But even if he did know something about the child, where did June get the photograph in the first place? Did June think Mark was hiding something?

Molly was never sure if she really didn't see it herself, or perhaps she just didn't want to believe it, but her first husband had been a very controlling man. Initially she told herself that she was happy to do whatever Mark asked of her. For the most part they were just small favours... *No big deal*, she would tell herself. But as time went on, Molly found herself missing out on too many things that were important to her. Sometimes it was because of Mark's work, which she understood, but more often it was because he expected her to change her life to suit his. And like so many women who found themselves in this situation, Molly got in the habit of accommodating her husband's schedule to the extent that she hardly recognised how his demands were impacting her life.

A prime example was the trip to China to visit her sister. Twice they had planned to make the trip and both times Mark cancelled it. Once was because of a medical conference he had agreed to attend and the second time his excuse for not going was because he wanted to wait until the weather in China was warmer. By that time Molly was nearly eight months pregnant and well past the point where her doctor would permit her to travel such a distance.

Molly's disappointment over not getting to see June and Sam was evident to everyone who knew her, including Mark. When he realised how much the visit meant to her, he swore they would make the much-anticipated trip after the baby was born and was old enough to travel. But as it turned out, that visit would never happen.

Reaching over the side of the tub Molly shut off the music that only moments ago had soothed her. As she opened the faucet, she shouted over the sound of the running water. "Damn it Mark! Why didn't I just go and visit my sister when I had the chance to? Why the hell did I always wait for you to say it was the right time?"

With tears streaming down her face, Molly was finally ready to allow herself to be honest about her life with Mark.

***

Dr. Mark Connor's face was exactly the one you would want to be looking at if you were unfortunate enough to find yourself in a hospital trauma unit. Tall, strikingly handsome, with sun-kissed blonde hair and piercing blue eyes, Mark had the look of the lead character in every romance novel written, except for one thing. He was very real.

They met by chance during a charity golf tournament while both were attending university. Mark was in his final year of med school and Molly was completing a master's in public relations.

The attraction was immediate and intense. When they decided to get married before graduation, family and friends encouraged them to wait just a bit longer. It wasn't that they didn't make a lovely couple. Just one glance at them and you knew you were looking at two young, beautiful, intelligent people who were obviously very much in love. It was just so unlike Molly to rush into something as important as marriage.

Molly's mom, the consummate Roman Catholic mother even suggested the unthinkable by advocating that they live together for a while, at least until they got to know each other's ways. But their desire to be together was so fervent that you might as well have tried to hold back the tide than to stop the young couple from becoming man and wife.

And so it was, on a beautiful spring day in 1989, Molly Halloran and Mark Connor stood in a tiny chapel and said their vows, promising to love and respect each other all the days of their lives.

June travelled home for the wedding to stand with Molly as her Maid of Honour. Although it was clear, at least to her parents, that

June shared the same apprehension as the rest of her family about their rush to get married, she never said a word about it. June even mentioned to her mom how Molly and Mark looked like an advertisement for a 'happily ever after' movie.

The night before the wedding June and Molly slept in the same bed as they had done so many times as children. They chatted late into the night with June asking countless questions about her brother-in-law-to-be. June listened, as she always did, smiling as Molly talked about Mark. Yet, without June having uttered a word of criticism, Molly had a strange sense that her sister harboured some sort of misgivings about the man Molly was going to marry.

The wedding took place the next morning as scheduled and to the casual observer a handsome groom and his beautiful bride with eyes locked on each other and hands tightly clasped took the first steps into their life together.

Two months after their wedding, the Connor and Halloran families came together once again. This made it was a trip to Montreal to watch their children graduate from university. Both families were delighted, and silently relieved, to see the two looking every bit as in love as they did on their wedding day.

And why wouldn't they, they were still newlyweds? They had successfully survived all the stress and hoop jumping associated with completing their respective degrees. Both had graduated at the top of their class and they were each being actively courted by head-hunters in their respective fields. Ah, if only things were as simple as they appeared to be!

In reality, even though Molly and Mark were still basking in the honeymoon phase of their marriage and were overjoyed to have finished university, that infamous "love and respect" vow was already facing its first real challenge.

Mark had been invited to do his residency at McGill Hospital by none other than the Chief of Staff. Molly was happy for her husband and proud of his success. It was just that she had hoped they would be returning to Cape Breton to work, as they had always planned.

To make matters worse, Mark would not even discuss the fact that he had also received a very attractive offer to do his residency at The Queen Elizabeth Hospital in Halifax, which, while not on the island, was at least in Nova Scotia. Obstinately Mark insisted that he simply couldn't turn down the opportunity to work with world-renown researchers in the field of infectious disease control, especially at the oldest and most respected medical faculty in Canada.

He argued that Molly was being selfish and short sighted, maintaining that she knew his plan was to someday work overseas, most likely in a third-world country. But what hurt the most was that Mark just naturally assumed Molly would adjust her career plan to whatever and wherever Mark decided to go. But this time, Molly had plans of her own and she was prepared to fight for them.

When the dutiful wife card didn't work, Mark tried to change her mind by using guilt. "Molly," he admonished using that defiant tone that she never noticed before they were married, but heard far too many times since. "Are you really telling me you wouldn't be willing to put your education to use in a country that has so little and needs so much? I think June would be very disappointed in you."

"How dare you to even suggest that June would want anything different for me than what I would want for myself and how dare you exclude me from plans that impact both our lives?" Mark, completely unaccustomed to having Molly disagree with him, especially so vehemently, was shocked into silence. For a moment he thought about trying to comfort her and even apologise for making her feel neglected. Instead Mark did what apparently was to become Mark's go-to option throughout their marriage. He left her alone and returned to his lab at the hospital, thinking, *Maybe tonight once she's had time to think this through, she'll be more reasonable.*

Equally surprised that she had found the courage to tell Mark how she felt, Molly did indeed spend the rest of the day thinking about the argument. Of course, she remembered that it was Mark's dream to work with Doctors Without Borders, and she *was* beginning to feel a bit selfish. By mid-afternoon Molly had convinced herself that Mark wasn't really being disrespectful or dismissive of her feelings. She decided that he was being adamant about her coming away with him because he loved her and didn't want for them to be apart. She remembered how upset and worried her own family had been when June chose to work so far away, and she wondered if that was also how Mark was feeling.

Molly promised herself she would talk to him again tonight and, hopefully, each would be able to better understand the other's perspective this time.

Mark returned around seven o'clock that evening and he came bearing flowers and dinner. He had stopped at the Italian restaurant she loved and ordered all her favourite dishes. *Good start* mused Molly. *Now, fingers crossed that the rest of the evening goes as well.*

When dinner was over, Molly mentioned to Mark that she would like to talk some more about their earlier discussion. Supressing a frustrated sigh, Mark agreed and the two moved into the living room.

"I am sorry about how things went today," Molly began. "Of course, I know how important your career is and I really am proud of what you are proposing to do with your life. It's just that now we are a married couple and you have to remember to include me in discussions about life decisions that affect both of us."

Surprised, but pleased that Molly was being so reasonable, Mark responded, "I'm sorry too, Molly. It's just that we have both been so busy with school these past few years; I guess I'm just not used to stopping and checking in with anyone. I promise I'll try harder."

Satisfied that they were making some headway, Molly moved on. "There will be plenty of time to figure this out over the next year. But Mark, there is one thing that I am very sure about. If you truly are committed to accepting the McGill Medical School residency, I will be starting my own job search right away and you might as well know, I'll be looking for work in Nova Scotia."

Before Mark could object, Molly continued. "There isn't a snowball's chance in hell that I am going to land a public relations job in Montreal, or anywhere in the Province of Quebec for that matter. Not unless the bilingual requirement has been relaxed to the point that it includes being able to speak a few words of Gaelic."

Mark knew Molly was right and he also realised that given the number of hours he would be expected to work over the next year, maybe things would be better between them if Molly did return home to work… at least for the time being.

When they went to bed that night, Molly wasn't certain if she felt better or worse. They weren't fighting anymore and that was a good thing. But in reality, this discussion had ended with an agreement that after only a few months of marriage Mark and Molly were going to be living apart. Not really how Molly had envisioned their first year together.

In the morning, Mark was already gone to the hospital before Molly awoke. He left a note saying he would be late tonight and not to hold dinner for him. He ended the message with, *I'm sorry and I love you so much* which made Molly feel marginally better. *No use dwelling on this anymore today*, Molly reasoned. With her decision made, she knew it was time to stop talking about working in Cape Breton and start looking for an actual job.

She began by perusing various employment search engines on the computer. *Certainly, there must be a public relations agency somewhere in Atlantic Canada that would be interested in hiring a person with my skill set and charming personality*, she thought. But as she tried to concentrate on the job descriptions and list of qualifications, Molly felt her mind wandering back to the previous day, specifically to the outcome of their argument. *Did we really both agree to do this or did I just cave to Mark's wishes, again?*

Chapter 8

Snapping back to the present, Molly shivered in the now cold bath water. She had lost track of how long she had been in the tub. As she was about to step out, the bathroom door, which she had left ajar, opened with a jolt. In walked Patrick stripped down to his boxers, carrying two glasses, a bottle of chilled wine and the wearing the same grin that he always wore when he thought Molly was suggesting a joint bath.

Seeing her tear-stained face, Patrick left the ice bucket, bottle and glasses on the vanity and fell to his knees to caress Molly as her body shivered uncontrollably in his arms. Without questioning her, he removed the plug from the tub and helped her to her feet. Patrick wrapped Molly in one of those ridiculously large bath sheets that she loved so much and carried her to their bed. Once he had her tucked in, he climbed into the bed beside her and enveloped her in his arms. And although his loving gestures brought on a new flood of tears, Patrick knew with certainty that holding his wife close to him and not saying a word was the correct course of action.

When her tears gave way to sobs and finally to soft sniffles, Patrick let his lips come to rest on Molly's brow before beginning a journey down her body. By the time the exotic string of kisses reached her lips, Molly had lifted her arms and wrapped them around her husband's neck. She clung to Patrick, moulding her body to his and returning his kisses with the same passion. A moan escaped her lips as Patrick's hand caressed her throat and then her breasts before coming to rest tantalisingly low on her abdomen. Once he arrived at this magnificent haven, Patrick's fingers stopped moving. He could already feel the heat that emanated from Molly and knew from having made love with her so many times before that if he didn't stop right now, he would rob both of them of the languid pleasure of the mind-blowing sex they had shared since the first time they came together.

As for Molly, who was usually the more patient and controlled of the couple, she had absolutely no intention of waiting to feel her husband inside of her tonight. After the emotional roller coaster she had ridden all day, there was only one thing that could give her the escape she so badly needed... and that thing was currently pressed firmly against her thigh as Patrick held her close.

Not willing to wait another second, Molly pounced on top of her husband in a svelte catlike move and sat astride him. The intake in Patrick's breath told her that he was as ready as she was. When she could feel his movements grow stronger against her, Molly raised herself to a kneeling position, keeping barely an inch between the two parts of their bodies that now ached to be united as one. With painfully teasing motions, Molly deftly moved closer and closer to Patrick's erection until he could feel her heat transfer to him as though she had lit his body on fire. Straining to bridge the last millimetre of space that remained between them, Patrick took possession of his wife. With his hand firmly planted on Molly's lower back, he lifted her slight frame and lowered her on top of him. Molly eagerly complied.

Once joined, they moved in unison as if sharing one body and one soul. Giving and taking in equal measures, asking nothing more from each other than the love they so willingly shared. Molly's name escaped his lips as he felt her moist heat envelop him. The air in their bedroom was filled with her essence, a smell that Patrick could only describe as sinfully sensuous and he filled his lung ravenously with her perfume. With efficient, deep thrusts he watched his beautiful wife as she let him bring her to the blessed release she craved. When her breathing began to settle, Patrick once again began to move inside her and in mere moments felt his own release as he poured himself into Molly.

Time stopped as in the aftermath of their lovemaking Patrick and Molly held onto each other, touching, kissing and murmuring words of endearment as they returned to earth together.

Now was the time for talking and Patrick patiently waited without saying a word until Molly raised herself on one elbow and began. "Someone told me once that grief demands an answer but Patrick, there is no answer for what I feel. Just when I think the pain is easing, something always happens that reminds me June is gone forever and that I missed the opportunity to see her one more time before she died."

Patrick knew how she punished herself for not making the trip to China to visit her sister as she had planned. There was no point in reminding her again that it was not her fault. He knew this because she had told him that it was Mark's choice, not hers, to cancel the trip. Instead, Patrick encouraged her to continue with her story. Molly took a deep breath and told Patrick about finding June's note and about the mysterious picture. Patrick, for his part listened intently until she invited him to read it himself.

A brief flash of something close to recognition crossed Patrick's face when he stared at the picture of the child, whom he guessed to be about two years old. But it was fleeting and no matter how long her stared at the old photo he could not pinpoint what it was about the child that had triggered the feeling. "And to make matters worse," Molly continued, "the only other person I could have talked to about this was Mark and he's dead too." Molly fell back into the blankets they had just made love on, eyes closed and lost in her own thoughts.

Patrick knew that Molly's first marriage was unsettled in many ways. He never questioned her about her time with Mark, beyond what Molly was willing to discuss. He knew that they met young and married very quickly and he knew that for most of their short time together, Mark and Molly lived apart. Now that was something Patrick could never wrap his head around. He could no more imagine his life without Molly than he could fathom not keeping his son Cole with him when his mother left them both to *find herself*.

With Molly nestled into his arms and breathing evenly, it was Patrick turn for reminiscence, as his thoughts turned to the darkness of his own first marriage.

What the hell kind of person walks away from her husband and especially her two-year-old boy with nothing more than a note saying she was sorry but lately she just hadn't been feeling fulfilled in her life? For the love of God, who even talks *like that?*

Patrick's blood still boiled when he thought about the day a subpoena was delivered to his door informing him that, Pamela Susan O'Neil (née: Donovan) had filed for divorce. She was not requesting alimony or support and she agreed to relinquish custody and visitation rights for one Cole Patrick O'Neil. A court date was set, and the hearing took less than fifteen minutes for the judge to award full custody of Cole to Patrick. The estranged Pamela Susan Donovan did not make an appearance in court and since that day she had not attempted to see or even contact her ex-husband and child.

His new father-in-law, Molly's dad, had an old adage he liked to use to describe such behaviour. With a wink at Patrick, he would say, "Remember, my boy, Hell is only half full". Patrick smiled and agreed that would be an appropriate comeuppance for his ex-wife.

For the hundredth time Patrick reminded himself that it was Pamela's loss, not his. That said he returned his attention to a matter that was far more important to him… Molly's dilemma. "Mol," he said gently to her when she finally opened her eyes and sat up in their bed. "I can't even imagine how you must be feeling right now, and I really don't have a clue what was on June's mind when she told you to discuss the picture with Mark. God, who would have imagined that within one year, your husband and your sister would be gone!"

Pulling Molly firmly into his embrace and placing his forehead on hers, Patrick whispered to her. "Baby, we've both been through a lot and I promise you we'll figure this puzzle out just like we did all the others... we'll do it together."

Chapter 9

1989 – 1992
"Home I'll be. Home I'll be. Banish thought of leaving. Home I'll be" – Rita MacNeil

It was barely three weeks since the decision had been made that Mark would remain in Montreal while Molly moved back east. As he stood next to the fully packed Volvo that Molly would be driving to Cape Breton, Mark seemed to be hit with the full impact of the change that was about to take place in their lives. For the first time in their marriage, Molly felt like her husband was actually second-guessing himself.

As he watched Molly mentally going through the final checklist, Mark saw no obvious signs of stress or doubt on her face as she prepared to leave. In fact, during the last few days, she seemed positively excited about the upcoming trip. Molly had already secured a public relations job in Cape Breton and her parents were happy that she was going to be staying with them, at least temporarily.

In two weeks' time, Molly would begin working with the recently established Enterprise Cape Breton Corporation. The best part of her new job was that her primary responsibility would be to advise the federal government on regional economic development initiatives for the island. Over the previous years, Cape Breton had suffered a huge economic loss as a result of downsizing and closures in its steel mill and coal mines. Once a thriving region, which had successfully sustained itself with resource-based industries for many years, the island and its people were now struggling to adjust to the reality of living and working in a new Cape Breton, one that would require different training and skills for its workforce.

Mark kissed his wife goodbye one more time and told her to drive carefully. "There are lots of crazy drivers on the road and I want you to be safe." He reminded Molly to call him that evening to let him know when she arrived at her friend's place in New Brunswick. An eight-hour drive the next day would have her at her parents' house where she would be staying, at least until Mark came home for a visit and they found an apartment. With a final hug and U2's *Where the Streets Have no Name* playing on the car radio, Molly headed east while Mark walked into their Montreal loft, which somehow didn't seem so much like home anymore.

Without knowing it at the time, the precedent of saying goodbye and waiting for Mark's return became the blueprint for the rest of their time together. After three months of "living in", Molly moved from her parent's house and bought a small home in Boularderie Island overlooking the beautiful Bras d'Or Lakes. She loved her job and quickly became a valuable asset to ECBC. For the most part, she was content. Although she missed her husband tremendously, she was busy at work and she had loads of family and friends to support her.

During that first year, Mark returned to Cape Breton whenever his schedule would allow, which wasn't nearly as often as either of them would have liked but they always made the best of whatever time they had.

Before the year ended, Mark had earned a post-doctoral fellowship and a chance to join Doctors Without Borders. They cried in each other's arms the night he told Molly he would be stationed in the Sudan. Mark told her how much it pained him to be away from her and he hoped that she could understand why he had to go. With a heavy heart, Molly gave her blessing and with that, any hope of them being together as a couple in the near future vanished.

Molly settled into her new home and community. People in the small town had lots to say about the attractive young woman who lived alone. They thought it strange that her husband, the doctor, was rarely, if ever, around. Out of respect for Mark and their marriage, Molly never complained to anyone about her situation Then one evening while having dinner at her parents' home, Molly found herself no longer able to carry her burden alone. While washing up the dishes after a delicious meal, she confided to her mother that she was unhappy and admitted that she was feeling very conflicted about her marriage to Mark.

Usually a confidant speaker, Molly stammered a little as she confessed that on one hand, she was proud of her husband and admired his commitment to his work, while on the other hand she resented the lack of interest he showed for her and their still-new marriage. Even though she understood the significance of the work Mark was doing, it did nothing to erase the loneliness of being ten thousand kilometres and a six-hour time difference away from the man she loved. She was also acutely aware that many of their friends – and especially Mark's family – regarded Mark as a saint; a handsome, gifted deity who forfeited the comforts of home and family to help those in need.

Dr. Mark Connor specialised in the treatment of autoimmune disease specifically immune thrombocytopenia, where the body attacks its own platelets. The focus of his work was the impact of the disease on women who, according to Mark's research, were three times more likely to be affected than men. And as if the syndrome wasn't punishing enough in and of itself, the hardest hit target group for autoimmune disease was young women in their child-bearing years. Pretty hard to compete with that level of dedication to humanity… so Molly didn't try to. She sucked it up and hoped that someday Mark would also have time to focus on being her husband.

Each time Mark came home, Molly sensed more stress in her husband. Initially he would seem happy to be home. In fact, it seemed like he couldn't get enough of her. He was reluctant to leave her side, and specifically her bed. But inevitably, within a few days of being home, she could feel a wall starting to form between them. He would begin to talk about the progress he and his team were making in one area, but instead of feeling some level of accomplishment in what they had achieved, Mark's focus would shift to the next conflicted area. When that happened, Molly knew he would be leaving soon. It seemed as though Mark's heart and his mind were torn between being with her and being where he felt that he needed to be.

More and more, his time in Cape Breton with Molly felt like a scheduled appointment while his true home was somewhere else, halfway around the world. When the time would come for Mark to leave, as she knew he always would, Molly struggled with her feelings about her husband, which ranged from pride to anger. Eventually those feelings changed to guilt as she found herself missing him less each time he went away.

Molly's mother listened attentively as Molly described how she was feeling. Alternating between knowing nods and handing Molly the next pot that needed drying, she encouraged her daughter to continue telling her story. Of course, her mother knew Molly was in pain and it hurt her not to be able to help. She had often shared her feelings and concerns with June when they talked on the phone and although June agreed with her mom, she adamantly insisted that they both butt out until Molly was ready to talk.

Well now the door was open, and her mother was more than ready to have her say. Without a disparaging word against Mark, she reminded Molly that her life and dreams and expectations were every bit as important as her husband's. With hands still wet from washing dishes, she hugged her youngest child and pleaded with her to take some time to think about what she needed from Mark. She made Molly promise that she would see a counsellor while Mark was away this time and when he returned for June's wedding in the spring perhaps, they should think about seeing a therapist together.

Breathing a sigh of relief, Molly hugged her mother back and held on for a very long time. She always felt better after talking to her mom. She should have realised that she didn't have to deal with this alone and vowed to do just what her mother suggested. That night on her way home, she even purchased a journal to help her organise her thoughts.

Chapter 10

You could feel the excitement mounting among the Halloran clan as winter descended on Cape Breton Island. June was coming home for the holidays that year and, heaven help them all, she was bringing a man to meet the family. She had mentioned her friend Sam several times, but everyone assumed he was just another of June's many acquaintances. So the family was quite excited to finally meet him and find out why this particular friend was bring-home-for-Christmas worthy.

Mark was also going to be home for Christmas and this time, he would be staying for three weeks, making this visit the longest time he and Molly would spend together since she left Montreal more than a year ago.

Although the family kept busy with cooking, decorating and preparing for their guests, time seemed to pass excruciatingly slowly. Everyone was anxiously awaiting the arrival of June and Mark who would be traveling from China and the Sudan respectively. Mark's parents would also be joining the Hallorans for the holidays. Spirits were high and everyone in both households agreed that this was shaping up to be the best Christmas ever.

When the big day finally arrived, the Hallorans could hardly contain their excitement. June took her car to the airport in Sydney while her mother and father followed behind in their ten-year-old Chrysler New Yorker. With three adults plus all the luggage and gifts that would most likely be accompanying the travellers, Molly's parents decided two trunks would be better than one.

As the ecstatic convoy headed out, they realised that the drive to the airport was probably going to take a little longer than usual. Winter road conditions in Cape Breton tended to be sketchy at the best of times and the recent ice and snow didn't help matters in the least. They were further delayed by the bustle of last-minute Christmas shoppers streaming in and out of the city's only mall, which was located on the same highway as the airport.

Molly, who was used to big-city traffic, smiled as she waited at a red light thinking about her parents in the car behind her. Whereas most cities suffered through rush-hour traffic, her father would be complaining loudly to his wife about the "friggin' congestion" and asking rhetorically if anyone in Sydney ever heard of a "damn car pool". Nope, her dad was not a man who dealt with traffic well or with patience.

As a result, the group arrived at the airport just moments before the airport clerk announced the on-schedule arrival of Air Canada Flight 1977 from Halifax. The real Christmas miracle was that Mark's plane was now due to arrive early and would be on the ground in just over an hour. Everyone agreed it made more sense to wait at the airport. In addition to not having to make two separate trips, it would give them time to kiss and hug June repeatedly and of course to begin the inquisition of the unsuspecting Sam Friedman III.

There being a total of one arrival gate at Cape Breton's only airport, it was not at all surprising that the Hallorans were front and centre when June's smiling face appeared at the door of the plane, her man in tow. *That's another thing I love about living here*, Molly thought as she watched her sister descend the stairs. *This is one of the few airports where you can see the passengers the second they disembark.* As if reading her mind, her parents shouted at the same time, "Look, there she is. I don't think I could have waited another minute to wrap my arms around her." In an instant, the otherwise calm airport exploded with the sounds of excited greetings, tears, hugs and kisses.

At one point during the ensuing chaos, a kindly older gentleman whose job was to welcome passengers to Sydney gently guided the Hallorans away from the doorway in order to let the other travellers enter. Hardly noticing the intrusion, the family continued on with their welcome festivities. Once June's face was finally devoid of any makeup from kisses and tears of joy, all eyes turned to the striking dark-haired man standing off to the side of the commotion. Moving as one unit, the Hallorans stormed Sam.

He had been an only child and June had prepared Sam as well as possible for the onslaught of questions he was sure to receive from her family. Sam handled it like a real trooper. It was immediately obvious to the family that he was very much in love with June and it appeared that the feelings were reciprocal. The joy in her parent's eyes made Molly certain that her mom was already planning the marriage of her older daughter... and the couple didn't disappoint. Before their luggage arrived at the baggage carousel, Sam and June announced that they were indeed engaged and were planning to get married the following spring.

So busy and noisy were the Hallorans as they celebrated the wonderful news that they missed the announcement of the next awaited flight. Molly, being the first to realise that Mark's plane had landed, broke away from the group in just enough time to see her handsome husband walking down the stairs and across the slippery tarmac.

Molly was in Mark's arms the second he cleared the door. When the greeter realised this was yet another member of the exuberant clan's entourage, he was quick to run interference and move the couple out of harm's way before they created another human roadblock. Watching as they passionately embraced, the kindly volunteer realised that the other travellers could have ploughed them over where they stood, and neither would have noticed. "Oh, to be young and in love," he murmured.

"OK you two," Molly's father jokingly reprimanded as he put a hand on each of their shoulders. "Give a guy a chance to welcome his first son-in-law home".

"*First?*" asked Mark with a look of confusion on his face as both in-laws enveloped him at the same time.

"I'll explain everything on the drive home," Molly assured him once her parents had released their grip. With a quick introduction to Sam and an air kiss exchanged between Mark and June, the gang left the airport arm in arm and proceed to their respective vehicles.

Christmas miracle number two occurred as the procession turned onto the street where the Halloran house shone brightly with festive lights. Right on cue, Mark's parents were pulling up to the front door as the others approached the driveway. With horns honking a welcome to each other and family members spilling out of their respective cars, a new round of kisses and hugs ensued. This time, Molly took control and ushered the happy gang up the walk and into the foyer of her parent's home.

As June walked into her childhood home, her senses were assaulted with so many familiar sights and smells it brought happy tears to her eyes. "Oh Mom," June proclaimed. "You really outdid yourself."

Fresh evergreen boughs and wreaths decorated with holly berries adorned the archways and every flat surface in the house boasted trays of delicious looking food. With a flip of a few switches Dad brought the rest of the magnificent décor into view. Soft candles cast a subtle light throughout the living and dining rooms while the fireplace mantle housed a bustling Christmas village scene.

The only piece of this idyllic scene not yet complete was a huge fir tree, which stood naked in front of the window patiently waiting for family and friends to decorate its branches. Boxes laden with Christmas ornaments, old and new, were stacked beside the tree and everyone was looking forward to participating in the Halloran tree-trimming ritual.

This first task, however, was to get people out of the hallway and settled into what would be their home for the holidays. June and Sam would be sleeping in June's old room. Mom and Dad, not entirely sure of the extent of their relationship had a plan B in place in case Sam turned out to be just an acquaintance, which clearly, he was *not*.

The Connors clan was camping in with the Hallorans as well and Molly took them upstairs to the guest room, which had been prepared for their arrival. Although Molly and Mark would be staying at their own house in Boularderie Island, they wouldn't be leaving for quite a while. For the next few hours, there was a lot of celebrating to be done.

By the time the group had reconvened in the living room, the drink cart was stocked, and Christmas music filled the room. Everyone was in a festive mood and ready to trim the tree. Carols were sung, and eggnog was served. By the time the fir tree was dressed in its Christmas finery, it was hard to imagine that some of the guests had only met hours before. It looked, felt and sounded like one big happy family.

Upon final inspection of their work, it was decided that it was time to set the angel on the tree, a privilege that was assigned to Sam, as the newest member of the clan. Sam, realising the significance of the honour that was bestowed upon him, took extra care to make sure the celestial being sat both straight and steady. He chuckled to himself when he imagined what his parents would think of their orthodox Jewish son presiding over such an event.

While the decorating committee was busy refilling their eggnog mugs and patting each other on the back for the fine job they'd done, Dad disappeared for a moment and returned carrying a huge red envelope, which he places on the coffee table for all to see. "Being a true believer in the value of the repetition of rituals," he announced, "I would like to invite all those present to join the Hallorans in the hangin' of the green.". Assuming this must be an old Irish tradition, the guests gathered around waiting to see what he would extract from the envelope.

The family, of course, knew exactly what was coming.

As was tradition, the last decorations to go on the tree were the family pictures. Inside the mystery package was a series of photographs all set in gaudy green plastic frames. Each had been taken on Christmas Eves over the years and the only criteria for making it into the envelope was that the picture had to be truly hideous.

As her father carefully removed the first framed photo from the packet, Molly and June simultaneously lunged in a futile attempt to grab it from their father's hand. "Oh, dear God in heaven!" they yelled in unison as they stared down at a picture of June at age thirteen doubled over laughing at two-year old Molly in her new Christmas pyjamas over which she proudly wore June's first training bra. Molly had found the garment in the clothes hamper and thought she would look very grown up if she had a bra like June. Laughing as hard again as she did in the picture, June proclaimed, "Nothing like sharing our *actual* dirty laundry on Sam's first visit."

Impervious to his daughters' mortification, picture after humiliating picture was selected from the envelope and hung on the tree until everyone in the room was exhausted from laughter. "Glad you enjoyed the show," Molly cajoled. "You can be sure that each of you will be making your own embarrassing contribution to next year's tree. Dad is never without his camera over the holidays." True to his word as June spoke, Dad was busy capturing a shot of Sam stuffing a large piece of Mom's famous rabbit pie into his mouth… a sure keeper for the collection.

A tinkling noise from the Christmas bell told the group it was time to move into the dining room where they were treated to a delicious meal, lovingly prepared by Molly and her parents. When the diners agreed they could not eat or drink another morsel, tired but satisfied they decided it was time to call it a night.

It had been obvious to everyone for the past hour that Molly and Mark were anxious to finally be alone together, so it was not surprising that they were the first to leave. After kissing everyone goodnight and promising to be back the next day, the two ran to their car arm-in-arm.

Chapter 11

That night felt like a beautiful dream to Molly. They hardly made it through the front door when they were naked and tucked into their bed for a long night of talking and passionate sex. In the morning when she finally awoke, it was to the sounds and smells of Mark making their breakfast, which he served to her in bed.

Molly made a quick call to her mom to let her know that they may not get back to the house until later that evening. Satisfied that they had lots of time, the happy couple resumed their marathon lovemaking session that had begun the night before. Finally sated, Mark and Molly enjoyed a leisurely shower and then put on another pot of coffee, which they took to the sunroom.

While they took in the beautiful winter scene outside the window, Molly told Mark that she was seeing a counsellor, marking the first time in their marriage she felt comfortable and confident enough to tell her husband the truth about how she had been feeling.

The look of shame on Mark's face when he listened to what Molly had been going through was palpable. What he hated the most was the realisation that he was the cause of her anguish. Rather than judging her, as Molly expected he might, he encouraged her to keep meeting with her counsellor and promised that he would attend a session with her before he left.

Her next appointment was scheduled between Christmas and New Year and Mark didn't just accompany her, he was fully engaged in the meeting. He talked openly about how his behaviour precipitated much of what Molly was feeling and he listened as the counsellor suggested things they could both work on as they moved forward. Molly was overjoyed with the outcome of the meeting and, for the first time in a long while, encouraged about their future.

The remainder of the Christmas season was every bit as wonderful as she hoped it would be. They spent lots of time at her parents visiting with June and getting to know their new brother-in-law-to-be. When Mark's parent's left for Halifax on Boxing Day, they thanked the Hallorans and said that they'd enjoyed every second of their stay. Mark promised he would call them the next day and he would stop in Halifax for a visit before he returned to work.

Mark continued to be affectionate and patient with Molly and she felt a sense of peace that she had not experienced for a long time. *At last,* she thought, *the loving man I married has returned to me.* When he did appear withdrawn or distracted, it didn't last for long. Even though Molly was aware of the change in Mark's behaviour at such times, she didn't press him about it, convincing herself that his mood probably had to do with work.

Three weeks passed like a blur; an amazingly blissful, erotically sensual, outrageously happy blur.

The only part of the holiday that Molly wished had gone better was June's obvious indifference toward Mark. They were cordial whenever the family was together, which was often, but there always seemed to be an underlying tension between them. "Perhaps I'm imagining things that aren't really there," Molly confessed to her mother when they had a few private moments together.

Always the diplomat, her mother listened without comment, remarking only that, "It would be a pretty dull world if we all felt the same about everybody and everything." Molly nodded in agreement but that niggling feeling never really left. She loved them both so much and wished they would become closer.

"You're right as always, Mom," said Molly, kissing her mother on the cheek. "Mark will be leaving in a few days, and I don't intend to waste one precious second." Dismissing her morose thoughts, Molly focused on making the best of the time they had left. Shutting themselves off from the rest of the world, the young couple spent their last few days locked in their home and in each other's arms.

And then in what felt like the blink of an eye, Molly and her family were back at the airport; this time to say goodbye to Mark.

June and Sam had left a week earlier in a tearful departure. Knowing they would be home again in a few months for their wedding made the parting a little more bearable. Saying goodbye to Mark, on the other hand, felt very different and Molly clung to him until the last call for boarding was announced. "I'll miss you too, baby," Mark crooned, and he kissed her tears away. "But I'll be back before you know it." Although he promised to try to get back for the wedding, Molly was not holding her breath. By now she was accustomed to having plans changed because of Mark's schedule.

Molly really hesitated to put any undue pressure on her husband. She was very aware that conditions in the Sudan were worsening. When Mark's team initially moved into Nuba in Southern Kardofan, their mission was to provide medical assistance in remote regions with poor access to healthcare, and to people affected by outbreaks of disease, and natural disasters.

By the mid-1980s, the country's economy was in danger. For many years, the primary industry was agro-pastoral farming, which sustained both livestock and farming on the same tract of land. The threat came from the rapidly increasing number of illegal, mechanised farms. Contrary to the government's orders, these large unregulated farms continued to push for higher yields. With no regard to preserving the land, the fertile rangeland had all but disappeared, leaving nowhere for livestock to graze.

For many years, the country had been plagued by civil unrest. But now, mounting unemployment as well as the loss of homes and farmland resulted in a mass exodus to the south. Not surprisingly, the outcome was a renewed and increasingly violent civil war. Mark and his team would be in Nuba to help with the resettling efforts.

He called Molly as soon as he arrived at the new location to let her know he was safe. This was something he had never done before, and Molly appreciated the gesture, especially knowing how busy he was and how difficult communication could be in such a remote region.

Mark was also diligent about making sure they talked at least once a week, more if he could manage it. Their conversations were longer and so much more relaxed. Although she missed him more than she could imagine, Molly was happy. She continued to meet with her counsellor who was pleased with the progress she was making. Even Molly's parents couldn't help but comment on how wonderfully content their daughter looked and sounded.

Chapter 12

It was early February and Molly did indeed feel pretty terrific. She was absolutely thrilled about two things; she and Mark were continuing to make headway with their marriage and she was pregnant.

When she told him the news, Molly though Mark was going to fly through the phone line. She wished she could have seen his face when he learned he was going to become a father. Because if his face looked anywhere as happy as his voice sounded, then Mark Connor was one happy man. "Honey!" Mark exclaimed when he finally got over the initial shock, "I don't care what I have to do to make it happen... but I am absolutely coming home." Molly was overjoyed, and they decided they would wait until he came home for the wedding before telling the rest of the family. They agreed this was news that they wanted to deliver together.

If Molly were asked to recall the happiest time of her life to that point, it would be the day they shared their wonderful news with their families. Mark stood proudly by her side with tears streaming down his cheeks as Molly delivered her prepared speech. "Listen up everyone," Molly began, and the family turned their attention from wedding preparations to the couple standing before them. "We love you all so much and we are so happy today to introduce the seven newest members of our family."

"*Seven!*" the word erupted from every member of the group like lava spewing from Mount Vesuvius.

June was the first to regain something of her composure. With exactly the level of tact Molly had come to expect from her sister, June bellowed, "Have you lost your mind girl? What the hell are you talking about?

While the group waited for a response, Mark and Molly walked over and kissed their respective mothers and said, "Two new grandmas and by default two papas, one aunt, one uncle and let's not forget the star of the show, one bouncing baby girl or boy and that makes seven! *We're pregnant!*" they shouted together.

Now Molly and Mark weren't sure what they expected in terms of a reaction to their news, but it certainly wasn't the one they got. Silence, unmitigated, stunned silence hung on the slackened jaws of all present while everyone waited for someone else to say something. Finally, Molly's father stepped forward and wrapped his arms around his daughter and son-in-law and with his voice cracking from emotion he whispered through tears of pure joy, "My baby girl is going to be a mother. Thank you both for this wonderful gift."

Then it happened, the proverbial penny dropped. To say that all hell broke loose would be a disservice to hell's own fury. The room filled with laughter, tears and congratulatory slaps on the back. Molly's father rushed to the kitchen and returned with his prized bottle of Middleton twenty-five-year-old pure pot-still Irish Whiskey. "It's the best in Cork County or maybe even the world," he declared with pride.

When he had poured a dram for everyone and of course a big glass of milk for the mother-to-be, they toasted the wonderful news before returning to the business at hand, the upcoming wedding plans

The marriage of June and Sam was a simple and beautiful ceremony. St. Theresa's Catholic Church was decorated with the greens and blossoms of spring. Father O'Brien, who had baptised both June and Molly, officiated at the mass alongside Rabbi Barach.

The music was a mixture of Celtic and traditional hymns as well as the lovely Jewish wedding song, *Yedid Nefesh*. And while everyone in the church was moved by the poignant service, it may as well have taken place in a tool barn as far as the bride and groom were aware. From the moment that they joined hands at the altar until they kissed at the end of service, the two never took their eyes off each other. Both Fr. O'Brien and Rabbi Barach agreed it was a rare and blessed pleasure to have the opportunity to unite a couple so totally committed to each other and so much in love.

The twenty-four hours following the wedding were like a marathon. Family and friends gathered at Mark and Molly's beautiful property in Boularderie where a magnificent wedding brunch was waiting for them. The temperature was unusually warm for a spring day in Cape Breton and the guests took full advantage of the chance to eat outdoors under the canopy that had been erected the night before. As with all Cape Breton outdoor events, plan "B", which meant picking up the party and moving it indoors was already in place. But there was no need for a plan "B" today. The sun shone on the bride and groom as if to mark the beginning of a bright future.

As the brunch tables were moved out, the entertainers moved in. For the rest of the afternoon and into the early evening the sounds of fiddles, guitars, penny whistles and of course singers could be heard for miles up and down the Bras d'or Lakes. Before the celebration came to an end, it seemed as though the entire populace of Boularderie had joined family and wedding guests for an impromptu *cèilidh*.

When June took the floor for the final waltz with her father, the band moved into a stirring rendition of *Oh Danny Boy*, which was followed by absolute silence. Everyone, especially the bride and her dad, needed a moment to regain their composure. Then within a minute the band, once again broke into a series of jigs and reels that had the raucous crowd back in full force on the makeshift dance floor.

For the final number of the evening, June called on her mother and sister to join her. The Halloran clan knew what was coming as they and the rest of the wedding guests were treated to mother and daughters kicking up their heels to the traditional Irish step-dance tune, *The Pubs o' Dublin*. When the music ended, the guests began to disperse. With arms wrapped around each other against the chill in the air, Molly and Mark stood at the end of the driveway and bid their guests good night.

The bride and groom would be spending their wedding night at a hotel in Sydney before heading back to the airport where they would begin their long flight home. When the plane was ready to board, and all other goodbyes were said, June embraced her sister. "Thank you for being there for me," she said. "I couldn't imagine a more perfect day or a better Maid of Honour. I love you, little Molly."

Promising that she wouldn't cry, Molly bit her lip as she choked out "I love you too, our June." And with a last hug for everyone, Mr. and Mrs. Sam Freidman made their way across the tarmac to the waiting plane. "We'll see you in Dongtan soon," Molly mouthed as June turned to look back and waved to her family one more time.

Mark put his arm around Molly and led her to their car, both knowing full well that they would be back at this airport in three more days, this time to say goodbye to Mark. "Come on, sweetheart," Mark said as he helped his wife into the car. "Let's make the best of the time we have left." And that's exactly what they did. Mark and Molly visited the gynaecologist and watched with awe as the doctor performed an ultrasound of their child. Each was given a copy of the picture and Mark put his immediately in his wallet.

On the drive home, Mark surprised his wife by informing her that he had made an appointment with the counsellor for the next day. He told her that the first visit was helpful, but he felt that they would both benefit from a follow-up visit before he left.

Overall, Molly felt the session went very well. In fact, the only time Mark seemed reticent to participate was when the talk turned to June and Sam's wedding. The tension between Mark and June seemed to intensify each time they were together and with the baby on the way, Molly desperately wanted her family fully intact.

Molly waited until they left the office before she broached her concern with Mark, who assured her there was nothing wrong between him and June. He said it was such a quick trip and he didn't want to cut into June's time with her family. He leaned over and kissed Molly on the cheek and asked her not to worry.

Their remaining time together was spent making love and planning for the arrival of the baby. Mark made Molly promise to take pictures of her belly every week, so he could watch his child grow. In fact, he was so excited about anything and everything to do with the baby that Molly didn't have the heart to tell him there wouldn't be any noticeable change in her size for quite some time. She loved how happy Mark was about becoming a parent and she silently prayed that they would figure out a way to be together as a family, under one roof, once the baby arrived.

Wednesday morning dawned under dark, cloudy skies, which matched Mark's mood as they prepared to head to the airport. Mark said his goodbyes to everyone else last night at a family dinner at Molly's parent's house. He would be spending a day in Halifax with his own parents before flying to Sudan. When they kissed goodbye this time, Molly was struck by a sense of sadness she could not explain. *Maybe it's just the baby hormones kicking in,* she surmised.

The one thing she was very happy about was that Mark had agreed to return in two months, so they could make the trip to Dongtan to visit June and Sam. He even promised to arrange for extra time off, so they could have a nice long holiday. Thoughts of being together with her sister, her husband and her new brother-in-law, all of whom she loved dearly, would just have to sustain Molly until they could be together again.

And of course, the fact that there was a precious new life growing inside of her would keep her mind and body plenty busy in the meantime.

Chapter 13

The first time the trip to Dongtan was postponed, Molly understood completely. The civil unrest in Nuba had escalated and there was simply no way for Mark to get away. Of course, she was disappointed, but she wanted their time together to be perfect and that wasn't likely to happen if Mark's mind was elsewhere. Mark said he felt certain things would improve within the month and he would be free to travel.

But when one month turned into three, Molly was finding it increasingly more difficult to stay positive and patient. She was well into her second trimester and she knew her window for long-distance travel would be closing. By the third postponement, Molly was so far along in her pregnancy that making the trip to China was no longer an option.

A visit to her doctor the following week resulted in the final and definitive verdict. "Molly, I am strongly recommending that you wait until after the baby arrives to make this trip. You are in excellent health and the baby is doing very well, but I cannot in good conscience give you permission to travel. And before you even start thinking about it, the airlines are not going to let you board the plane without a letter from me."

Molly was angry and upset when she left her doctor's office. She complained to her parents and again that night on the phone to Mark. Not surprisingly all three agreed with the doctor, leaving Molly with no choice but to cancel the trip and wait for the baby to arrive.

Molly spent a restless night and when Mark called the following morning to check on her, her mood had not improved. Try as he might, Mark was not able to get her to accept how dangerous it would be for both her and the baby to travel to a foreign country when her due day was so close. He promised her again that the three of them would get to see June as a family, as soon as the baby was old enough to make the trip. By the time they said goodbye, Molly was feeling a little bit better.

Before they signed off, Mark wished her a Happy Canada Day. The next day would be July 1st and Mark knew how much his wife loved celebrating her country's birthday. "Try to cut back on the hotdogs and fried onions," Mark teased, "I don't want my baby addicted to that garbage you eat." Molly said she'd do her best and promised to drink milk instead of beer this year.

***

Exactly one month following the Canada Day celebrations, Molly received another phone call from Nuba. This time it was from the Chief of Staff at the Mother of Mercy Catholic Hospital where Mark worked.

Dr. Kent Granton was a friend of Mark and Molly. In fact, Kent was the driving force behind Mark's decision to join Doctors without Borders. Not that Kent pressured him in any way. Mark's desire to be part of that organisation was because he had the utmost respect for his friend and former professor at McGill University. During his time in med school the two had often discussed the need to bring advanced western medicine and technology to third-world countries. So when the opportunity came for Mark to work with his mentor, he jumped at the chance.

"Kent," Molly sang into the phone when she recognised his voice, "it's so nice to hear from you." But the words were no sooner out of her mouth than she realised that there would be nothing nice or good about this call.

"Oh, my God, Molly, I'm so sorry". Completely overcome with emotion, Dr. Kent Granton wept as he told Molly her husband had been killed by an anti-government rebel gang that morning. Mark had been walking to the clinic, as he did every day, when a man pulled up alongside him on a scooter. Those who saw the incident said Mark had a smile on his face when the man stopped him, and it looked as though Mark was about to shake the man's hand. In an instant, the sniper pulled a gun from the waistband of his trousers and fired three bullets into Mark. "Molly," Kent continued, his voice now barley a whisper, "Mark died instantly. He was only a few metres away from the clinic and some locals who knew Mark well carried him to my office, but he was already gone. The gunman was the seventeen-year-old son of a known insurgent. After he shot Mark, he turned the gun on himself. Molly," Kent pleaded brokenly, "please tell me what I can do help you."

Molly made only one request before she ended the call. "Bring Mark home."

The funeral service for Dr. Mark Connor had to be moved to an auditorium in order to accommodate the throngs who came to pay their respects. Molly stood next to the urn that held the remains of her husband, and received condolences from family, friends and colleagues, plus a multitude of people she had never met before.

The local paper ran a full-page feature that morning outlining Mark's numerous achievements in the field of autoimmune disease control in the Sudan and China, as well as the tragic circumstances surrounding his untimely death. As mourners streamed by, Molly personally thanked each person for coming. She refused to sit down, even for a minute. Her parents worried about her but knew better than to add to her angst by insisting that she take a break. Widowed and in her seventh month of pregnancy, Molly's parents knew the best thing they could do for their daughter was to be with her throughout this ordeal and be ready to catch her when she fell, which seemed inevitable.

June was not able to make it home for the funeral on such short notice and her absence was like a physical pain to Molly. Although they had talked on the phone every day since Mark's death, it wasn't the same as having June by her side. During each conversation, June reminded Molly to try to concentrate on the beautiful child that she and Mark had made. The baby would be born soon and in him or her, a piece of Mark would live on. Molly said she would try but both sisters knew that along with Mark, a piece of Molly had also died.

The upside (if you could call it that) of unmitigated grief is its power to numb the mind and body and Molly used that to get her through the wake and funeral. With her family at her side Molly moved stoically through all the rituals, apparently saying and doing the right things at the proper times. People commented on how strong a woman she was and how she would be "just fine", in time. Molly heard their words and all their kind sentiments but instead of comforting her, they only added to her pain and guilt.

Molly and Mark's marriage, though short in duration, had been filled with extremes. Separated, almost since the beginning of their marriage, they learned to cram life into the brief times they were together. As a result, they loved fervently but they fought with equal passion. And while there were times where she missed Mark more than she could imagine, those feelings were often countered with doubt and anger. Too many times Molly felt betrayed by Mark's broken promises, and it was difficult to forget how many times she had put her plans and dreams on hold in order to accommodate his. Without a doubt, during their last year together things between them had seemed to be better. But even then, she wasn't certain if Mark was happy with her or with the notion of being a father. And now he was gone, and Molly would never have the opportunity to resolve these uncertainties.

Chapter 14

Early in the morning of December 4th, Molly awoke with a pain that could only mean one thing. It was time to become a mother. As she had promised, she called her parents who proceeded to make what may have been the fastest trip ever from Sydney to Boularderie Island. Molly insisted that she could drive herself to the hospital and meet up with them there, but by the time she was halfway through making her case, her parents were already on the road, so Molly checked her hospital bag, which had been packed for over a month and sat by the door to wait.

The drive to the hospital was uneventful, for the most part. Molly's mother sat in the back seat, holding her daughter's hand and reminding her to breathe through her contractions, which were already pretty regular. Molly's father, for his part, sang Irish lullabies as he manoeuvred the car along the snow-covered roads. Molly could see his hands tremble slightly. She noticed he was sweating a bit despite the cold weather, and it touched her heart to realise he was worried about his little girl.

It was quiet when they reached the hospital and Molly was admitted immediately. She and her mother proceeded to the maternity ward while her father stayed with the desk nurse to complete the registration. He had decided weeks before that when Molly's time came, he didn't want her to have to be subject to questions about the baby's father. It was less than two months since Mark's funeral and understandably Molly was still pretty raw.

Once settled into the ward, Molly's labour progressed rapidly. With her mother at her side, the kindly Dr. Tucker at the business end of the delivery table, Molly pushed for all she was worth. In just under four hours the new mother and her beautiful, screaming baby girl met for the first time.

A thorough examination confirmed that the baby girl weighing in at a mere 6 pounds and 1 ounce and measuring all of 17 inches in length was hale and healthy. Once she was cleaned and swaddled, Dr. Tucker passed the baby to Molly to hold and nurse. With tears in her eyes, Molly kissed her mother's hand, which was busy patting the tiny, fuzzy blonde head that was already looking for her first meal. "Mom, her name is Ava," said Molly. "It means strength and this little one will need plenty. What do you think of the name?"

"I love it," replied her mother. "And so will your dad. Ava Gardner is his favourite actress and he'll think you named her for his secret love." Ava's only reaction to her naming was a belch befitting someone twice her size. Then with a contented crooked smile the hungry baby resumed her first attempt at nursing.

Molly was discharged from the hospital three days later and insisted that her parents take her and Ava back to Boularderie to their own home. The nursery was ready, and Molly saw no use in postponing the inevitable, which was that she was a single parent. So she might as well get used to it as soon as possible.

Ava was the perfect baby. She was pleasant with everyone who came to visit… and there were many who came. She was a very good, albeit intense, eater and she slept through most of the night. Molly and Ava quickly fell into a routine and for the first time since Mark's death, Molly knew she and her daughter were going to be fine.

Each day Molly dutifully talked to her baby about Mark and showed her pictures of her daddy. Ava grew up knowing her father through those photos and the wonderful stories of his life and work. *How beautiful it must be,* Molly thought, *to have so pure a relationship with someone that can never be tarnished by life's transgressions.*

When Ava was six months old she got her first tooth. She was already crawling and making regular attempts to pull herself up to a standing position. She could mimic sounds and Molly was almost certain that on a couple of occasions she heard Ava say 'Mama'.

And then one Saturday morning while marvelling at the skills of her beautiful daughter, Molly's mother and father arrived at her door, unexpectedly. The look in their eyes was something Molly could not describe. Without a word of greeting, Molly's mother took the baby from her arms while her father sat beside her on the sofa. Her fear and confusion turned immediately to pain and horror as he spoke. "Molly, my love, our June is dead".

Wrapping strong arms around his youngest daughter as if to try to shield her from the devastating news, Molly's father told her what they knew. "Sam called this morning. He said she died of something called Addison's Disease. That's all we know. Molly, please get the baby ready and come home for a while with Mom and me." With a pain in her heart that would scarcely allow her to breathe, Molly and Ava followed her parents to Sydney. She stayed with them until after June's funeral and then she and her daughter went home to try, one more time, to pick up the pieces.

That was twenty-three years ago and for the pain she still felt it might as well have been twenty-three minutes ago.

Chapter 15

2015

On Cape Breton Island it's a well-known fact that if you don't like the weather, just wait an hour or two. Clearly, weather forecasting is an imperfect science at best, and very few places on earth push the envelope for ambiguous forecasts as far as Cape Breton does.

For starters the island, like many other locations in the Maritime provinces, lies on the track of several major weather systems. When you throw in the effects of the cold Labrador current and the Gulf Stream as well as the Les Suetes winds that rip through the western and northern coast of the Cape Breton highlands, then it's not so hard to imagine why weather is so unpredictable and quick to change.

But in this instance, the meteorological team who forecast the Nor'easter for the first weekend of January was spot on in their predictions. The storm began late in the evening with light snow and a bit of wind. By midnight, the snow was falling with a purpose and the winds were gaining momentum. The storm continued overnight and by morning you couldn't see across the street… assuming you still had a window that you were able to see out of.

Being born and raised on the island, Patrick and Molly knew exactly what kind of day was in store for them. The snow was scheduled to continue until late afternoon with persistent wind squalls throughout the day. "Well my dear," Patrick proclaimed as he peered out from their bedroom window, "there isn't a snowball's chance in hell, no pun intended, that we are going to see a snow plough on these roads anytime soon. We might as well make the best of a day indoors." With a cunning smile he jumped back into bed, where he happily spent the next hour making love with his wife.

"Mmm" Molly sighed contentedly, "I only know of one thing that could make this day any more perfect." Although Patrick may have wished his wife were suggesting another hour of earth-shattering sex, he knew her too well to assume her greatest desire now was anything other than hot, strong coffee. Rolling out of bed, Patrick slipped on a discarded pair of sleep pants and lumbered downstairs to, once again, satisfy his wife's passion. *Might as well make some of my famous scrambled eggs while I'm here*, Patrick decided.

Feeling at peace with the world, Patrick flipped on the radio and sang along with the Foo Fighters' *Congregation*, the best song in years, in his opinion. He smiled to himself as he realised that Molly would call that song garbage and then try to convince him that *Unchained Melody,* by The Righteous Brothers, was far better. *Funny how we can be so compatible in some things,* thought Patrick, remembering his sated and still naked wife, *and so far apart on others.* He laughed to himself as he recalled just how much he loved those differences.

Breakfast tray in hand, Patrick kissed his sleeping wife awake and proceeded to climb back into bed where they enjoyed their meal in blissful silence, happy enough just to be together on this stormy day. "Pat, I've been thinking about last night," Molly said as she finished the last of her coffee and reached for the carafe for a refill. Pat knew the pain she felt whenever she relived that terrible time in her life that took her first husband and her sister from her, especially the fact that she never got to visit with her beloved sister before she died.

Pat put his arms around her and gently kissed her. "I know this is so hard on you, baby, and now with the confusion around the picture and June's note, I'm sure it's even worse. I just wish there was something I could do to lessen your grief."

June turned around in his arms, so she was facing him. Looking directly at Patrick with those enormous dark green eyes he loved so much, June surprised him by saying, "Actually, I think there is something that might help me to reconcile this sorrow, once and for all."

Patrick, who would gladly walk across a bed of nails for his wife immediately said, "Just tell me what you are thinking about Molly, you know I'll do my darnedest to make it happen."

Molly was silent for a moment and when Patrick saw that she was biting on her bottom lip he knew she was having second thoughts about telling him what was on her mind. *"Please* baby," Patrick pleaded as he took her hands, "it will be better for both of us if we talk about it."

Molly took a deep breath, looked into Patrick's eyes one more time for moral support before she began. "Pat", she blurted out before she had a chance to change her mind again. "I know we have been talking about our anniversary trip to Hawaii for nearly two years and I really do want to make that trip again with you but…" Molly paused again to gulp in another deep breath and some courage "but, would you consider going to Dongtan instead?"

"OK, wasn't expecting that," Patrick said as he absorbed what his wife had just told him. He took a moment to collect his thoughts before answering.

Molly, assuming his hesitation meant that he had no intention of entertaining such a crazy notion, quickly continued, "Never mind Pat. It was a bad idea. Of course we'll go to Hawaii as we had planned. I'm sorry I even brought it up."

"Whoa, lady!" Patrick cautioned, moving toward Molly and taking her face in his hands. "You're going to dislocate your tongue with all this speed talking."

Molly relaxed a little when she realized Patrick wasn't angry with her. "Now let's take a breath and start again" Patrick suggested. "Dongtan is a bit of a departure from a trip to the Hawaiian Islands… and I hear the beaches aren't quite as nice. So I'm really going to need you to fill me in on the missing pieces."

Once Molly started talking, the floodgate sprang open and words poured out of her. Patrick sat close to his wife, never letting go of her hand. The only time he spoke was to encourage Molly to continue with her story.

During the next hour Patrick listened as his wife described the pain and guilt she had carried with her for over twenty years. Molly had often mentioned in passing that June and Mark Connor did not have a close relationship, a situation Patrick knew was difficult for Molly. What he was not aware of was the deep impact their unresolved estrangement continued to have on his wife.

The stories he was hearing today tore at Patrick's heart. He wondered how Molly had managed to keep this hurt bottled up for so long and he cursed himself for not recognising that his wife was in such pain.

Over their years together, Molly had implied to Patrick that she blamed Mark for driving a wedge between her and her sister. She also admitted there were times when she hated him for the way he acted around June. But today Patrick was hearing Molly admit that she felt like a failure as a sister and as a wife for not being able to resolve the matter.

She went on to tell Patrick that when the family had gathered for June and Sam's wedding, it seemed like things had improved somewhat between Mark and June. Happy to have some semblance of harmony restored, Molly didn't broach the subject with either of them. She loved them both and yet it always felt as though she was walking on eggshells whenever her husband and sister were together. However, it was June's wedding day and Molly had vowed to make sure it was perfect in every way.

All these years later, it was still difficult to believe that in the mere blink of an eye those two vibrant, young lives ended. And with their death any opportunity for explanations or reconciliation also died.

Of course Molly mourned the loss of her husband. It pained her profoundly to know that he would never see the wonderful child they created. But the cause of Molly's greatest sorrow was, and continued to be, not having had a chance to say goodbye to her sister. Molly loved June unconditionally and it was clear to Patrick from all of the family stories he heard that the feelings between the sisters were mutual. Although she didn't talk about June so much, as the years slipped by, there were times when Patrick noticed a sad and distant look in his wife's green eyes and he knew without asking that she was thinking about her sister.

In fact, Molly had that look right now and Patrick knew he couldn't stand to see her hurt this way for another second. "Molly, I do want to take you to Dongtan. If there is something there that will bring you peace of mind, let's not waste any more time. We'll book our flights as soon as you are ready. But please baby, promise you'll let me be there for you."

In that instant, Molly's eyes changed from a look of sorrow to one of pure love and gratitude. "Thank you, Pat," she said, very moved. This was her last comment before she lay back down on their bed where, emotionally exhausted, she fell asleep.

Leaving only long enough to make another pot of coffee, Patrick returned to their bed, where he sat with his laptop and watched his wife sleep. He thought as he watched her in repose that she already looked more relaxed. Maybe it was just wishful thinking on his part, but either way, he was happy to see her sleep so soundly.

Patrick used the time while Molly slept to begin some research on flights to China. He also checked into accommodations in Shanghai and Dongtan. He was not surprised to discover that there were plenty of both, which was great because he wanted to let Molly be the one who decided where they should stay. Not wanting to lose whatever momentum they had gained during Molly's disclosure, Patrick suspected that she would be more likely to proceed if at least some of the travel plans were already in place. However, he decided he would wait and see how Molly was feeling after she awoke before he shared the information.

A slight movement of blankets told Patrick that Molly was rousing. Closing the computer, he lay on their bed beside her. One sleepy eye opened and then another and the first thing Molly was aware of was Patrick's gentle touch on her arm and his soft kisses covering her face. "Welcome back sleepy-head" Patrick teased as Molly continued to slowly wake up.

"How long was I out?" Molly asked, surprised to see that it was already beginning to get dark out.

"No longer than you needed to be," Patrick answered as she snuggled deeper into her husband's strong arms.

They remained locked in their loving embrace until the first signs of evening's darkness filled the room. No words were spoken between them and none were needed. But when the sounds of two grumbling stomachs overtook the scraping noise of the snow ploughs that were busily reopening the roads, Patrick suggested Molly get her pretty little ass out of bed and start thinking about what they should have for dinner.

A quick scan of the refrigerator and cupboards told them their best chance for sustenance was at the Cedar House, a local restaurant not far from their home where you could always get a delicious, home-cooked meal and a dessert that was well worth the calories.

With the decision made and no need to fuss over what to wear, they shared a quick shower, threw on jeans and a t-shirt, ski jackets and boots and within thirty minutes Patrick had shovelled out his driveway and was heading for the freshly ploughed North Sydney Highway.

Chapter 16

As always, the Cedar House did not disappoint. Molly chose her favourite, fish and chips while Patrick went straight for the daily special of fishcakes and baked beans. They split a piping hot bowl of lobster bisque just to tide them over until their meals arrived. A piece of chocolate cake with boiled icing and a cup of coffee finished the feast and the two departed the restaurant full and satisfied. "See you soon!" the staff called out as they were leaving. Molly and Patrick were regulars and they loved the long-time employees nearly as much as they loved the food.

As they drove home Molly asked Patrick if he would mind making one more stop before they called it a day. The Cedar House is located at the Seal Island Bridge near the base of Kelly's Mountain. Less than a kilometre away, a sharp right turn off the highway onto the New Campbellton Road leads to a quaint little village called Cape Dauphin where Patrick and Molly spent many sunny summer days with Cole and Ava when they were younger. Even now, on those rare occasions when both children were home during the summer months, one or the other was sure to suggest a visit to the 'cape', just for old time's sake.

As luck would have it, a single lane had been cleared on the road and Patrick carefully manoeuvred the car along the snowy path.

Located on the east coast of Cape Breton Island, Cape Dauphin divides St. Ann's Bay from the Great Bras d'Or channel. Although there is little else to see along the road, the cape itself boasts a profusion of caves and caverns, the most notable being The Fairy Hole. Etched into the side of a steep cliff that is relentlessly battered by the Atlantic Ocean, the entrance to the Fairy Hole is a wide cavern that quickly funnels down to a series of tiny crawl spaces.

Most children born on Cape Breton Island can recount at least one of the historical or mythical stories linked to The Fairy Hole. According to Mi'kmaq legend the cave was the home of Glooscap, a Mi'kmaq hero. The story goes that one day while out in his canoe, two women on shore taunted Glooscap. Angered by their provocation Glooscap broke his canoe into two pieces. These two pieces are said to be the Bird Islands, which can be seen if you look off to the right from the shore. His rage not quite complete Glooscap went on to turn the aberrant women who had insulted him into stone. Legend has it that the two stone pillars that now guard the cave represent the fossilised remains of Glooscap's two unfortunate tormentors.

But Molly did not bring Patrick to the cape to reminisce. In fact, dwelling on the past was the last thing she wanted to do tonight. Molly was finally ready to embrace her future, free of all the sorrow and regrets that had been her constant companions for far too long. She knew the dark seclusion of the New Campbellton Road along with the unrelenting sound of the pounding waves of the Atlantic Ocean was exactly the right setting to begin her restoration.

"Pat," Molly began, staring into her husband's eyes once he had parked their car. "I do want to go to Dongtan and not only will I let you help me through this… I really *need* you to be there with me. Patrick pulled Molly closer to him. He now knew with certainty that she would be receptive to looking at the itinerary he had begun working on. "Done and done," said Patrick. "Now let's get the hell out of here before Glooscap pays us a visit."

It was past 10 o'clock by the time Patrick and Molly got home, too late for any more discussion and far too late to even think about sharing his recently found travel information. Instead the two climbed the stairs to their bedroom and jumped in bed and were asleep before their head hit the pillows.

Molly was first to awaken the next morning. She lay still, not wanting to disturb Patrick who was sound asleep, at least that's what the thunderous snoring that emanated from his side of the bed suggested. She was happy to have a few uninterrupted minutes to think about the yesterday's events. As difficult as the day had been, she was truly happy with the way things were turning out. Perhaps finding June's letter and especially the picture of the mystery child was just the kick in the pants she needed to get her moving.

In a strange way Molly was already starting to feel better than she had in years, or, if not better, at least more in control. She still wasn't able to make the connection between June's letter and how it related to Mark. Happy to let go of that part of the mystery, Molly simply chalked it up to another fact in the long list of things she didn't know about her first husband.

Slipping quietly out of bed, Molly looked one more time at her sleeping husband before she made her way to the coffee pot, which was beckoning to her from the kitchen below. "God, I am one lucky woman," Molly whispered softly as she remembered how graciously Patrick took the news about yet another change in their anniversary trip, choosing instead to focus on Molly's needs. She knew she would never forget this act of selflessness, but now it was her turn to do something nice for her husband.

Patrick O'Neil was the opposite of a fussy eater. Molly had yet to hear him say no to any meal he was offered, and he seemed to enjoy each one to the fullest.

More than once Molly witnessed her trim, fit husband hoe into the wildest culinary concoctions she could imagine. No pepper was too hot, no cheese too strong, and, God help us, no haggis too horrible for Mark to chew up and swallow. But if he was forced to pick a favourite meal, Molly knew with certainty that it would be breakfast.

Closing their bedroom door, Molly descended the stairs and made her way to her kitchen. Oh how she loved this room, so bright and sunny, especially on a glorious morning such as this.

During a recent renovation, Molly had the contractors knock down the dining room wall, leaving her with a large eat-in kitchen.

In proposing this overhaul to Patrick she argued, "The last time I saw you eat at the dining room table was at the stag party you hosted for Cole. And if I'm not mistaken the meal was pizza and beer." Patrick groaned at the memory, vividly recalling the colossal hangover he and his son had sported the following morning. It was true that the dining room was the least functional space in the house, unless you counted the number of times its chairs were used as coat racks. Knowing he had been blessed with a wife who was an amazing cook and pastry chef, Patrick mused, *What a fool I would be to do anything that would detract from Molly wanting to spend lots of time in her kitchen.*

Molly moved around her new granite island, complete with its sunken bronze Spanish-style sink. She loved the look and feel of the smooth counter top, not to mention the fact that there was enough working space to prepare a meal for an army. As a special treat for both Molly and Patrick they'd included a customised wine refrigerator as part of the design. Clicking the remote for her ever-present iPad, the room instantly filled with the harmonies of the Canadian Tenors. Singing along with the Tenors to Leonard Cohen's *Hallelujah*, Molly began to prepare a breakfast feast.

Totally absorbed in her project, Molly let out a shriek when Patrick appeared behind her and wrapped his arms around his wife. "Jesus, Mary and Joseph, Pat!" Molly howled, "You scared me half to death. What the hell were you thinking sneaking up on me like that? I thought you were still asleep!"

"*Sneaking!*" Patrick shot back, "With all the singing and pot banging going on, who could sleep? And anyway, even if the noise didn't wake me, the delicious aromas wafting up the stairs certainly would have." With that said, Patrick turned Molly around in his arms and kissed her deeply. "Good morning gorgeous" he continued, "Did I mention lately how much fun it is to be married to you?"

"You are absolutely incorrigible" Molly replied, "but I love being married to you too." And with a smile on her face, Molly returned to making breakfast while Patrick poured them each a cup of coffee and sat on a stool at the island to watch the master at work.

Before long the two were seated at their new kitchen table enjoying chilled mimosas, creamy blueberry crepes and Molly's famous sausage and egg casserole. When the meal was over, Patrick handed Molly the draft itinerary he had put together the day before and invited her to take her coffee into the atrium, where he would join her once he cleaned up after breakfast. "I really do love you" Molly called over her shoulder as she left for the beautiful sunlit room, coffee and notebook in hand.

By the time Patrick finished his chores and joined Molly in the atrium she had not only read the material he gave her, she was already putting together a lengthy to-do list for the proposed trip. Looking up from her notes, her eyes glistening from the love and emotion she was feeling, she made a solemn promise to her husband. "I swear to you Pat, before our next anniversary we will have our trip to Hawaii. I don't know how to thank you enough for pulling this information together. The one thing you can be sure of though is when we do return to Kaua'i, you will have your wife back, whole and healthy."

"No thanks needed," Patrick answered promptly, "but I'll be holding you to that promise… Now let's get started."

Chapter 17

The very first item on Molly's to-do list was to alert the troops. "Let's begin with Cole," Pat suggested. "He'll be the easier of the two."

Cole had graduated from Law School in 2010 and had accepted a position with a well-established law firm in Halifax. They knew Cole would listen carefully to what they had to say and probably even offer some advice about travelling in a foreign country.

When their daughter-in-law Laurie answered the phone, Patrick could hear his son and granddaughter singing 'inky dinky spider' in the background. Kelly Ann's tiny giggles melted his heart and brought a tear of pride and joy to his eyes. After speaking with Laurie for a few moments, Cole came on the line. "Hey Dad, what's up? I never hear from you this early in the day. Is Mom OK?"

"Your mother is just fine," Patrick assured him. "In fact she's right here. I have you on speaker phone and we have something we want to talk to you about."

"Fire away," replied Cole. Having grown up with these two as parents, Cole felt prepared for anything they might throw at him. Patrick began by describing how Molly had found the letter and picture from June. He went on to tell his son that they were considering making a trip to China instead of their thrice-planned Hawaii vacation. Cole was well aware of how painful his aunt June's death was on his mom and it broke his heart to know that it still made her so sad.

"Whew, that's a lot of stuff going on," he said when his father finished the story. "Mom," had raised, "Do you think this trip will provide some closure for you?"

"Yes darling, I really think this is something I have to do," she answered.

"Then go for it Mom," Cole responded encouragingly. "When are you leaving and what can I do to help? Oh and one more thing, I'll be looking forward to a very cool gift from Dongtan." Expecting nothing less from their boy, Molly and Pat told Cole they would be in touch with him as soon as they completed making their plans. Everyone said their goodbyes and Laurie brought the baby to the phone to make kissy noises to her grandparents.

"One down and one to go," said Patrick. "Are you feeling brave enough to call Ava yet?"

"*God,* no!" exclaimed Molly. "I think I'll take a little break first and give her a call this evening. Besides, when have you ever known our daughter to be up before noon on a Saturday morning?"

Ava was also living in Halifax just a few blocks away from Cole. She had worked for nearly two years in a rural hospital in Cape Breton after completing her master's degree in nursing. Like the father she had never known, Ava was drawn toward helping people, especially those in the greatest need. When she learned that a mainland Nova Scotia University had established a degree in Global Health, she was quick to apply and was promptly accepted.

The programme was designed to provide nurse practitioners with training in the area of social and cultural determinants of community health and to encourage a broader understanding of their implications on preventing infectious disease. Ava would be completing her studies in June and she was already considering an offer to work in Tanzania. But for all her intelligence and compassion—and the Lord knows she had plenty of both, Ava still had the innate ability to turn into a drama queen at the drop of a hat.

So rather than making the second call right then, Molly and Patrick had another cup of coffee as they enjoyed the warmth of the winter sun shining through the windows of the atrium. "It's hard to believe how ass-freezing cold is it out there," Patrick proclaimed as he stretched his long body to capture as many of the sun's precious rays as he could. Molly knew it wouldn't be long before her husband was asleep in his sunny nest. She had seen this scenario play out many times in her marriage.

"Baby" she said before his eyes slammed shut, "why don't you have a little nap? I have an errand I have to run."

"Mmm" was all Molly heard before the soft snoring began, indicating her husband was down for the count.

It wasn't so much an errand that Molly was off to. In fact, she was on her way to have yet another discussion about the upcoming trip. Molly shivered as she scraped the ice from last night's frost off her windshield. *Patrick was right*, she thought as she got into the car, *it is damn cold this morning*.

With her iPad tunes for company, Molly drove out Highway Number 4. In no time at all she could feel the sun shining brilliantly through the windows of her car making her forget for a moment that it was still the dead of winter. The snow ploughs had done an excellent job of clearing away the mess from the previous storm, leaving the streets bare.

Signalling to make a left turn, Molly guided her car through the gates of the cemetery that housed the grave site of her parents. She regularly visited the resting place of her mother and father since they passed away, three and five years ago, respectively. Unlike June, who wanted her ashes spread all over the world, Molly's parents had left specific instructions about their final arrangements. After fifty years of marriage, they fully intended to spend the rest of eternity together. In fact, according to their joint will, whoever checked out first was perfectly willing to sit in their urn and wait for the remaining partner to expire, at which time they would be buried together in the same plot with one headstone. It was Molly's dad, or at least his ashes, which took up residence in the top drawer of the guest room where he waited two years for the love of his life to join him.

Bundled up in her winter coat, fur hat, scarf and mitts, Molly took one last sip of her now cold coffee and made her way down row 125 to her parents' grave. As she walked the short distance, Molly glanced ahead two rows to the left. "Good morning Mr. and

Mrs. Powers," she chimed as she passed the headstone of the couple who once lived around the corner from her parents. "Strange how these things work out," Molly mused to herself, "Dad never liked Mr. Powers in life. He must be royally pissed to be stuck with him as a neighbour again."

Continuing along the path, Molly quickly forgot about the nasty Mr. Powers as her eyes fixed on the snow-white marble stone that marked the place where her parents lay. Initially, she had despised the idea of any type of burial, but Pat reminded her it was what they had wanted. Cole and Ava agreed with their dad and added that it would be nice to have an actual place where they could come to visit with Nan and Pop. Of course they were correct, and Molly was happy she was able to visit make regular trips to the cemetery.

"Hey, you two," Molly called out as she approached the plot where their ashes were buried. Her eyes misted over as she ran her hand along the smooth marble stone wondering if the sensation of loss ever really left. "So, here's the deal" she announced in quiet but determined voice, "last night I found a letter from our June. It was really quite vague and mysterious. The strangest part was that she had attached a picture of a little girl whom I had never seen before. We were apparently going to talk about it when I visited her in Dongtan… but of course that never happened. In her letter June suggested that Mark could fill me in on some of the details, which also wasn't to be." Clearing her throat, she continued. "Mom, Dad, I'm just so tired of dealing with all of these gaps and missing pieces from my life. Pat and I are finally going to take that trip to Dongtan. I don't know if I'm going to find any answers there. I just know I have to try."

Her soliloquy complete, Molly stood for a while, taking in the peace and silence and then she bid her parents goodbye and returned to her car. Wishing she had left the engine running, Molly sat for a moment and enjoyed the instant gratification of heated seats while she waited for the windshield to clear. Obviously Molly knew that she didn't have to trek all the way out here to talk to her deceased parents. But somehow it made a difference when she stood on the ground where they lay. And besides, she always felt better for having made a connection with them.

By the time she arrived home, Patrick was awake and talking on the telephone. One look at his frazzled appearance told Molly that the caller was none other than Miss Ava. "Honey, your mom just walked in." Patrick looked relieved and thankful for the support as he switched to speakerphone.

"Mom, have you lost your mind?" Ava shrieked before Molly even had a chance to say hello.

"Well hello to you too sweetheart," Molly replied. "You will be happy to know that my mind is completely intact. Now slow down for a minute and tell me what has you so riled up."

Ava took a breath. "Mom," she began again, this time more slowly. "Dad said you cancelled your Hawaii trip *again*. He said you were heading off on a wild goose chase to China. As for the picture of the kid, for God sake, it was taken nearly twenty-five years ago, and nobody even knows who she is. You must know there isn't a snowball's chance in hell that you'll find her and even if you did, what would you say to her?"

Ava continued her rant for another few minutes, recounting the dangers of travelling so far away on their own with no real plan in place. When she finally came up for air. Patrick was quick to jump in. "Ava," he said in a firm and understanding voice, "we love that you are concerned for our safety and you're absolutely right about this being a big departure from the anniversary trip we had been talking about. But sweetie, please try to understand how important this is to your mother and to me. Finding Aunt June's letter so long after her death is probably the last chance, we'll ever have to answer the questions that have been haunting your mom for so many years. And even if the trip proves fruitless on that account, we will have had an exciting adventure in a part of the world that neither of us has visited before."

Ava was silent for a moment longer. When she did speak, it sounded like an entirely different person on the other end of the line… a much younger and less self-assured girl. Ava's previous bluster had turned into soft sobs.

"Daddy, you know how much I love you and Mom, and I only want you to be happy…" She paused again as if searching for the right words. "It's just that…well it's never been a secret in our family that aunt June was not a big fan of my birth father." She took another breath. "I know this will sound childish and probably even selfish but even though you are my dad," Ava choked out the last words through her tears, "Mark was my father and it sounds to me like the real reason for this trip is to find another reason to prove that aunt June was right about him."

Exhausted and emotionally drained, Ava stopped talking. Of the three people in the conversation, it was Molly who was first to find her voice. "Ava, my beautiful, brave girl, I can't even imagine how difficult it would be to only know the man who was your birth father through stories and pictures. But there is so much of Mark in you that you really have to look no farther than yourself to know the man he was. Your father was a gifted doctor and a kind and caring man. He dedicated his life to helping others. Yes, there were times that I wished he had chosen a different path, but that was only because I missed him so much and longed for us to be together as a family. Mark spent his life trying to make the world a better and safer place and he died doing what he had been born to do. Sweetheart, the happiest day in your father's life was the day I told him I was pregnant with you. He told everyone he met that he was going to be a father and I know his greatest regret would be never having had the chance to know and love you as Daddy and I do. You are a strong and beautiful young woman and I couldn't be prouder of you than I am right now for having the strength to tell us how you are feeling. Ava, this trip we are planning is not to discredit your father. It is an opportunity for me to find peace and bring closure to the two greatest losses of my life."

Unable to continue, Molly unashamedly let her daughter and her husband hear the pain and sorrow she had kept bottled up inside for far too long. Patrick wrapped his arms around Molly as he spoke to his wife and daughter. "Ava, please try to understand that this is something your mother needs to do, and I want to be there for her. And by the way, it's because of your father that I have you. Honey, I'm the luckiest man on earth because of Mark Connor and I promise you I'll never forget that."

This time the ensuing silence was broken by the sounds of tearful laughter. "Oh my God" Ava choked out. "What a pathetic bunch of cry-babies we are. I love you guys and of course I think you should make the trip. It will be an awesome experience. And just for the record, it's Cole and I who are the luckiest people in the world to have you as our parents. I'll give him a call tomorrow to let him know that I'm totally on board with this and I'll be sure to tell him what a jerk I was tonight... not that he'll be surprised." The family said their goodbyes agreeing to keep in touch as Molly and Patrick finalised their plans.

"Want a drink?" Patrick asked as he hung up the phone.

"Hell yes!" Molly replied, practically sprinting toward the wet bar.

Chapter 18

The next morning dawned sunny, bright and extremely cold. Molly awoke early and rather than giving Patrick a little nudge to let him know she was conscious, she took the time to rethink the events of the previous day.

Snuggling deeper into the fluffy goose down duvet that covered their bed, Molly reflected on how sincerely blessed she was to have this family of hers. It was true that they didn't become a family in the traditional manner and yes, they certainly endured some tough times as each struggled to find their place in this newly blended clan. But by hook or by crook they managed to bond together as a strong and loving unit, resilient enough to withstand any obstacle the world saw fit to throw at them. And while Molly waited for Patrick to wake up, she silently prayed that they would be able to deal with this next adventure with the same fortitude as they did with all those that came before.

As if he had read her mind, Patrick's eyes popped open and he smiled at his wife and said, "Good morning my love. Are you ready to plan a trip to the Far East?"

"I've been ready for twenty years" Molly replied. "Let's do it."

It had become tradition in the Connor-Halloran household that Patrick and Molly's bedroom served as the legislative chamber for the most important discussions of their marriage, and today's topic most definitely met the criteria. "Breakfast" they said in unison and within minutes the kitchen was in full production.

Patrick, notably the best bacon fryer of the two, was draped in his greasy 'Kiss the Cook' apron and before long the aroma of thick Canadian back bacon filled the air. Molly, on French toast duty, was adding cinnamon and nutmeg to the orange juice and egg mixture that soon would provide a bath for thick slices of French bread.

While the main courses cooked, Patrick brewed an extra-large pot of coffee while Molly cut up fresh fruit… clearly the only healthy food choice in the meal. Molly arranged the food on two plates and Patrick did a quick clean-up. "What a team we are" Molly said over her shoulder as Patrick followed her up the stairs to their bedroom. "I hope things go as well in the boardroom," she continued as she motioned toward the breakfast trays that stood by each side of the bed.

For the next twenty minutes the only sound that emerged from the room was the clatter of forks and knives striking plates mixed with the occasional, "Hmm that's good," which emanated from both diners, with equal regularity.

"Ready to begin?" Patrick asked as he moved the breakfast dishes aside and topped up both coffee cups.

"I'm already there," replied Molly as she produced a pencil and notebook.

"I guess a list is as good a place as any to begin." Patrick smiled at Molly sitting up in the bed with a nest of pillows behind her and glasses perched precariously on the end of her nose. His wife was the consummate list maker. "I think that's a great way to start." Patrick climbed back into bed and meeting was officially called to order.

The effective teamwork continued as they had hoped and in what seemed like only a few minutes they had produced both a to-do list as well as a go-forward strategy. Patrick expanded on the information he had found online, and Molly came up with a few more questions about travel and accommodations that Patrick agreed to look into.

Molly, for her part, was going to begin by contacting Sam Friedman and tell him what they were planning. Sam had stayed in contact with his wife's family over the years. Even though it was initially hard for Molly to talk to Sam without June chattering away in the background of her mind, she was so thankful that he continued to make the overture to stay connected. They only talked a few times a year now and Molly initiated as many calls as Sam. It was always nice to hear from him and it made her so happy to know that June's projects were thriving.

Molly hated that Sam had never remarried. When Molly broached the subject with him a number of years ago, Sam simply replied that in his heart, he was still very much married to her sister. Molly understood completely and never brought the topic up again.

They continued to plan and talk for another hour until both agreed it was time to stop making lists and start dealing with some of the tasks they had already identified. They had not yet set a definite date for the trip. That would have put undue pressure on both of them and really there was no point.

Before declaring the meeting adjourned, Patrick announced that he had one more thing on his mind. One look at her husband and she knew full well what he was thinking about. Happily, she felt exactly the same way. Turning to face each other, Patrick wrapped his arms around Molly and brought his lips to hers. For the remainder of the morning they made slow, leisurely love, giving to and taking from each other in equal measures. Sated from their lovemaking and bursting with love for her husband, Molly lay in Patrick's arms until the ringing telephone reminded them it was time to return to reality and to restart their day.

The phone call was from Patrick's best friend Ryan. "Hey buddy. Hope I didn't get you out of bed," Ryan joked, not imagining that anyone would actually still be in bed at noon.

"Nope," Patrick lied, "I was just sitting here waiting for your call. What's up?"

"Got a little problem with my garage door opener. Could be frozen from the cold. But whatever it is, the friggin' door just opens randomly on its own. Any chance you could drop over and have a look at it?"

"Be right there" Patrick responded good-naturedly.

Looking down at his beautiful, still naked wife who was now lying on top of the sheets, stretching like a contented kitten, Patrick groaned as he pulled himself out of bed. "If you are trying to tempt me to get back in there, you're doing all the right things," he told Molly as she ran her fingers up and down his back. Giving her a quick kiss, he grudgingly got dressed and put together some tools to deal with Ryan's possessed garage door.

"You're a good man," Molly called after him.

"I'm a damn fool" Patrick yelled back, laughing, as he stepped out the door into the freezing cold and made his way to his friend's house, three doors down the street.

Molly took her time getting out of bed and after a steaming hot shower she was ready to start her day, which she realised with a sense of true contentment, was already half over. She thought about calling Sam but remembering the eleven-hour time difference she knew it would be midnight there and much too late to call. She decided to try him around 8 o'clock that evening. Sam would be up by seven in the morning and she could talk to him before he left for work.

Determined not to waste what was left of the day Molly took a deep breath, opened the door leading to the basement where she had pledged not to leave that level of her home until the infamous Christmas boxes were put away. After all, with the trip to China becoming a reality, who knew if or when the she'd get around to it again?

One quick look at the floor told her that the mess hadn't diminished over time. Pausing only to pull her unruly auburn hair back into a ponytail and turn on her music, Molly put on her game face and prepared to attack the chaos. She chose a selection of Motown music for today's job, hoping the upbeat rhythm would keep her moving.

The first song to play was *My Guy*, by Mary Wells. "Well that's appropriate," Molly muttered. "If anyone can get me going and keep me moving it's definitely my guy!" Still basking in the glow of their early morning escapade, Molly hoisted the first box to its proper shelf with a satisfied grin. A dozen songs later, Christmas 2014 was done and done.

As her anthem to a job well done Molly, accompanied Marvin

Gaye in a rousing rendition of, *Ain't no Mountain High Enough.* Picking up the earlier discarded broken badminton racket, which she now used as a microphone, Molly decided to keep forging ahead with the clean-up project. Who knew what else she might find?

By the time Patrick arrived home from helping his friend, Molly had filled five large garbage bags with all manner of junk and refuse. "Wow!" exclaimed Patrick when he found his wife standing next to the fruits of her labour. "Is that what our basement floor looks like? I don't know what inspired you, but I'm sure glad you went with it." Molly's smile and soft blush told her husband exactly what her motivation had been, and it made him so happy to know that Molly still wanted him the way he wanted her.

"Come on my love," Patrick offered. "Let's get cleaned up and I'll take you out to dinner. I think we both did enough for one day."

Chapter 19

Another of the many things Patrick loved about living in a small city is that dinner reservations are rarely required. Even on weekends when it is busier than usual, most establishments would try to fit you in. As it happened, a few new restaurants had opened in Sydney and Glace Bay recently and Patrick and Molly decided to try one. They selected a little café and wine bar that was getting some great reviews. By the time they finished appetizers and wine they agreed Talo's was going to live up to its reputation.

While waiting for their entrée to arrive, Patrick filled Molly in on the mystery of the self-opening garage door at Ryan's house. "Well you know what he's like, Mol," Patrick said as he rolled his eyes. Molly smiled and nodded. Ryan and Pat met when he began dating Molly. Given that Molly and Marie were best friends since childhood, the two men slipped easily into a close friendship… one where they quickly learned to push each other's buttons.

Patrick told Molly that by the time he arrived, Ryan was on the phone vehemently registering a complaint with a Sears representative, where he bought the unit. While Ryan was busy yelling at the unfortunate sales person who answered his call, Pat walked across the street to his other neighbours, the Roses, who had also installed a new Sears garage door opener. When Patrick asked Mrs. Rose if she had been having any problems with her door, she replied that she did notice that her garage door was opened on two occasions when she was she and her husband were sure they had closed it.

Asking to borrow the Roses' remote control, Patrick immediately went back to Ryan's and took possession of his as well. Patrick stood on the edge of the road between the two homes and pressed the button on one unit. Both doors opened in unison. As a double check, he tried the button on the other opener, which caused the two doors to close, confirming his suspicions. Apparently the sending units on both machines had been programmed with the same code. Patrick removed the back from the Rose's opener, changed one number in the pre-set code and the problem was solved.

Molly who was already laughing as Patrick recounted the story, nearly chocked on her wine when he told her what happened next. "When I walked back in, Ryan was still on the phone chewing out the poor bugger from Sears. So, I took the phone from him and to the clerk telling him that my friend had a little too much to drink and I thanked him for being so patient. I told Ryan there was absolutely nothing wrong with his door opener and got him to try it a few times, so he could see that it was working OK."

"Oh my God Pat, did you eventually tell him what was wrong with it," Molly asked, laughing.

"Hell no," replied her husband. "It's way more fun to keep him guessing. And besides, he deserves it for dragging me away from my bed after my day got off to such a magnificent start." Molly shook her head and smilingly declared, "You two will never grow up."

The amusing tale was quickly forgotten as the waiter made his way to their table with two plates full of food that smelt wonderful. Molly had ordered the maple mushroom chicken and Patrick was having beef tips in red wine gravy. Both meals were served with a medley of fresh veggies and basket of mouth-watering homemade bread. The two ate their meals in near silence, speaking only to comment on how delicious everything was or to offer each other a taste from their respective plates. When the meal was finished, Molly and Patrick decided to bypass dessert and instead enjoyed one of the gourmet coffees, which were fast becoming a specialty of the restaurant.

Over coffee Molly told Patrick that she was going to call Sam once they got home. Before leaving the restaurant, they discussed a few options for dates for their trip. They agreed it was important to go at a time that would be convenient for Sam. They also wanted to make sure that they didn't put any pressure on him to solve the mystery of June's letter. They just hoped that he would be available and willing to show them around the city June had loved so much.

Patrick paid the bill and they both took a moment to tell the owners how much they enjoyed their meal. Too many small businesses in Cape Breton have been forced to close because of the economy and a declining population. They sincerely hoped Talo's would survive and prosper. For their part Molly and Patrick promised to tell all of their friends what a great experience they had. They said goodbye to the staff and reluctantly made their way out into the cold January night, where snow was now softly falling.

The drive home took them past the Sydney airport. Molly looked at the sign as they drove by and was immediately overcome with a feeling of trepidation and excitement. "Pat," she said nodding toward the airport road, "We're really going to do this China thing?"

"Yep" was his only response.

They arrived back at their house at half past seven. Patrick put the car in the garage and told Molly he would be in as soon as he cleared the snow off the front steps. Using the time to get her thoughts together, Molly made a quick note outlining the points she wanted to cover during her conversation with Sam. She was still feeling somewhat apprehensive about discussing the rationale for the trip with Sam, so Molly was glad she had her list to refer to.

Hearing Patrick banging the snow off his boots at the door, Molly rechecked the country code for China and placed her call. Sam answered on the first ring, "Hey, how's my favourite sister-in-law?"

"Oh Sam," Molly responded. "It's always so nice to hear your voice. Pat is here too so I'm going to put you on speaker phone."

Sam had taken to Patrick the first time they spoke. It was obvious to Sam how much Patrick loved Molly and that made him a good guy in Sam's book. The two fell into their usual easy banter as they caught up on the news and ribbed each other about the recent performance of their respective hockey teams. Molly enjoyed listening to two of her favourite men talking this way. As always, she wished June was there to be part of the conversation. Whatever misgivings June harboured about Mark, Molly knew she would have loved Patrick.

When the banter subsided, Molly reminded Patrick that Sam was probably on his way to work and they should get to the reason for their call. "Please tell me you are finally coming for a visit," Sam intoned before Molly had a chance to begin.

"Well, that's cutting right to the chase." Molly answered. "That is exactly why we are calling."

During the next ten minutes, Patrick and Molly told Sam about finding June's letter and the picture that was attached. Sam listened attentively not saying a word until the two had finished their story. "OK" said Sam when they had relayed all the information they had. "I didn't know about the picture, but June told me about the letter when we were on the plane to China after our wedding. Molly, I know it was her intention to discuss what she knew with you when you came to Dongtan." Sam's voice drifted off for a moment. Molly knew he was remembering why that trip never happened. "Mol," he began again when he found his voice. " I really thought that you would have found that letter a long time ago. I guess I just assumed that you chose not to say anything to me about it after June died."

Molly told Sam that she found the letter and picture quite by chance only a few weeks ago. "Then listen to me guys," Sam said determinedly. "I can think of a hundred reasons why you should come to Dongtan. And this is just one more. Please finish making your plans and let me know when to expect you. There is no bad time to come. I am already looking forward to your visit." Molly thanked Sam and promised to call him soon with their travel arrangements.

Hanging up the phone Patrick looked at his wife and responded again to the comment she had made during the drive home from the restaurant. "Yep, we really are going to do this."

Chapter 20

Sleep eluded Patrick and Molly that night. They were both understandably excited about their upcoming adventure and it was difficult to settle their minds. No sooner would one begin to nod off that the other would come up with a question or a comment about the trip and the two would be wide awake again.

It was nearly 10 o'clock before they awoke the next morning and they did so with a start. Both normally early risers, Molly was the first to stir. One bleary-eyed glance at the clock on her bed table and she was giving her sleeping husband a shove. Reluctantly dragging himself to consciousness, Patrick propped himself up on one elbow and checked the clock himself. "So much for getting an early start to our day," he commented as he lowered himself back to a horizontal position and enjoyed feel of the late morning winter sun shining through their window. "I think this is my favourite part of retirement," he continued. "This and never knowing or caring what day of the week it is." But one more not so gentle shove from Molly told him that his leisurely morning had abruptly ended.

Although they were both tired from the night before, their late-night discussions proved to be fruitful. In fact, somewhere between midnight and one they had managed to select a date for the trip. As a result of many conversations with June and Sam over the years, they were aware of the weather in South-East China during the different seasons. And although they weren't looking for or expecting Hawaii weather, Patrick remembered Sam talking about how cold and wet January and February could be. At the end of a cold Cape Breton winter, more bad weather was something they absolutely wanted to avoid. Summer in Dongtan, on the other hand, was very hot and besides, they didn't want to postpone the trip any longer than necessary.

The compromise was mid-March. By then the daytime temperatures would be in the low twenties and the weather not quite so rainy. This timing also worked out well because it gave Molly a full five weeks to prepare. They still weren't certain how long they would be staying, and Molly wanted to spend time with both of their children and of course little Kelly Ann, before they left. She was at that stage where they changed every day. Molly didn't want to miss any of it.

"Well, now that the date is selected," said Molly as she prepared breakfast, "I guess the next step is to book our tickets." Patrick agreed and said he would take care of that. He told Molly he had some errands to run in town and could easily drop by the travel agency while he was out. Molly happily concurred saying she had a thousand things to do while he was gone.

It was nearly noon by the time they finished breakfast, showered and dressed for the day. Before he left, Patrick asked Molly if she wanted him to have some copies made of the child's picture that June had attached to her letter. His thinking was that it would be helpful to leave a copy of the picture with anyone who might be able to help discover her identity. "That's a wonderful idea," Molly replied as she ran upstairs to get retrieve the photo.

June's letter and the picture were in the bottom drawer of Molly's jewellery chest, where she often stored important documents. Taking the yellowed photo over to their bed, Molly sat down and, once again, stared into the eyes of the little girl. "Who are you and what is your connection to my family?" Molly had repeated this same mantra a dozen times since she made the discovery. Even though Patrick thought he recognised something the first time he saw the photo, there was nothing overtly familiar to Molly about this child. At least nothing that she dared to let herself imagine.

Molly put the photo in an envelope and gave it to Patrick. "Have a good day Pat," she called out to him as he tucked the envelope inside a folder he was carrying and left to do his errands. Molly promised herself she was not going to dwell on the mystery child today. She reasoned there would be lots of time for that when they got to China. Waving goodbye to her husband, Molly went into her office to begin the trip list. Now that the date was set, she was really looking forward to getting started.

Patrick's first stop was Tim Horton's, the local coffee shop. Although there was a Tim's on darn near every corner in the city, he drove a few kilometres out of his way to go to his favourite location. Patrick parked his truck in the lot, opting not to take advantage of the drive through. He always ran into someone he knew at Tim's and besides that, he actually believed you got a better cup of coffee if you were standing in front of the lady who was preparing it for you.

As he picked his steps carefully across the still icy parking lot, Patrick's attention was drawn to the table nearest the window where three of his neighbours, including Ryan, were waving at him. "Hey Pat," one of the men called out when he entered the shop, "Grab a coffee and join us." Patrick knew he had a lot to do that day, so he ordered his coffee to go. That way he could have a quick visit with the guys and then get on with his day.

Pat took his coffee black, unlike the double-double that Ryan drank. Why anyone would put that much cream and sugar in a cup of coffee was beyond his comprehension. "You might as well have a cup of warm sweet milk as drink that crap," Patrick was fond of telling his buddy. Then he would boast, "This is the way *real* men take their coffee," which always started a spirited exchange of words between the two friends.

Coffee in hand Patrick joined the table and conversation that was already well underway. Today's topic was the state of the streets and sidewalks after the most recent ice and snow. "I don't know why the hell we pay taxes," one of the men was saying as Patrick sat down. "I nearly broke my neck climbing over the snow bank in front of the post office today. And when I came out, one of our city's finest was getting ready to put a ticket on my car for not feeding the parking meter. Well, you can be sure I told him what kind of chance there was of me paying that ticket!"

"Good for you Bill," cheered the other three men who readily agreed that people should not be ticketed when the city hadn't even bothered to clear a footpath to the parking meters. Then in turn, each man at the table recounted a story about icy sidewalks, snow banks so high you couldn't see oncoming traffic and a myriad other tales of winter on the island. Bill brought the conversation to an end by grumbling to whomever was listening, "Why the hell do we even stay here?"

"Well, there is a simple solution for that problem," Ryan reminded the group. "We're all retired now. We should be heading for points south right after Christmas and not coming back until the snow is gone." Patrick could see where this conversation was headed. He also knew that not one of those present, himself included, would leave Cape Breton for more than a month at a time. As such, he decided this was a good time to take his leave.

"Molly has me running errands today," he announced as he got up and put his jacket on. He took what remained of his coffee with him, said goodbye to his friends and headed for the door.

As he was walking away Ryan called out, "Thanks again buddy, for fixing my garage door."

"No problem, my friend," replied Patrick as he thought, *Add one more thank you to my bank account.*

From the coffee shop, Patrick continued on to Wal-Mart where, after a bit of struggle, he managed to make several copies of the photograph. Realising this was clearly not his forte, he asked the assistant if she could help make an enlargement of one of the copies, thinking perhaps he or Molly would notice something in a larger picture that wasn't visible in the original. The assistant informed him that the photographer would be in later in the day and said that he was much more adept at working with older pictures. She took the picture from Patrick and told him he could pick up the enlargement the next day. Patrick paid for the copies and thanked the young lady for her help.

His next stop was one he hadn't mentioned to Molly. Patrick had an acquaintance who worked for a technology company specialising in genealogy. In a telephone conversation the day before, Patrick explained to his friend he was trying to identify a child from a photograph. Paul Blanchard had started his company four years earlier upon retiring from the crime division of the RCMP after thirty years of service. If anyone could trace this photo using modern technology, Patrick felt certain Paul was the guy.

His office was on the second floor of an insurance company in downtown Sydney. Walking up the single flight of stairs in the rather dated building, Patrick knocked on the door bearing Paul's name. Not getting a reply he knocked a little harder causing the door, which was already ajar, to swing open. Once inside, Patrick let his eyes scan the darkened room until he found Paul totally engrossed in looking at one of the ten computer screens whose blue light cast a soft, almost surreal, shadow across the room. "Oh my God!" Patrick said out loud. "You really are a total geek!" Laughing and rising from his chair to shake Patrick's hand, Paul replied, "Well that's a fine way to greet someone when you're looking for a favour."

The two shook hands and Paul invited Patrick to have a seat. "Easier said than done," declared Patrick as he moved mountains of books, manuals and empty coffee cups from any flat surface that might serve as a place to sit.

"Let's see what you have," Paul began.

He studied the photograph under a light and then again using what Patrick assumed to be a magnifying device. "Any idea where or when the photo was taken?" Paul asked. Shaking his head, Patrick explained that given the timing of June's last visit to Cape Breton and the fact that the child in the picture looked to be about two or three years old, he guessed it would have to have been taken somewhere in the range of twenty to twenty-five years ago. Patrick also informed Paul that June and her husband had been living in Dongtan at that time and although the child did look to be of Asian descent, he really couldn't be sure.

"OK, not much to work with," Paul said. "Leave it with me and I'll run some tests." Patrick thanked Paul telling him they would be leaving in just over a month and anything he could come up with would be far better than what they currently had. "Don't despair buddy. With the advances in technology and genealogical research, who knows what we might find. Although, it's probably a good idea not to mention anything to Molly just yet. No need to get her hopes up unnecessarily." Patrick agreed wholeheartedly, thanking Paul again and telling him he would keep in touch.

His last stop was the travel agency. Patrick had made an appointment earlier that morning, so they would have a chance to get some information ready for him before he arrived. As he hoped, the appointment was brief. There weren't a lot of options for flights traveling from Halifax, Nova Scotia to Shanghai, China and Patrick was pleased that the agent had found one with only two stops. He had his choice of days when the flight was available, and Patrick selected March 15th. The Ides of March seemed like as good a day as any to embark on this adventure. He asked the travel agent to email the details for him and Molly to review and within twenty minutes of arriving, Patrick was back in his car and heading for home.

Chapter 21

It was clear that Molly was also having a busy and productive morning, as was evidenced by the wonderful aroma that greeted Patrick as he opened the front door of their home. A consummate multi-tasker, Molly always cooked or baked when she was in full-bore planning mode. She adamantly believed that working with her hands allowed her to clear her mind. Having been the beneficiary of numerous work-related cooking jags over the years, Patrick had no reason to doubt her logic. The smell of cinnamon and nutmeg told Patrick that today was a baking day. Taking off his coat and boots he hurried to the kitchen to kiss his wife and volunteer to be her taste tester.

"What an amazing sight," Patrick proclaimed as he entered the kitchen. "A stunning woman and a counter full of delectable goodies. What more could a man ask for?"

Molly looked up from the mountain of paperwork that had somehow accumulated around her. "Cut the bullshit and put the kettle on and I just might let you try one of these sticky buns," she teased.

Over tea and pastry they filled each other in on their day's progress. Patrick had already printed the itinerary the travel agent emailed to him and Molly studied it while she sipped her tea. She was pleased that this piece of the planning went so well, and she was absolutely delighted with the flights Patrick was able to get. Meanwhile, Patrick reviewed the lists that Molly was working on and said a silent prayer of thanks that his wife was so well organised.

"So, we fly out of Halifax four weeks from Saturday and I want to spend at least three days with the kids before we leave." Molly told Patrick. "That means we have less than a month before we head out and plenty to do in the interim." "Then we better get at it," Patrick agreed, grabbing another sticky bun before he left the kitchen.

That evening they spent two hours quietly sitting on the sofa, eyes fixed on their respective laptops. One of the first items on the to-do list was to search for accommodations in Shanghai and Dongtan. Patrick agreed to take on that task.

Because they weren't certain how long they would be staying, Molly suggested he look at lodging options that offered long- and short-term rentals. For her part, Molly was compiling a list of hospitals, orphanages and other agencies that might be able to help uncover the identity of the mystery child. For most of the evening, the only conversation between them was when they exchanged computers so one could see what the other had found.

Satisfied that they were making some headway Patrick proposed they shut off the computers for the night and take a break. "We can't do it all in one day," Patrick said, knowing full well that his wife would keep working all night if he didn't stop her. "Let's get out of the house for a while," he suggested. "My neck is stiff from bending over the computer and my head is spinning from looking at hotels." Molly, who had just found another small hospital about an hour outside of Dongtan promised she would stop working as soon as she recorded the information from her latest find.

Patrick knew from experience that it would be more than a few minutes before Molly was ready to call it a night. Standing up to stretch his legs, he decided to give his friend Ryan a call to see what he was up to.

Ryan's wife Marie answered the phone with a cheerful hello, assuming it was Molly calling for a chat. "Hi Pat," she said. "I'm surprised you're not glued to the television watching the game. Ryan certainly is."

"Oh crap, I forgot all about it!" Patrick bellowed into the phone. "I hope you're up for company, because Mol and I are on our way." Laughing, Marie replied, "The back door is unlocked. See you soon.

And tell Molly to bring over some of whatever she was baking today. I could smell it as I walked by your house this morning."

A Montreal Canadian hockey fan since birth, Patrick never missed a game. And tonight they were playing Toronto, Ryan's favourite team. *Damn,* thought Patrick. *I must have been totally involved in our trip planning to have missed an opportunity to torment Ryan about his last-place Leafs.*

Grabbing his jacket and Molly's from the closet and picking up what was left of the pan of sticky buns, he rushed into the living room, where Molly was still engrossed in her research. "Work's over baby. I forgot about the hockey game and Marie just invited us over for a visit."

Recognising what could only be described as anguish on her husband's face over missing the first period of the game, Molly closed the computer, put on her coat and boots and barely caught up with Patrick as he sprinted for the front door.

Ryan and Marie were their best friends and she was happy to spend a few hours catching up on the news while the boys fought over hockey. No sooner had they crossed the threshold of their friend's house than Patrick had his boots off, gave an air kiss to Marie as he flew by her and bounded onto the sofa to join Ryan. "You're missing a great game, buddy," Ryan said, winding him up. The Habs are down one already. Want a beer?"

Marie brought in two cold beers and a bag of chips and set them down on the coffee table. "Thanks dear," the men said in unison, not even looking up from the television to see whose wife had delivered the treats. "Don't forget to save us some dessert!" one of them yelled as she left them to their game.

In the kitchen Molly had already put the kettle on for tea and set out the buns on a plate from her friend's cupboard. She smiled as she thought about how comfortable she always felt roaming around Marie's house. Each was as familiar with the other's kitchen as she was with her own. While Molly waited for Marie to return, she decided now would be a good time to tell her about June's letter and the trip they were planning.

"They should be good until intermission," Marie reported as she took her seat at the kitchen table. "Did I ever tell you how much I love being waited on in my own home?"

"Only about a thousand times," Molly replied. "Kick back kid, you deserve a break and anyway I have something I want to talk to you about."

Marie listened attentively as Molly told her about the photo, the letter from June and the upcoming trip. The entire time she talked, Molly fussed around the kitchen busying herself with unnecessary jobs. Twice, Molly picked up Marie's teacup and wiped under it with a cloth.

Marie never uttered a syllable throughout the one-way conversation, but instead watched her friend closely while nodding encouragingly so that she would continue talking. When she was done, Molly looked at Marie for the first time and what she saw on her best friend's face surprised her.

"You knew about this, didn't you?" Molly asked in disbelief. "Why didn't you stop me? And more importantly, why the hell didn't you say something earlier?" Not sure if she was feeling anger or embarrassment, Molly plopped down on a chair and covered her face with her hands. Rising from her own seat, Marie bent down and gently took both of Molly's hands in her own.

"Yes I knew some of the story. Ava called me last night after you spoke with her. She's just worried about you, dear. She completely understands what you are doing and why, but she's scared. As for why I didn't mention it sooner, well as I said, I only spoke to Ava last night and besides, this wasn't my story to tell… it's yours."

While Molly listened to her friend's explanation, she began to sip her cooling tea and pick at the gooey sweet that Marie had slid in front of her. Seeing that she was somewhat placated, Marie returned to her seat and continued. " I haven't told Ryan any of this yet and I wasn't sure if Pat mentioned it to him. But I can tell you one thing. I think it's a wonderful idea. The trip alone would be fantastic. Not to mention how nice it will be to have a visit with

111

Sam." Molly looked a lot more relaxed now, so Marie went on. "And, if you do happen to find out some details about the picture and the information June was planning to share with you, well that will be a bonus."

"Thank you" said Molly getting up to pour two fresh cups of tea. "This is why you are my best friend."

"As you are mine" Marie answered, smiling tenderly at her. "Now you bring me one more of those sinfully delicious buns and I'll promise you undying loyalty 'till death do us part."

"That better not be the last one," roared Ryan and he and Patrick emerged from the family room. "It takes a lot of energy to coach all of those players from the sofa. Isn't that right buddy?" Yeah, yeah," Patrick replied good-naturedly. "I'm not sure how those two teams got as far as they did without Coach Ryan's assistance. And I really can't even imagine how they survive the untelevised games when you aren't there to scream obscenities at the TV."

Ryan picked up the wet dishtowel Molly had been using, snapped his friend smartly in the ass with it and declared. "Make yourself useful putz, scoop up the rest of those buns while I grab two more cold ones." 'You got it," Patrick replied, reaching for the plate, "and hurry up you old codger, the third period just started."

"Remind me again why we love them," Marie asked as the boys hurried back to their lair. "I don't know about you my friend, Molly replied. "But for me it's all about the sex. I mean did you *see* that ass?"

"Oh dear God!" moaned Marie rolling her eyes. "You're as bad as they are."

With the drama of upcoming trip out of the way the four friends enjoyed the rest of their evening together. The girls even joined their husbands in the family room for the end of the game. Upon their arrival, the Montreal Canadians were down two to one with twelve minutes left in the game. Ryan was in his glory relentlessly ribbing his friend about what a pathetic bunch of losers the Habs had thrown together this year.

With three minutes to play, the Canadians tied the game, which added an entirely different dynamic to the atmosphere in the family room. And then five minutes into overtime the pathetic bunch of losers scored the winning goal, at which point Patrick jumped from his seat and performed his victory dance while Ryan spewed obscenities and vowed, he would be rooting for the Black Hawks next year.

Chapter 22

Back at home Molly and Patrick were ready to crash. Exhausted from the day's events, they were both happy to ignore the mess they had left in the kitchen and the family room, promising to clean it up tomorrow. They shared a quick shower and were tucked in bed with the lights out within half an hour of leaving their friends' house.

As they lay in their bed, Patrick reached for Molly's hand. This intimate gesture was something they shared every night since their wedding day. Neither remembered how the practice began but both avowed it was a habit they never wanted to break.

Although their children had been gone for quite a few years now, Molly still marvelled at how quiet the house was as night. No more banging of utensils from late-night lunches. No more ringing telephones and no more giggles emanating from downstairs as Cole, Ava or sometimes both entertained friends. Molly loved the solitude and privacy she and Patrick shared as a result of their now empty nest, but God, she missed the sounds of a house full of family sometimes. And tonight, as she lay in the stillness of the night, was one of those times.

She must have inadvertently sighed out loud because Patrick immediately raised himself up on one elbow and asked her if everything was OK. "Just missing the kids," she replied. But now that she knew her husband was also awake, she decided to enjoy the unexpected company. As she sat up in the bed, Patrick did the same, knowing that once Molly was up there was not much chance he would be going to sleep anytime soon.

"Pat," Molly asked, her voice a bit hesitant. "Did you happen to mention anything about June's letter or the trip to Ryan?"

"Yeah, I did" he replied.

"What did you tell him and what did he say?"

Patrick thought for a moment because he really didn't remember too much about the conversation. "Well, I told him you found a picture of a little girl attached to a long-lost letter from your sister and that we were going to China to see if we could find out who the child was and why June wanted you to have the picture." As for Ryan's response, Patrick didn't have to wrack his brain over that piece of the conversation. Ryan replied as he always did. "Cool."

"That's it... he just said *cool*?" Molly asked, dumbfounded. "He didn't ask anything about the picture or comment on finding June's letter after so long?"

"Nope. Not another word." Now, Molly understood Ryan was one of the least meddlesome people she had ever encountered. Lord knows how many times she heard Marie say that every house on the street could disappear and unless someone brought it up first, Ryan would never mention it. But given the gist of this news and knowing the Hallorans and O'Neil's as he did Molly was truly shocked that he wasn't more inquisitive.

Pretty sure that there was more to the story, Patrick continued, "I'm guessing that you and Marie talked about this as well. What did she think about our news?"

Molly repeated the conversation she and Marie had, including the details about Ava's call to Marie. "Well, Ryan sure didn't know that part. Or at least he didn't mention it." Patrick was a little surprised that their daughter had shared the information with Marie. He knew the two were very close, but Ava had seemed just fine at the end of the conversation he and Molly had with her earlier in the week. Now he was beginning to wonder if she really *did* have more concerns about the upcoming trip than she had raised. One look at Molly and he knew she was worried too.

"OK. Here's what I think we should to do." Patrick suggested, taking control of the conversation before Molly let herself become overly upset. "We'll be in Halifax for a few days before we leave for China. That gives us nearly a month to gather whatever

115

information we can. Hopefully, by the time we visit the kids, we'll have a few more pieces of the puzzle solved, and we'll have some concrete information to share with them. In the meantime, let's just keep in regular contact with Ava, as we always do."

Molly relaxed immediately knowing Patrick was right. She and Ava were always open with each other. From the time she was a very young child, Ava told Molly everything. Thinking back on those days, Molly remembered times when she wished Ava would have chosen not to be quite so forthcoming with every detail of her life, especially during her teenage years. But for now, the memories of those sometimes shocking disclosures offered Molly a gentle reminder that if there was anything really bothering Ava, she would tell her mother. Molly reasoned that Ava's call to Marie probably provided her with an opportunity to vent to someone else she loved and trusted. And as Patrick pointed out, they would be spending time with their daughter soon. Until then, Molly would be careful to listen to what Ava was saying and even what she was not saying. Molly vowed to make sure she always left the door wide open for Ava to speak her mind.

Satisfied with the plan, she settled back into the bed and turned to face Patrick, who was already more than halfway asleep. "Thank you, my level-headed husband. You know this is why I keep you around, right?" Molly joked.

"Really?" Patrick shot back, no longer sleepy. "I thought it was because of *this*."

In an instant, Patrick gathered Molly into his arms and pulled her close to him. Kissing her gently at first and then more deeply as she quickly matched his passion, Patrick threw back the duvet that covered them, removed her nighty and stared at his wife. She had always been a beautiful woman, everyone said so and Patrick was proud to be her husband. But this Molly, the one that lay naked and aroused before him, was someone he didn't have to share with anyone and he was thankful for this gift every day.

As familiar with her body as he was with his own, Patrick tenderly and expertly touched and caressed Molly until she pleaded with him to become a part of her. With excruciating control, Patrick lowered himself on top of, and then finally into, his wife. The fiery heat he felt as he entered her told him Molly wanted him as much as he did her and he felt humbled by the vulnerability they showed each other.

After so many years together, it amazed Patrick that he still felt this way every time they made love. He was also astounded by the fact that once they came together, neither could wait more than a few minutes before they succumbed to the release they both so urgently desired. Molly cried out his name as an orgasm rocked her body. Patrick forced himself to wait until her shudders subsided before he exploded inside her, breathing her name like a sacred oath.

Lying in each other's arms they fell asleep soundly and together as the moonlight peeked through the curtains and poured over them. When they awoke the next morning Molly and Patrick laughed as they untangled legs and arms until they discovered where one person ended and the other began. "I love you," they said in the same breath and with a peaceful mind and a satisfied body, they began a new day.

Chapter 23

Patrick cleaned up the kitchen mess left over from the night before as Molly prepared breakfast. Over hot porridge and blueberries they shared, smiles, small talk and sections of the morning newspaper. Most of the news in the local paper covered stories and events they heard on television or through social media days before, but they read them anyway.

They always began by scanning the obituaries. Patrick said he did it to confirm he wasn't among the dearly departed, to which Molly would chastise him for being so callous. Molly, who also read the obituaries, did so because there was rarely a day when she didn't know someone attached to at least one of the names listed. It was yet another reality of living on Cape Breton Island... everyone knew each other's family.

The entire process of reading and discussing the newspaper generally took no more than half an hour, and that included looking at what was on sale at the two main grocery stores. And then for comedy relief, at least once a week you could count on a misprint where a wedding announcement would be included with the obituaries or vice versa. This always provided a good laugh for the readership... well perhaps not for the bride and groom or the family of the deceased. Oh yes, Molly and Patrick did love small-city living.

With breakfast and the news covered, Patrick headed out to run a few errands and meet Ryan and the guys for coffee. Molly, who was still carrying a few post-holiday pounds, planned to hit the gym and then take care of some business in town. Marie mentioned joining her at the gym when they were together last night, but Molly would believe that when she saw it. When it came to exercise of any description, Marie was the consummate poster child for the old adage that the 'road to hell is paved with good intentions. Molly had a few things to do before she left and if she heard from Marie, well that would be great. But she sure wasn't going to hold her breath waiting.

Molly showered, dressed and got her gym bag ready. She decided to leave a quick message for Ava, even though Molly knew she would be in class by now. Ava would get the message when she finished for the day and, hopefully, call home that evening. It was while she was leaving a message on her daughter's phone that she heard the front door open and Marie calling out, "Come on old girl. Get your ass in gear. I thought we were heading to the gym." Shocked to hear her friend downstairs, much less ready to go, Molly made a mental note to herself to buy a lottery ticket while she was out, because clearly today was a day for unprecedented events.

Grabbing her gym bag, Molly ran down the stairs to join her friend before Marie had a chance to change her mind and back out. Molly kissed her on the cheek as she slipped into her winter coat and boots. "Let's do this," she said as they headed down the driveway to Marie's waiting car.

Molly snuggled into the heated seats in her friend's BMW. For as long as they knew each other, Marie had the coolest ride in the neighbourhood. As far as clothes, jewellery or travel went she couldn't care less. According to Marie, she wore jeans and leggings most of her life and anyway, she had plenty of clothes stuffed in the back of her closet to get her through the odd times when she had to dress up. Of course, Ryan supported her totally. Not only did he love the idea from the cost savings perspective, he also hated to get dressed up. Having a wife who felt the same way meant he never had to listen to her complain about his sparse and sometimes tattered wardrobe.

But when it came to automobiles, there was no room for discussion: Marie loved her cars. She took as much time as was needed to find her dream ride and once found, she bought it. Her last car was a Lexus and the two before that were Corvettes. All were current-year luxury models and the Vets were both ragtop convertibles. Though clearly not the most practical choice for Cape Breton, Marie didn't care. When winter arrived, the car was put on blocks in the garage and Marie borrowed whatever Ryan happened to be driving at the time.

This morning Molly welcomed the warm, leather seats and excellent sound system as they made their way downtown to the gym. "So..." she asked, once they were underway. "What's this all about? You're never up this early in the morning and you sure as hell never joined me at the gym before." Marie gave her friend a sideways glance that suggested Molly might want to consider changing the topic.

"What is it?" Molly continued, now concerned that perhaps something was wrong. Marie took a deep breath, looked straight ahead and answered. "Last night, after you and Pat left our house, my husband mentioned how terrific you looked...not once, but three times. Don't get me wrong girlfriend, you *do* look amazing, but I want to be sure that big, lovable lug of a man sees me that way too!"

Marie was a strikingly beautiful woman and it was clear to anyone with two eyes that Ryan was besotted with her. However, it was a known fact that her friend avoided exercise like the plague. So if Ryan's comment prompted her to get a little more active, Molly wasn't going to argue. "Honey, you are a knockout and everyone knows Ryan stills gapes like a teenager every time he looks at you. Think of it this way. A few weeks at the gym and you'll look even hotter cruising around in your new Beemer."

With that, Marie stepped on the gas, cranked up the music and set off with a vengeance to sign up for her first ever fitness programme.

For anyone who grew up in Cape Breton, it comes as no surprise that a) it is difficult if not impossible to keep a secret in a small community and b) news on the island travels faster by word of mouth than by any know form of social media.

Molly and Marie had scarcely set foot inside the locker room when one of the neighbourhood busy bodies approached them. "Wow Marie. Is that really you in a gymnasium? I can hardly believe my eyes!" Before Marie could launch into an equally rude reply, the woman continued. "And you, miss *world traveller*," she addressed Molly. "Word is that you and that handsome husband of yours are heading off to the Far East. I can't even imagine why anyone would go there when the world is in such a mess. I was telling my George last night that it would take a team of wild horses to drag me off Cape Breton Island."

Winking at each other Molly and Marie replied in unison, "I'm sure that could be arranged dear." Continuing to their lockers, giggling like two school children, Marie announced. "I'm already glad I came Mol. I've wanted to get my tongue on that meddlesome old bitch since the day she moved into the neighbourhood."

For Marie's first session, Molly suggested they try a gentle flow yoga class. She knew and liked Paula, the instructor, and felt that this was the best way to ensure that her friend didn't bolt from the class never to return again. Although Molly was used to a higher intensity class, she was happy to give herself a break and enjoy the slower-paced session. Her week had been so mentally draining that the thought of listening to Paula's calming voice as she loosened her tense muscles and joints would be just what the doctor ordered. And Paula didn't disappoint.

Throughout the session, Molly kept an eye on Marie and was pleased to see that she was trying all of the poses. Whenever she would seem confused or unbalanced, Paula would show up at her mat and soothingly talk her through the process. During the last ten minutes when they were in *Savasana*, the resting pose, Molly was pretty sure she could hear snoring coming from the direction of Marie's mat.

As the session ended and Paula read the closing mantra, Molly felt a sense of peace and tranquillity that she hadn't experienced in quite some time. It was true that she still had some apprehension about making the trip, but she knew for sure that it was the right thing for her to do. She repeated the last line of the mantra, "Let peace fill our heart, our world and our universe" to herself one more time, then rolling to her side she winked at her friend and gave her the international sign for 'let's go get a coffee'.

Despite the economic downturn that had plagued Cape Breton in recent years, the one anomaly Molly found difficult to comprehend was why Tim Horton's coffee shops survived. There were three locations within walking distance of the fitness centre, all of which boasted a thriving business.

Marie added another Looney to the parking meter as they walked past the BMW on their way to Tim's. She grumbled, as she always did about why the municipality charged people to park downtown when they were crying for more business. Yep, Marie would spend $80,000 on a car without batting an eye but the thought of paying one dollar to park it would send her into a tailspin.

Inside the shop, they ordered their coffee and an oatcake to go along with it before selecting a booth near the back of the store. As it turned out, there timing was perfect. Their arrival was right in between the on-the-way-to-work and the mid-morning coffee break crowds, so the store was relatively quiet.

For a few moments the friends sat in silence sipping coffee and letting the hot, sweet liquid warm their insides. Molly and Marie had always been the kind of friends that did not have to constantly talk in order to communicate. But today was different. Molly had something on her mind that she wanted to discuss with her friend. As if reading her thoughts, Marie waved her hand in front of Molly's face as she said, "Earth to Molly. Come on, I know there is something bothering you, so you might as well spit it out."

Taking one more gulp of her coffee Molly told Marie that she was worried about Ava's reaction to their upcoming trip. And that fact that she had called Marie to discuss it made Molly even more concerned that Ava was holding something back.

"Oh honey," Marie said taking Molly's hand in her own. "I'm so sorry. I didn't think Ava's calling me would upset you. Yes, she mentioned the trip, but she didn't seem overly concerned by it, other than the obvious apprehension about you and Pat being so far away on your own. Really Mol," Marie continued, "If I thought for a second that anything was amiss with Ava, I would tell you immediately."

"Of course you would," Molly responded, already more relaxed. "I didn't mean to suggest otherwise. I guess the thought of opening up this Pandora's box has me more rattled that I realised."

Marie was probably the person in Molly's life who knew more about her marriage to Mark that anyone else, including her family. Friends since high school, the two shared their most intimate secrets with each other. Although Molly had a wonderfully open relationship with her mother, there were times when she chose not to disclose certain information about Mark for fear of needlessly upsetting either of her parents. During these times Marie served as her sounding board, always knowing just what to say, or not say, depending on the circumstances.

Marie often admitted that despite the girls' close friendship she never really felt like she got to know Mark at a personal level. His tragic death occurred before she married Ryan, so they really didn't hang out as couples. And of course, Mark was away so often. On those rare occasions when he did come home, he understandably wanted Molly all to himself.

If asked to describe Mark to someone who had never met him, Marie would probably use words like, handsome, intelligent, secretive and aloof. In retrospect Marie realised it was strange that she never considered this before. *Was it possible that Mark did have something to hide? Is that what her friend was referring to when she mentioned opening Pandora's box? Poor Molly, no wonder she was feeling frazzled.*

Her head swimming with these thoughts, Marie didn't even notice when two people joined their table. "Earth to Marie," Molly intoned, mimicking the same phrase Marie had used on her earlier. "Sorry," Marie said offering a half smile, "I must have zoned out after my exhausting day at the gym."

"Spoken like a true rookie," one of the women teased as she and her friend took the two remaining seats in their booth.

The four women chatted amicably until Marie remembered the parking meter, which was most likely out of time. "Shit! Got to run. Nice talking to you," Marie announced as she grabbed her coat and Molly's arm before racing down the road in enough time to watch a police officer ticketing her precious Beemer. "Shit," she repeated. "I knew this exercise thing was going to be more trouble than it was worth!"

Chapter 24

Marie extracted the newly written ticket from her frozen windshield and gave it to Molly to file in the glove compartment along with the unpaid speeding ticket she was issued the week before. She was glad now that she hadn't mentioned the first one to Ryan, rationalising that she might as well deal with both transgressions in the same conversation. Ryan would only laugh and tell her to get her butt down to city hall and pay her fines, knowing how much she hated giving the municipality one red cent.

Starting the car, she listened with pleasure as the finely tuned engine purred to life. Within minutes the seats were once again warm, and the heater had cleared the frost that had already started to form on the windshield. Before putting the car in gear to pull away, she turned to face Molly.

"Listen honey. I know this trip is like a long overdue mission for you. I'm sure whatever you find out is going to be better than going through the rest of your life wondering and worrying. You are a strong and intelligent woman and Patrick will be there to support you every step of the way. Just promise me one thing." Taken off guard by Marie's speech, Molly asked what her friend wanted her to promise. "Promise me that you will not blame yourself, in any way shape or form for whatever it was that June wanted to tell you."

"I promise" Marie vowed, "and thank you for being such a wonderful friend."

While the girls were driving home, Patrick was arriving at a different Tim Horton's, located on the other side of town. He was a little later getting there than he expected and was happy to see that Ryan was still there waiting for him. "Hey buddy, sorry I'm late,"

Patrick apologised as he ordered an extra-large coffee. "Can I get something for you?" Ryan called back that he'd take anything that had icing on it, so Patrick chose a double chocolate doughnut with candy sprinkles for his friend.

An otherwise healthy-living person, Ryan had a sweet tooth the size of his expanding belly. He had spent his entire life eating whatever he pleased with no negative consequences, until one day not so long ago, when middle age snuck up and bit him in the ass, literally! Marie tried to encourage him to reduce his intake of sweets but between Molly's constant deliveries of baked goods and Ryan's regular trips to Tim's, it was an uphill battle.

"Thanks," said Ryan, biting into the doughnut and enjoying the sugary rush. "So, where did you get to this morning?" Patrick told his friend about dropping into Paul Blanchard's office earlier that week. As Ryan listened Patrick explained that he had given Paul a copy of the child's picture that was attached to June's letter and asked him to investigate. "

"Wow man, this really is a big deal, isn't it?" Not meaning to belittle the situation, but Ryan had assumed the mystery behind the kid's picture was just curiosity on Molly's part, not something that required a *private investigator*. "What did he find out?" Ryan inquired, now fully engaged in the story.

"Not as much as I hopped for," Patrick answered, with a definite note of disappointment in his voice.

According to Paul, in the absence of any other data the picture itself did not provide enough clues for conducting this type of search. The detective told Patrick that the most effective methods for photo identification today are through the use of facial recognition software. Given that the picture was quite old, and the subject of the photograph was very young, it would be highly unlikely that any viable match would be possible through this means.

"Well that sucks. Did he have any suggestions as to what your next step should be?" Ryan asked hopefully. Patrick recounted everything else Paul had told· him including that he would keep working toward identifying the type of photographic technique that had been used to create the picture. Apparently, it is also possible to narrow down the time period when the photograph was taken. "Paul thinks our best bet is to try to track down more information once we get to China… *if* that's even where the child is from. He has contacts all over Asia and while he's working on this end, he is going to put us in touch with people who can help us over there."

Ryan hated to hear his pal sounding so discouraged. He knew from Marie of the deep funk Molly slipped into after losing her husband and sister in such a short period. Ryan was delighted when Molly met and married Patrick. Not only did he bring a light back into Molly's life, he quickly became Ryan's best friend. Now he felt concerned that revisiting these sad memories would drive Molly back to that dark place where she lived for far too long.

"Buddy, you know I'm not an overly schmaltzy guy," Ryan said, already sounding uncomfortable with the conversation. "But there isn't anything I wouldn't do for you and Mol. Same goes for Marie. So if there is any way can help out, please ask us." Patrick nodded, not sure if he could trust his voice to speak. Both sat in silence finishing their drinks when Patrick announced they better get out of here before they got a loitering violation. Glad for the excuse to change the subject the two friends walked to their respective vehicles promising to get together to watch the hockey game Saturday night.

"My place this time," Patrick called out as he unlocked his car.

"You got it buddy," Ryan replied. "I'll bring the beer."

On his way home, Patrick stopped at Wal-Mart to pick up the photograph he was having enlarged. He thanked the technician, paid the cashier and slipped the envelope into a file folder without looking at it. He decided it would be better if he and Molly examined it together.

Over dinner that evening, Patrick told Molly about his visit to Paul Blanchard's office. Not certain what her reaction would be to this intervention, he was pleased when Molly agreed that it was a terrific idea. Patrick also told her about the copy of the photograph that had been professionally enlarged, explaining as Paul had to him, that the enhanced image might provide more clues to assist them in their investigation. Although they were going to examine the new material in greater detail later that evening, she really did want to have a quick peek at it now. Patrick reached for the file folder and handed her the envelope. This time, Molly's reaction to the picture was immediate and visceral.

Pushing aside her plate, Molly reached for her reading glasses, which were always close by. As much as she despised that fact that she needed them more often these days, she wanted to get a clearer look at the child's image. Patrick watched the expression on his wife's face as she studied the picture in silence for several minutes.

When she was finally ready to speak, she looked up at Patrick and uttered, "There *is* something familiar about her. I know you saw it as well Pat. I remember a flash of recognition in your eyes when you first looked at the picture. I didn't see anything at that time, so I didn't bother to bring it up. But now I can see it too.

It was clear that Molly was becoming more upset as she spoke. Patrick could hear a growing sense of urgency in her voice and for a moment he was sorry that he even told her about it. Reaching across the table to retrieve the picture, he returned it to the envelope and confirmed, "You're right, something did catch my eye when you showed it to me the first time, but it was fleeting. Mol, I looked at that the picture a dozen times since then and I'll be darned if I can put my finger on whatever it was, I thought I recognised. Listen honey, let's finish dinner and we'll look at it together," Patrick suggested.

Molly nodded her agreement, but her attention had already shifted to back to the picture. Picking up her fork, Molly moved food aimlessly around her plate, no longer interested in the meal she had prepared.

Patrick helped clean up after dinner and even managed to distract Molly with some stories from his visit with Ryan that morning. Molly laughed, as she always did whenever Patrick recounted the tales and adventures of these two best friends. She was glad that Patrick had a person like Ryan in his life and she knew the feelings were reciprocal. However, the second they were finished in the kitchen, Molly took the file folder and headed into the living room where she, once again, removed the picture.

Patrick left her alone with the photograph and her thoughts while he put on a pot of tea. As much as they both loved their coffee, if either of them had a cup of the wonderful black liquid after five o'clock, they would be up half the night.

By the time he joined Molly she was so absorbed in scrutinising the picture that she hadn't even hear him enter. She jumped when he placed a cup of tea on the table in front of her, nearly spilling it on the notebook by her side.

Although he would have preferred to enjoy his tea and dessert before beginning this task, he knew that Molly would not be able to rest until they put their heads together and tried to figured out the next piece of the puzzle. Grabbing a double chocolate brownie that Molly must have baked that afternoon, he put on his glasses and sat next to his wife on the sofa.

"OK," Molly began, "Let's start by taking another look at Mishi's picture."

"*Mishi*? Who the hell is Mishi?" Patrick asked almost afraid to hear the answer.

"Oh, I named her" Molly replied as if that should have been obvious. "I was tired of referring to her as the child in the picture. It just seemed so cold and impersonal. And anyway, Mishi means *lost* in Chinese and that's how I have come to think of her."

"OK, Mishi it is," Patrick concurred.

The notes that Molly had made prior to Patrick joining her turned out to be a list of facial attributes shared by members of her family and Mark's. Not knowing where to begin otherwise, she figured her own back yard was as good a place as any. Also, given that she and Patrick both recognised something familiar when they looked at Mishi's face, confirmed to Molly that her own family was probably the place to start the search. At the very least they might be able to eliminate a family connection, at which point they could redirect their focus elsewhere.

Patrick picked up the notebook and began to read. Molly's list started with her parents, her sister June, herself and Ava. The next grouping consisted of Mark Connor, his parents and the names of people Patrick did not know but assumed to be relatives of Mark. Although it had been quickly scribbled down in point form, Patrick was able to deduce the following:

Molly's father was pure Irish, all the way from his twinkling blue eyes and rusty red hair to his broad chest and muscular legs. Patrick remembered meeting Mr. Halloran for the first time. Even though Molly was already a grown woman, Patrick had the distinct impression that his father-in-law was willing and more than able to snap him in two if he ever harmed the man's precious baby girl.

Looking at Molly, it was plain to see that she was her father's daughter. Of course, Molly's hair was a beautiful shiny rich auburn and her eyes were more green than blue, but there was never a doubt that the two were related.

Similarly, Mrs. Halloran and June were like two peas in a pod. Not only in appearance but their mannerisms as well. Both were tall and slender. They shared the same fair skin and straight blond hair. Even the shape of their lips when they smiled was identical. Although Patrick never met June, he did have the pleasure of knowing Molly's mom. He distinctly remembered the first time he saw a picture of both women together. He actually had to look twice to ascertain who was who.

Moving on to her notes on Mark Connor. Molly had written by his name that he had honey blond hair and deep blue eyes. The first time Patrick saw a photograph of Mark, he knew who it was without asking. Mark was the male version of Ava. Mark's mother was a tiny woman with black hair and deep brown eyes. Molly mentioned she had been a ballet dancer in her younger years and always described her a delicate beauty. As for Mark's dad, well it was pretty clear that both Mark and Ava inherited their good looks from Mr. Connor Sr. Not that guys spend a lot of time checking out other guys' appearances, but even Patrick had to admit these two men were good-looking dudes. As for the rest of the names on the list, the characteristics were pretty much a repeat or combination of those already listed.

"Good job, Mol," Patrick announced when he finished reading her notes. "This was an excellent idea. It gives us a great place to start our search. And it will be a very useful piece of information to pass along to the investigators, if need be."

For the entire time Patrick was reading the list, Molly continued to examine the picture. Suddenly, she looked up and handed the photo to Patrick. "Pat, can we move on to something else? I really don't want to do this any longer. I don't even know what I'm looking for anymore." Molly sounded and looked exhausted. "It's just a picture of a little girl, probably of Asian descent who is likely twenty-five years old now, assuming she is still alive, and I have no real reason to believe she is related to me. The only people who may have any information about her are dead. Why am I even doing this to myself? And now I've involved you in it. Oh Patrick, I wish I could just let this go, but I can't."

As much as he hated to see Molly this way, Patrick was glad for the opportunity to finally have his say on the matter. "I want you to listen to me Molly," he said with firmness in his voice that she hadn't expected. When he knew he had her full attention, Patrick continued. "You are right, we don't know a damn thing about the child in this picture and yes, Mark and June are no longer here to tell us anything about her. But we *are* leaving for China in a couple of weeks and it seems to me that if there is any chance of learning more about the child's identity, it's going to happen while we are there. Look baby," Patrick went on, his voice now sounding loving and gentle, "between Sam and the investigators that Paul Blanchard is going to contact on our behalf, we have plenty of resources to help us solve the puzzle. In the meantime, can we just look forward to the adventure of this exciting journey we are embarking on? Oh, and finally, you are *not* dragging me into this. I wouldn't miss it for the world."

Molly felt better already. "Thank you, my love," Molly smiled, reaching for his hand. "We do have lots to look forward to." As she leaned over to kiss her husband, Molly wondered how the hell she got so lucky to find a man like Patrick.

Chapter 25

When Molly awoke the next morning, she felt like a new woman. Gone was the persistent headache and knot in her stomach that had been plaguing her since the day she discovered June's letter. The feeling of nervousness she carried around had also lessened, but most of all Molly was at peace because she knew with certainty that Patrick was in this with her for the long haul.

She jumped out of bed as soon as her eyes were opened. Giving her sleeping husband a soft kiss on the forehead, so as not to wake him, Molly headed straight for the kitchen, raring ready to start her day. "Get that coffee pot on, girl" she told herself, "You've got a trip to plan."

Her first task was to have another look at the file Patrick brought home with him yesterday. She found it on a table by the sofa where they had been sitting the night before. As she hoped, in addition to June's letter and the copies of Mishi's picture, the file also contained the results of Patrick's earlier research.

The first entry in the file was a list of hotels and inns in Shanghai and Dongtan. In typical Patrick fashion, the information was scribbled on the back of a Christmas card in her husband's hen-scratch handwriting. After a quick attempt at deciphering the script, Molly was pretty sure the list included hotel names, room rates and amenities. She also found a paper with travel dates and flight information.

Satisfied that their planning was off to a good start, Molly returned to the kitchen where the coffee pot sat waiting to be ravished by its caffeine-crazed owner. As she enjoyed her first cup, by far the best one of the day, Molly pulled out the list she had been working on and continued jotting things down as they popped into her head.

For starters she planned to call Ava and Cole and settle on a time that would be good to visit with them before she and Patrick left for China. It was so convenient having both children living in Halifax. In addition to getting to spend time with them together, they also got a chance to see their precious granddaughter, Kelly Ann. And as an added bonus, it was so much easier and cheaper to get a flight out of Halifax than it was to leave from Cape Breton Island. Plus they could leave their car at one of the children's houses.

Sam Friedman had already said he was available anytime they chose to come, so it was just a matter of letting him know the date they would be arriving. If she was successful in getting hold of Cole and Ava tonight, they should be able to start booking plane tickets by tomorrow. Molly knew there was still plenty to do but she was pleased with how this part of the plan was coming together.

No sooner had Molly closed the file and started to think about making breakfast than Patrick appeared in the kitchen. Clad in sleep pants and a well-worn sweatshirt Molly smiled at her dishevelled husband and said, "Good morning handsome... come here often?"

"As often as I possibly can," Patrick replied with a lewd and lascivious grin on his unshaven face. He wrapped his arms around Molly, kissing her on the neck and placing one hand over her breast while stealing her cup of coffee with the other. Before Molly could react to either action, he sauntered off to the front door to retrieve the morning paper.

"So, what can I do to help?" Patrick asked as he strolled back into the kitchen. Molly suggested the first thing he could do was to return her coffee or at the very least pour her a fresh cup.

Relieved to see his wife looking happy and so much more relaxed, Patrick not only poured her a cup of coffee; he offered to make breakfast while she browsed through the morning paper. "Well I sure won't say no to that," said Molly happily.

The rest of the day flew by so quickly that neither could believe it was nearly eight o'clock in the evening. It seemed like every day since they retired was like that. For two people who worked so hard in their respective careers, neither could imagine that their retirement days would be so full. Both had easily moved into this new phase of their life and it was obvious to anyone who saw them that they were enjoying every second of it.

Molly ordered a pizza for supper since there was no way she was going to be doing any cooking. While waiting for the delivery, they decided to give the kids a call. This time, they would start with Ava. Molly was a little concerned that she hadn't heard from her in a few days. It wasn't as if they spoke every day but after their last conversation Molly just wanted to be sure Ava really was all right with the trip.

As Patrick was dialling the number, he was interrupted by the sound of a baby crying loudly.

"What the hell is that?" he yelled, startled by the noise.

"FaceTime message!" they said at the same time, remembering that Cole had set a wailing baby as their FaceTime ringtone after Kelly Ann was born. Still not fully accustomed to that particular branch of technology, Patrick dropped the phone and grabbed his iPad, frantically pushing buttons, for fear of missing the call.

Breathing a sigh of relief as the green light flashed indicating that the call was connecting, Molly and Patrick huddled in front of the screen waiting anxiously to see Kelly Ann, and of course, her parents. One second latter, the screen was filled with a chocolate pudding covered face, blowing kisses through the computer.

"How is my beautiful little girl?" Molly cooed blowing kisses right back at the baby, which made her giggle.

"I'm just fine, thank you," replied a voice in the background that could be none other than Ava, who could now be seen peeking around the baby's head. Delighted to have reached the whole family together, Patrick asked them to squeeze in closer, so they could see everyone. Cole carried the computer to the kitchen table, where there was more room to move. Laurie took the chair next to Cole with Kelly Ann on her lap, while Ava pulled up a stool and placed it behind and between her brother and sister-in-law.

Once in position, everyone began to talk at once and no one could make out a word anyone was saying. A shrill whistle from Molly brought the conversation to an abrupt halt. "Slow down! We want to hear from everyone," Molly assured her family when she had their attention, "just not all at the same time." As everyone turned to look at each other, Kelly Ann decided to take charge of the situation. "I talk," she announced in her sweet baby voice.

"Well that's a wonderful idea sweetheart" Patrick replied, "What are you going to tell everyone?" Without missing a beat, the precocious two-year-old replied, "Kelly Ann go potty."

"And we're out of here!" chimed in Laurie as she scooped up her baby girl and tore off for the bathroom. Kelly Ann had quickly learned how the reward system for a successful trip to the potty worked and she utilised it to her best advantage. On a good day, she could get M and Ms, gummy bears and two books read to her if she played her cards right. Ava, who had witnessed her scam on a number of occasions, swore that the little munchkin could pee on command if she wanted a treat.

"Well, perhaps while we are waiting for her highness to return from the throne, your Mom and I can let you know where we are with planning our trip to China. As Patrick spoke, Molly watched Ava's face for any tell-tale expressions or signs of misgivings. She thought she noticed a slight flinch from her daughter when Pat mentioned the trip, but it was there and gone in a second. Staring directly into her daughter's eyes while Patrick went over the tentative agenda including the days they would like to spend in Halifax before they left, she observed that Ava showed no signs of stress or irritation. Molly relaxed a bit, convincing herself that she had become so worried about how Ava would take the news that she was most likely looking for something that wasn't even there.

Cole was next to speak, "Sounds like you got a lot done since the last time we talked. Listen guys, as far as my schedule goes, just let us know the date you will be arriving and how long you'll be staying. Laurie has your room ready and waiting. If it's through the week, I'll be working but I figured you'd want the extra time to spoil your granddaughter."

Ava chimed in by saying, "Same here. I'm looking forward to seeing you both. I have no classes on Friday, so I'm free from Friday through Sunday. If there is anything special you want to do while you're in town, let me know and I'll arrange it. Anyway, I was just on my way home when Cole decided to call you, so I'll say so long for now and see you soon."

Patrick and Molly watched as Ava yelled her farewells to Laurie and the baby who were still in the bathroom, deep in negotiation over how many gummy bears she should get for a pee and a poop. Hugging her brother and blowing a kiss to her parents, Ava grabbed her jacket off the coat rack and was out the door.

Before Molly had a chance to ask, Cole jumped in. "Mom, Dad, she's working through it. Whatever was bugging her about you going to China… she swears she's over it. We talked about it for two hours last week and she really seems to be OK. I promise I'll tell you if she gets weird about it again."

Right on cue Kelly Ann toddled back into the picture. "I pooped," she announced proudly, with gummy bear juice running down her chin. Fighting to hold back their laughter the besotted grandparents told Kelly Ann what a good girl she was. They thanked Cole and Laurie for opening their home to them and said goodbye to their family, promising to see them all very soon.

Chapter 26

With just over two weeks until they were scheduled to leave, the O'Neil household became a hotbed of activity. The day after talking with their children on FaceTime, Patrick called the travel agency and booked their flights. He decided the best course of action would be to purchase an open-ended ticket, so they didn't have to commit to a return date or pay the exorbitant fees associated with changing a ticket.

The plan was to drive to Halifax two weeks from Thursday and leave their car with Ava while they were away. Ava said she would take them to the airport for their six-a.m. flight Monday morning. That would give them all day Friday alone with Ava and they would still have plenty of time to spend with Cole, Laurie and of course Kelly Ann. Patrick and Molly always looked forward to being able to spend time with both of their children together. Since Cole got married and especially since the baby was born, it was a rare occasion that the whole family was in the same place at the same time. Work, school and life in general always seemed to get in the way.

Patrick was delighted that they were staying at Cole's because Ava's apartment was quite small. It was also so easy to spend time in their son and daughter-in-law's home. Laurie loved company and she always planned something special for her in-laws when they came for a visit. She and Cole had finished a charming suite of rooms in their basement where Patrick and Molly felt totally at home. Ava ate dinner at her brother's most nights anyway and Patrick planned to take everyone out for a special meal on their last night in Halifax. Molly secretly hoped that, at some point during the visit, she could convince Cole to take his wife on date, and leave the very willing grandparents to babysit.

She didn't even want to think about how difficult it would be to be away from her little angel for a whole month. Kelly Ann changed so much each time they saw her and they both hated to miss any of those special moments. Molly quickly brushed those unhappy thoughts from her mind, choosing to focus on having four wonderful days with her family followed by a very exciting adventure with her husband.

Patrick had no trouble confirming their trip. He had used the same travel agency numerous times in the past and always found them to be helpful and efficient. The woman he spoke with earlier had started a file based on their first conversation, so it was really just a matter of rechecking the availability of the flights they wanted and booking their tickets. By the time he returned to the kitchen where Molly was still working on her lists, he had a printed itinerary in his hand.

Molly reviewed the schedule and was thrilled with their flight times and the short layovers. It was going to be a long trip, no matter how you looked at it, but Patrick had done a terrific job of getting them the best possible flights. Excited to let the kids know when to expect them, Molly immediately sent an email to Cole, Ava and Sam.

Patrick left her with the information and returned to his office where he moved on to the next item on his list: booking accommodation. Molly said she would be available to help if Patrick needed her for anything, but she was glad he volunteered to do the job himself. He had great taste in selecting hotels and he knew exactly what she liked and, more importantly, what she didn't like.

While he was otherwise occupied, Molly grabbed her jacket and a copy of the itinerary and made her way over to Marie and Ryan's. She knew her friend was home and she wanted to pass along the latest information on their trip. *Hmm, better bring a few snicker doodles with me*, Molly decided, knowing Ryan would expect a sweet treat.

Marie smiled and waved from her living room window when she spotted Molly coming up the walk. "Come in from the cold my friend," Marie said, opening the door and quickly closing it behind Molly to keep the cold air outside. The friends hugged, and Marie offered to hold the snicker doodles while Molly took off her boots and jacket. By the time she made her way to the kitchen, Marie had the coffee pot on and the treats were on the table.

They talked about the weather and the children for a few minutes before either brought up the trip.

"No use trying to avoid the elephant in the room," Marie blurted out, her not-so-subtle way of telling her friend to give her the update they both knew was the reason for the visit.

"Why do I always act this way when I talk or even think about the trip? You would think I was setting out to do something *awful*," Molly lamented as she added cream to her coffee. "I mean, this should be the trip of a lifetime," she continued, "But instead, I feel so... *damn it* Marie, I don't even know *what* I feel!"

Marie swallowed the mouthful of snicker doodle that she had been enjoying since her friend began talking. "You feel so uncertain? Confused maybe? Molly dear, you received what basically amounts to a letter from the great beyond," Marie reminded her friend. "And to top it off there's a freaking picture of a small human being that may or may not have some connection to your life. Honey, if you *weren't* freaked out over this, I'd be worried about you."

"Of course, of course, you're right." Molly thanked her friend for putting all of this turmoil in perspective for her.

"OK then," Marie resumed her mini lecture. "Now tell me what you have planned and more importantly, tell me what Ryan and I can do to help."

Breathing a sigh of relief and a quick prayer of thanks for good friends, Molly gave Marie a copy of the itinerary Patrick received from their travel agent. Since they had become neighbours and friends, the two families always watched out for each other's property when one was away. Because they knew each other's home as well as they knew their own, there was very little to discuss in terms of what to check on. Ryan would do a walk through every other day and Marie would tend to the flowers. They would turn different lights on randomly. Not that there had ever been a problem with burglary in their quiet neighbourhood... but these days you just couldn't take anything for granted.

Marie admitted that she was a little concerned about the O'Neil's not having a confirmed return date. She understood why they were leaving it open, but she knew she was going to miss her friend while she was away. Knowing when she was coming home would, at least, give her a timeframe that she could count down to. Molly promised that she would let Marie and Ryan know when they would be returning as soon as she knew herself. She also vowed to keep in weekly contact with her friends; even more frequently if something came up.

Back in her own home, Molly peeked her head into the office/den when Patrick was diligently pouring over notes. "Hey babe," he said when he saw her standing in the doorway. "You were so quiet out there, I though you left." Molly told him she had been visiting with Marie and that she and Ryan had once again, generously, offered to take care of things at their house and property while they were away.

"Awesome" Patrick replied using his wife's visit as a good excuse to stand up and stretch. Molly went on to tell him that Marie had a medical appointment in Halifax during the time they were away, and she planned to visit Cole and Ava while she was there. "We are very lucky to have them as friends and neighbours."

Patrick agreed wholeheartedly. "Though sometimes I think it's your baking and Ryan's inability to fix anything on his own that keeps the friendship alive," he joked, knowing full well that the two couples were truly best friends.

For the rest of that week and halfway through the next, Molly and Patrick worked like a fine-tuned machine completing the numerous tasks that needed to be done before they left. With only four days to go, they miraculously found themselves in the same room at the same time without a checklist in their hand. "Could it be that we are actually ready?" Patrick asked cautiously, almost afraid that Molly would produce another note from her pocket that would have them running in circles again.

Molly answered by lifting two wine glasses from the cabinet and heading for the refrigerator where a bottle of their favourite Sauvignon Blanc was chilling for just such an occasion. "Hell yeah," said Patrick as he followed his wife into the kitchen, corkscrew in hand.

Molly fixed a snack consisting of smoked Nova Scotia salmon on thin slices of toasted baguette with cream cheese, dill and a few capers on the side. Brie cheese baked with cranberry and almonds finished off the nosh tray. In the meantime, Patrick gathered up the information he had been working on, poured two glasses of wine and met Molly in the family room where she had set up a table, lit a few candles and turned on some easy-listening music.

"God, but I love the way we still have these picnic dates," a name Patrick had given to the impromptu rendezvous they had been enjoying since they first met. Kicking off their shoes and laying back against the mountain of throw cushions that adorned the overstuffed leather sofa, they lay in each other's arms for several minutes before Patrick handed Molly her glass and made a brief toast to commemorate a job well done.

No one spoke for the next half hour. The only sounds besides the soft melodies of Norah Jones album were the contented sighs of a tired but satisfied couple enjoying good food, fine wine and each other's company.

As Patrick scraped together the last dregs of the delicious lunch, Molly refilled their wine glasses and asked Patrick to update her on the research he had been working on all week. "Sure," Patrick replied as he accepted the glass Molly offered him. "I'll start with our accommodations." Opening the folder that had grown quite substantially since the last time Molly looked at it, Patrick removed a file containing several pages of information about lodging options in both Shanghai and Dongtan.

They decided earlier that they would enjoy a few days alone in Shanghai before venturing north to Dongtan. Patrick suggested she begin by looking at the hotels he selected from that area. Taking the file, Molly was more than a little impressed with what her husband had put together. In addition to location and pricing, Patrick included several pictures and a list of amenities for each accommodation.

As Molly flipped through the papers, she told Patrick they all looked wonderful and said she would be happy to stay at any one of them. She continued to feel that way until she came to the information for the last hotel on the list. Patrick watched with pleasure as her eyes widened. "Mother of God, Pat! This is amazing. Can we really stay here?" Without even looking, he knew she was reading about the Fairmont Peace Hotel. He knew because he felt exactly the same way when he first saw it.

Built more than eighty years ago, the Shanghai landmark had undergone a complete renovation and, as they could see from the pictures, the remodelled hotel featured a perfect blend of the original art deco-inspired furnishings with ultra-modern amenities.

Even the location looked to be ideal. Never having been there before, neither wanted to do too much exploring on their own, at least not until they were more familiar with their surroundings. According to the information Patrick provided, the Fairmont Peace Hotel was situated directly on Shanghai's famous waterside promenade, called the Bund. By simply walking out the door of the hotel, they could experience both the old and the new Shanghai, where distinctive modern structures stood adjacent to centuries-old colonial buildings. And if what the brochure said was true, it would be a terrific place to people watch.

"Can we even afford to stay here?" Molly asked, almost afraid that the answer would be no.

"I think we can manage a few days without breaking the budget." Patrick replied. At this point, he was prepared to mortgage the house if it meant taking Molly there. This was the first time she showed any real enthusiasm about the trip and he'd be darned of he was going to take that away from her.

"This is going to be spectacular," Molly exclaimed, jumping up from the sofa, spinning in a circle and laughing like a child. Becoming serious for a moment, she looked into her husband's eyes and said. "Whatever else we wind up having to deal with on this journey, I want you know how much I'm going to enjoy seeing this part of the world with you." Patrick hoped that there would be plenty of wonderful experiences for both of them, but even more than that, he wished that the trip would also provide some closure for Molly.

Too tired and excited to continue selecting accommodations, Patrick took the file from Molly and put it back in the folder. "Tomorrow is another day, my love," he said gently. "Let's put this aside for the night and go to bed." As she fell asleep, Molly dreamed that she waltzing in the arms of her husband on the iconic sprung-wooden dance floor of the Fairmont Peace Hotel.

Chapter 27

Patrick had scheduled a final meeting with Paul Blanchard for Monday morning. He invited Molly to accompany him to Paul's office, rather than hearing the information second-hand. That is, assuming there was anything new to report.

As they climbed the wooden stairs to the second floor, Molly agreed that Paul's office could have been taken directly from a Mickey Spillane novel. Like Patrick, she'd known Paul since he was an RCMP officer. She had the utmost respect for him then and she was confident that he would try his best to help them with the picture puzzle they were trying to piece together.

Upon entering the office, the two men shook hands and Paul greeted Molly with a big bear hug, while informing her, "If you ever get tired of that oaf of a husband of yours Mol, you know I'm only a phone call away." All three laughed knowing that Paul was completely in love with his wife...and besides, she was also retired RCMP and could easily put Paul on his ass, if she chose to.

After quickly catching up on each other's news, Paul got down to business. "Like I told Pat earlier, a single picture with no name or other identifying information is pretty hard to trace. However, I was able to do some further enhancements to the copy you left with me and the result was pretty good." Paul explained that the additional enlargement gave them a clearer picture of the background, which might help to pinpoint a location. He added that the child's facial features were also much sharper in the new photograph allowing him to detect birthmarks and other skin characteristics that could be useful in helping to identify the child.

Although it was clear that the child in the picture was of Asian descent, Paul asked Molly if she was certain that the little girl was from China. Molly explained that she wasn't really certain of anything. She described finding the picture and letter from her sister more than a quarter of a century after it had been written. Her eyes clouded over with sadness as she told Paul "My sister June was living in Dongtan at the time and my first husband, Mark, was in the Sudan. However, he often lectured in China because both countries were suffering from similar environmental challenges." Lowering her head Molly continued, her voice barely audible, "In her letter, June told me to ask Mark about the picture. Within months of writing the letter, both my sister and Mark were dead."

Knowing how difficult it was for Molly to talk about that time in her life, Patrick jumped into the conversation. "Mark worked for Doctors Without Borders and he travelled extensively. June's husband Sam is still in Dongtan and besides the picture, that's all we have to go on."

By the time Patrick finished speaking, Molly had regained her composure. "Look Paul," she said to their old friend. "We really hope that we're starting our search in the right corner of the world, but even if we come up empty-handed, I'll feel like I at least tried to fill in some gaping holes in my life that I have been tip-toeing around for a long time."

"Then let's do this," Paul said sounding more confident that he actually felt. "Please leave me all of your contact information so I can reach you while you are away. In the meantime, I am going to send this information to two excellent detectives who I've worked with before. I'll send you an email before you leave on Thursday with their credentials." As Molly and Pat stood up to leave, Paul came around the desk and put a big hand on both of their shoulders. "If this young lady is somewhere in the south of China, I promise you we'll track her down."

"Thank you, Paul," Patrick and Molly replied in unison. "We'll keep in touch." As they descended the stairs, they knew their friend would do whatever he could to help them.

Since they were already downtown, Molly convinced Patrick this would be a good time to do a bit of shopping. It was her plan to finish packing no later than the following evening and even though he vehemently disagreed, Patrick needed some new clothes to take on the trip. "For the love of God, Pat!" Molly admonished, "Would it kill you to buy some new socks and underwear?" Molly was confident that once she got him through the door of the men's wear store, she could convince him to pick out a few new shirts and maybe a pair of pants as well.

While loading up the trunk of their car an hour later, Molly mentally scratched, 'shopping for Pat' off her to-do list. She gave herself a little pat on the back for actually sticking to her list as much as she had... procrastinator that she was. Who knew, maybe she was turning over a new leaf.

A quick stop at the grocery store to pick up a few things she needed for dinner and they were headed home. Tonight was the last hockey game Patrick and Ryan would be watching together for a while and he was looking forward to the evening. "Maybe we should drop into the liquor store as well," he suggested. "A nice bottle of wine would go great with the roast beef you are cooking."

Marie and Ryan would be joining them for dinner and while the boys were watching their game, Marie had offered to help Molly with her packing; an offer Molly gladly accepted. For some reason, taking the suitcases out of the attic was the one job Molly couldn't force herself to do. The more she thought about packing, the more she realised this was going to be one of those trips where she would to have to be super judicious about what to take and what they could do without. Since Marie was so much better than Molly at such tasks, she was thrilled to have her friend's assistance.

Molly sat in the car while Patrick ran into the liquor store. While she waited, she thought about all they had accomplished in just one week. After they'd spoken to Paul, she felt more at ease about beginning the search for Mishi. More importantly, she knew she was ready to go on this trip and prepared to accept whatever the adventure had in store for her. The only thing Molly didn't allow herself to think about was how the enhanced picture Paul had shown them further confirmed what she had already recognised in the child's face.

Chapter 28

Unfortunately, things in Halifax weren't running quite so smoothly. During the preparation for her in-laws' visit, Laurie caught a bug that just wouldn't let her go. Although she tried valiantly for two days to fight it off, the nausea and headache won. Finally on the third day, Cole convinced his wife to go to bed and stay there until she was feeling better, insisting that his parents didn't expect or want her to fuss. Reluctantly, she gave in and took to her bed where she spent the next two days feeling absolutely miserable.

And as if that wasn't enough, Kelly Ann chose her mother's convalescence as the perfect time to burst into the terrible twos stage. Like everything else in Kelly Ann's short life, she undertook this stage with a vengeance. Aware that his parents would be arriving soon and completely at his wits' ends with his daughter's tantrums, Cole gave in and called for reinforcements.

"Holy crap," Ava exclaimed as she watched her sweet little niece turn into the Tasmanian Devil before her eyes. "What the hell... literally, is going on with her?"

"Are you kidding me," Cole shot back. "You don't recognise this? Ava, this is exactly what you were like when you were Kelly Ann's age. The only difference is that I expect she'll grow out of this, whereas you never stopped being a pain in the ass."

Instead of taking offence, Ava burst out laughing. "Wow, you really are strung out over, aren't you? Look I do feel sorry that all of this is happening to you at once, but I have to say, it's kind of nice *not* to be the one teetering on the edge for a change." Giving her big brother a hug and leaving him to deal with Kelly Ann's most recent mess, which was substantial, she scooped up the screaming baby and headed up the stairs.

Her first stop was at the parent's bedroom, where she gently opened the door and pointed to Laurie who was sleeping peacefully. Whispering into the baby's ear she murmured, "Mommy is sick, and she needs to sleep." Somewhat appeased that her mother was, in fact, still in the house, Kelly Ann's sobs subsided slightly. Together they proceeded to the bathroom where Ava filled the tub with warm water and lots of soapy bubbles. Stripping away Kelly Ann's peanut butter-covered pants and shirt, she plopped the sticky baby butt first into the tub. In an instant the crying ceased and was replaced by joyous giggles as her niece swam and splashed to her little heart's content.

As she sat on the floor beside the tub, Ava thought about what Cole said to her during his earlier rave. Not that she would ever admit it, at least not to her family, but Ava actually did remember some of the antics she pulled when she was younger. What she recalled most clearly was that an unexpected bubble bath was the perfect equaliser. In fact, she could close her eyes now and imagine her own mom and dad sitting beside the tub entertaining her while Ava calmed down from whatever she had been in a snit about.

Lost in her memories, Ava didn't realise that tears were falling down her cheeks until she heard a sweet baby voice asking. "Why are you crying Aunt Ava?"

"I most certainly am not crying," she replied with a smile. "Some little munchkin just splashed bubbles in my eyes." Her quick and positive response brought on another fit of giggles and plenty of splashing. "Screw the mess" Ava said under her breath and joined in the splash party, "I'll clean the bathroom later."

While the girls played bathtub games, Cole finished cleaning the walls where Kelly Ann had created a finger painting mural with crunchy peanut butter. Satisfied that Laurie wouldn't know what her kitchen had looked like an hour ago, he put on a pot of spaghetti sauce for supper and made some toast and tea for the patient. When he took the tray into their room, he was happy to see Laurie sitting up in the bed. Though still looking a little green, she said she was feeling much better. Laurie ate the lunch Cole prepared and even got to spend a few minutes with her squeaky-clean baby girl. Cole and Ava decided not to share the events that led to the unscheduled bath. The fact that Laurie didn't ask about it made the withholding of information even easier.

Laurie kissed the baby on her damp hair and looked up at her sister-in-law through sleepy eyes. "Thank you for coming over. You're the best." With each consecutive blink becoming longer than the one before she assured Cole that she would be feeling much better in the morning. Before anyone had a chance to agree, Laurie drifted off to sleep again. Taking that as their cue to leave, the rest of the family went downstairs to have their own meal.

Dishes done and mother and child asleep, Cole and Ava grabbed a beer out of the refrigerator and moved into the family room. "I really do appreciate your help." He said to his sister, "Oh, and I'm sorry about the pain in the ass remark."

Once again Ava laughed and told Cole that she took no offence. "Who knows," Ava quipped, still not ready to fess up, "there might have even been some truth to it."

Not wanting to disrupt her good mood, Cole cautiously asked her how she was feeling now that their parents' trip to China was drawing close. Ava took a sip of her beer before answering, "It's the craziest thing Cole. I have no logical reason to be upset about this and the last thing I want is to put any more pressure on Mom." She stopped for a moment to organise her thoughts. "It's just a weird feeling that I can't explain."

Cole didn't break eye contact with his sister, nor did he interrupt her. In a moment she continued. "I mean, think about it. Your mom just up and split when you were barely two years old and my birth father was killed before I was even born. That's a lot for any family to endure and yet we dealt with it and became a strong and loving family. Now suddenly, a random picture of a kid surfaces and our parents are travelling halfway around the world trying to solve some mystery. Don't you find that a bit strange?"

"Listen squirt," Cole fondly reverted to the nickname she hated when she was a teenager. "Whatever the reason, this is obviously important to Mom. Let's just try not to make this any more difficult on them than it already is. You know they'll keep us informed about any developments. I get that you find all this kind of weird but..." Cole stood up and moved out of her direct line of attack before finishing his sentence. "But I find *you* kind of weird and I love you all the same."

Apparently he didn't move away quite far or fast enough. With the speed and agility of a ninja warrior, Ava's fist connected solidly with Cole's forearm. "Yeah, I love you too shit head" she replied as she kissed him on the cheek before heading to the spare room. "Might as well spend the night," she announced. "God knows you can barely function without me."

Laurie was back to her old self by the morning, which was evidenced by the flurry of cooking and cleaning going on in the kitchen when Cole descended the stairs. While they were enjoying a quiet cup of coffee in the kitchen, it occurred to both of them at the same time that something was missing. "The baby!' they said in unison as they tore up the stairs to the nursery where they found an empty crib.

Before total panic set in, Ava called out from the guest room. "Looking for someone? Great parenting skills you two have." Ava admonished when her brother and sister-in-law rounded the corner into her room. "Now do you think you can manage to keep her safe until I'm out the shower?"

When she returned to the kitchen, Ava accepted the cup of coffee that was being offered to her. "Thanks, but I'll take mine to go," she answered. If Laurie was feeling as good as she looked, it was clear that Ava's services were no longer required. "I have some schoolwork to catch up on before Mom and Dad arrive. I really want to get that out of the way, so I will be free to spend time with them on Friday."

Chapter 29

Early on Thursday morning, Patrick had the car packed and they were ready to roll. Molly did a terrific job of eliminating unnecessary items and actually managed to get everything she wanted to bring into two suitcases. As for their stay in Halifax, one small bag was all they would need. Laurie always made sure their room was fully stocked.

Their tickets, itinerary, passports and other travel documents were in a separate envelope in Molly's carry-on bag. Patrick's job was to carry all the information that he and Paul Blanchard had acquired to date. In addition to the child's picture that was attached to June's letter, Patrick suggested it might be a good idea to gather up some other family photos, especially ones that included Mark and his parents. "Who knows," said Patrick. "They might even help to uncover another piece of the puzzle. And anyway, it won't take up much room to pack them."

Molly agreed, and Patrick added the extra pictures to his file, which he tucked into his old backpack. Molly shook her head every time her husband dragged the backpack out of storage. It had been with him since his college days and the grubby looking bag continued to accompany him every time he travelled. Patrick insisted that he couldn't find a new backpack that he liked as much as this one, declaring it had just the right number of pockets to store everything he needed and besides, it fit his back and shoulders perfectly. Having heard this argument countless times over the past two decades, Molly didn't even bother suggesting he get a new one any more.

While they were in the process of going through the final checklist, Ryan and Marie dropped over for one last visit. By mid-morning, the four friends were saying their final goodbyes. Marie held onto Molly an extra minute and reminded her to have a wonderful time. Ryan assured Patrick that the house would be in good hands. With one last flurry of waves, kisses and handshakes the O'Neil's pulled out of their driveway and headed for Halifax.

Willie Nelson's, *On the Road Again,* blared from the car radio as they pulled away. "Well, that has to be some kind of omen," Patrick proclaimed.

"I just hope it's a good one." Molly chuckled at her husband's trepidation. "*Now* who is the sceptical one? I thought I was the only person in our family who believed in serendipity."

The drive seemed to fly by and in no time at all they were crossing the Canso Causeway, which linked Cape Breton Island to mainland Nova Scotia.

"Have you noticed that since Kelly Ann was born, the trip to Halifax appeared to get shorter each time we visit?" Patrick remarked. Today's trek was particularly quick given all the exciting plans they had to talk about as they drove. The couple only stopped once on the way for a coffee and sandwich, not wanting to ruin the delicious meal they were sure Laurie would have prepared for dinner that evening.

Molly could feel her excitement mounting the closer they got to Halifax. She was so besotted with her granddaughter that at times she wondered if she was looking more forward to spending time with the baby than she was to seeing China for the first time. Either way, Molly and Patrick agreed they were at the beginning of a very exciting adventure.

Patrick was first to spot his son's house. "We're here," he announced as Molly jolted awake, hardly able to believe she had fallen asleep. As they signalled to pull into the driveway, the front door bust open and their family spilled out onto the veranda. And before the car came to a full stop, Molly was out the door and running up the stairs, arms outstretched.

As usual, Kelly Ann took on the role of official greeter. "Nana, Papa here," she squealed, her chubby legs kicking to get out of her father's arms and into Molly's. Patrick's heart melted as he watched his wife cradle their granddaughter. If he had one regret in his life it would be that he and Molly didn't have the opportunity to have a child together. Not that they tried to prevent it… it just wasn't in the cards for them.

"OK, its Papa's turn," Patrick said as he reached for the baby. With screams of delight, she jumped from Molly's arms into Patrick's where she nestled into his neck and told him, "I love you Papa."

"Well, there it is!" said the three adult children who were still standing on the steps. "What chance do we have to even get noticed when the munchkin here is clearly stealing the show?"

Cole opened the front door and welcomed them into the warm, delicious smelling foyer.

An hour later, as they sat around the dining room tables, pleasantly stuffed from the amazing meal they had just finished, Molly and Patrick shared a private smile. They were both so proud of their children and the life they were making for themselves.

Even after all these years, it was still hard to remember that Cole and Ava we not blood related. They continued to get along as adults the way they did when they were children, often finishing each other's sentences when they were telling a story. Adding Laurie and Kelly Ann to the family was truly the icing on the cake. As if reading her thoughts, Laurie chose that moment to ask who was having dessert.

"Are you kidding me?" Cole hooted. "When has anyone in this family ever said no to dessert? Unless, of course, Ava made it!" His comment got him another punch in the arm from his sister and a round of muffled laughter from the rest of the family. Molly was first to regain her composure.

"I'll help you in the kitchen Laurie," she said pushing her chair away from the table. The two women left the table together, leaving the disgruntled Ava to deal with her brother.

Tonight's dessert was another of Laurie's masterpieces, a white chocolate raspberry cheesecake and it looked divine. Molly got small plates and forks out of the cupboards while Laurie added the finishing touches to the raspberry sauce that was to be drizzled on top of the already decadent dessert.

The women worked side by side, each doing their own job when Molly put her arm around Laurie and said. "So, when were you planning to tell me that I am going to be a grandmother again?"

Cake server stopping in mid slice, Laurie turned to her mother-in-law, while backing her further out of earshot of the rest of the family. "How could you possibly know *that*?" Laurie asked looking as shocked as she felt. "I only just found out myself. Jeez, I haven't even been to the doctor to have it confirmed. What are you... some kind of psychic?"

"Nope" Molly answered, "just a mother who recognises the beautiful glow of pregnancy on a woman she loves like a daughter."

Eyes filling with tears of joy, Laurie threw herself into Molly's arms. "I'm so excited too. We've always planned to have at least two children. I was busting to tell you, but Cole suggested waiting until you came home from your trip. He didn't want you worrying unnecessarily about us while you were in China."

Molly knew that Cole was remembering the countless phone calls and visits she had made during Laurie's first pregnancy. "I guess I wouldn't have told me either," Molly agreed. "But now that the cat is out of the bag, are we going to celebrate the wonderful news?"

"Yes, we are," Laurie responded. "Why don't you do it after dessert?" she suggested. "I can't wait to see the look on Cole's face when you tell him you already figured it out.

Mother and daughter-in-law re-entered the dining room carrying plates of cheesecake that were now covered in raspberry sauce and garnished with fresh mint and shaved chocolate. Cheers and applause accompanied their entrance when the rest of the family got a glimpse of the treat that was yet to come. "Now how am I even supposed to compete with this?" Ava asked as she reached for her plate. "Is there anything you're *not* good at?" she said teasingly to her sister-in-law.

Before Laurie had a chance to respond Molly blurted out the news. "Well she's certainly good at procreation. Cole and Laurie are pregnant!"

"OK, way to bring a meal to a screaming halt." Patrick teased Molly, as they got ready for bed later that night.

"Oh, for goodness sake, Pat, it is absolutely wonderful news and I just couldn't wait another minute to share it with everyone." Patrick, who was just as happy as his wife, nodded in agreement. "It really is great news. Do you think maybe this one will be a boy?"

"Fifty percent chance," Molly told him. "We'll have to wait and see, just like the last time."

Tired from the day, they climbed into bed where they fell asleep instantly, neither of them moving a muscle for the next eight hours. As planned, they spent Friday with Ava, shopping, visiting her apartment and talking about school and her upcoming trip to Tanzania, which was now only a few months away.

Ava told her mother that she had recently heard from the Center for Disease Control in Africa. She learned that her work placement would be in a remote city called Dar es Salaam, where the residents were suffering from the effects of exposure to air and water pollution caused by untreated solid and liquid waste. Her job would be to work with the local schools to develop programmes to promote safe drinking water education.

Molly listened attentively to her daughter, but she shuddered inwardly wondering if she could cope with another member of her family putting their life in danger for this cause. She and Patrick were proud of Ava, but the memories of June and Mark were still fresh in Molly's mind.

After lunch, Patrick dropped the girls off at a spa, where Ava and Molly had booked a massage, manicure and pedicure. While they sat waiting for their nails to dry Ava thanked her mom for a wonderful day. She assured her mother that she was OK with the trip and apologised again for her initial reaction. Molly leaned over and kissed her daughter on the cheek. "I know baby and I love you for caring so much about us. But I don't want you spending your time worrying about Dad and me. You have exams to think about and that's where your focus should be." Ava promised she would try not to worry.

Saturday was a full out family day with meals and activities planned from morning until night. Laurie had to stop for a rest in the afternoon. Now that everyone knew about the pregnancy, it was easier for her to slip away for a little break when she needed one.

While Laurie rested, Molly and Patrick took Kelly Ann to see *Frozen* at the theatre, where she sat enthralled for two full hours. All the way home in the car and for the rest of the evening, she sang snippets from *Let it Go*, the theme song from the movie. At the end of each performance everyone clapped and told her she had a lovely voice.

Sunday dawned bright and sunny and extremely cold. "Not gonna lie to you," Patrick announced to Cole as they scraped ice from the windshield of his son's SUV. "I won't be missing this weather when we leave tomorrow." Laughing, Cole admitted that he wouldn't mind getting away to somewhere warm. But with Laurie being pregnant and Kelly Ann being…well, herself, there wasn't much chance of a trip south for him anytime soon.

The plan for the day was a family brunch followed by a sleigh ride at the Hatfield farms. Despite Laurie's objections, dinner that night was going to be takeout from Cole and Ava's favourite Chinese restaurant.

"This is nuts," Laurie protested. "First of all, I'm pregnant, not sick. I can easily whip up something for dinner. And secondly, you are going to be eating Chinese food in China for the next month. "Both great points, honey… but overruled," Cole told his wife. "You never let me eat fast food and this might well be my last MSG fix before baby number two arrives." Laurie begrudgingly agreed but made them promise to let her make appetisers and dessert.

Everyone enjoyed the day, especially Kelly Ann, who named one of the horses Elsa and sang, *Let it Go* to him several times during the sleigh ride. Fortunately, it was a private rental, so it was only the family who got to hear the never-ending performance.

Following an early dinner, Molly excused herself to give Kelly Ann her bath while the others cleaned up. Wanting to spend as much time as possible with her granddaughter, she let Kelly Ann play much longer in the tub. Once tucked into bed, Patrick joined them and read the baby her bedtime story. Kelly Ann's eyes were slamming shut by the time he got through the first two pages, but Patrick read on, not wanting this precious time with her to end. They both kissed the sleeping baby, wishing her sweet dreams and promising to visit her as soon as they returned.

Laurie met them in the hallway as Molly and Patrick were leaving Kelly Ann's room. Wrapping her arms around her in-laws she kissed them goodbye, wished them a wonderful trip and headed off to bed. Five o'clock in the morning was just a bit too early for her to get mobile these days, so she wouldn't be accompanying them to the airport.

Returning to the kitchen, Molly and Patrick joined Cole and Ava for a cup of tea before they headed off to bed as excited as two children on Christmas Eve. "Ready?" Molly asked Patrick, as she kissed him goodnight.

"Let's do it," came Patrick's familiar response. Five minutes later both were asleep.

Chapter 30

"Oh my God… it's pitch black out there." Cole told Ava as he scooped heaping tablespoons full of coffee into the percolator at three o'clock on Monday morning.

"Stop bitching," Ava shot back. "You were the one who insisted on coming to the airport with me to see them off." Neither sibling was much of a morning person, and getting up this early proved to be a daunting task for both of them.

Despite the darkness and the ungodly hour, they somehow managed to make four cups of coffee, which they poured into thermos mugs. Ava handed out cups to Cole and both of her parents as each one made their way to the car. With virtually no traffic on the roads, the trip to the airport went without incident and they arrived at Standfield International in plenty of time for the flight.

Molly was overcome with emotion as she kissed her children goodbye. Ava, for her part, did her very best not to give in to the tears and fears that she was feeling. Pat hugged Cole and Ava promising to contact them as soon as they arrived in Shanghai. With goodbyes said, there was just enough time to check their itinerary one more time and finish the last dregs of coffee from their mugs before their boarding announcement was called.

Joining hands, Molly and Patrick walked through the security gate and headed off to the waiting plane, feeling equal amounts of nervousness and excitement. Two stops and twenty-seven hours later their plane landed at Pudong International Airport in Shanghai, China.

As they made their way to the baggage claim area, Molly tried to calculate the time difference in her very tired head. Their flight left Halifax at seven o'clock Monday morning and she had previously decided not to change her watch until they arrived at their final destination. Squinting to see the time, she noted it read ten a.m. on Tuesday. Using her fingers to add the eleven-hour time difference, Molly concluded the correct local time to be nine p.m.

Everything she knew or had read about jet lag suggested it was best to try to adapt to the local time as quickly as possible. In this instance, even though it was still morning on their body, it was already night in Shanghai and Molly and Patrick were pretty sure they would be able to sleep once they arrived at their hotel. By the time they collected their bags and found transportation to the hotel it would be nearly midnight and hopefully, they wouldn't be too tempted to begin exploring the magnificent city that would be their home for the next month or more.

The airport was an impressive complex and finding the correct baggage carousel was a feat in itself. Pudong International consisted of two massive terminal buildings each encompassing countless stores, restaurants, services and specialty shops. The brochures she read prior to leaving Nova Scotia said the airport property covered more than fifteen square kilometres and standing among the throngs of travellers who were also waiting for their luggage, she could easily imagine that statistic to be true. In fact, Molly was so caught up in the wonder of everything going on around her that she was startled to see Patrick standing at her side with both of their suitcases and all of their carry-on luggage neatly arranged on one of the thousands of baggage carts the airport provided.

"Well, I guess the travel gods are with us tonight… or is it this morning?" Patrick asked Molly. "Our bags were in the first group to arrive." While his wife had been day-dreaming, in addition to collecting their luggage, Patrick also acquired information on ground transportation. Pushing the laden cart with one hand and directing Molly through the turnstile with the other, the couple made their way outdoors. At exactly quarter past ten the O'Neil's experienced the first sights, sounds and smells of Shanghai and they stopped for a moment just to try to let the reality set in.

Unbeknownst to Molly or Patrick, one of the many luxurious amenities provided by the Fairmount Peace Hotel was a chauffeur-driven limousine, which was parked outside the main doors of the airport waiting to take them to their hotel. "OK, this doesn't suck." Patrick whispered in his wife's ear as he noticed the card bearing their name and the name of the hotel. As they approached the smartly attired chauffeur, he smiled and greeted them, taking Molly by the elbow and assisting her in to the opulent vehicle. Patrick didn't wait for an invitation. He quickly ran around the other side and jumped in, sliding close to his wife and planting a kiss soundly on her mouth. With the utmost of discretion, the driver looked away and took his seat at the wheel.

The trip downtown took less than thirty minutes and Molly was almost sorry when they pulled up in front of the Fairmount Peace Hotel. Their chauffeur's English was excellent, and he regaled them with stories about Shanghai as he pointed out 'must see' landmarks along the way. Patrick told Molly his head felt like it was on a swivel as tried to take in all the sights that whisked by his window.

Molly smiled as she watched her excited husband looking this way and that. "I thought I would be the impatient one, Pat. Remember, we are going to be here for at least a month and there will be lots of time to see everything. All I really want to see tonight is our bed."

As she finished her sentence with a wide yawn, the driver pulled up to a spectacular marquee and in his most official voice announced, "Mr. and Mrs. O'Neil, it is my pleasure to welcome you to the majestic Fairmount Peace Hotel."

Before Patrick had a chance to tip the driver and thank him for the wonderful tour, both doors of the limo were opened, and the hotel staff sprang into action. Molly was presented with an exquisite bouquet of Chinese flowers. Pink Camellia and yellow Chinese roses surrounded one solid white orchid. Burying her face in the bouquet and breathing deeply, Molly wondered if this was really happening or if she had died and gone to heaven.

For Patrick, the welcome gift was a bottle of Fenjui Baijiu, China's most famous rice wine. Tired as he was, Patrick remembered reading that the alcohol content of Baijiu was somewhere between 40% and 60%. "Not tonight," Patrick told Molly, referring to the potent liquor. "I think I would prefer to remember my first night in Shanghai.

Next in line to offer his service was a porter who introduced himself as Fa Zhang. Moving with lightning speed, he greeted the O'Neil's with a formal bow before collecting all their belongings and then disappeared inside a nearby elevator.

The whirlwind continued at the reception desk where a swipe of Patrick's credit card and his signature was all that was necessary to complete the check-in process.

"Phew," breathed Molly, as they entered the same elevator Fa Zhang had taken a few moments earlier, "I think I could get used to this kind of service pretty easily. We haven't even seen our room and I'm already in love with the place."

Chapter 31

Whatever they may have expected of their accommodation at the Fairmount Peace Hotel became a complete underestimation when Patrick and Molly walked across the threshold of their suite. Any adjective that they could think of to describe the room could not hold a candle to what they experienced as they surveyed their surroundings.

In the centre of the room, a king-sized bed sat atop a raised platform. The ornate head- and footboard made the already large bed look absolutely enormous and extremely inviting. Running her hand over the silk duvet that covered the bed, Molly felt like she was touching a cloud. The bottom half of the bed was covered with a satin coverlet with ruffled flanges. A mountain of accent pillows from Damask bolsters to velvety, pin-tucked boudoirs made Patrick wonder where they would find room to sleep among all the silk and satin. But one look at his wife as she caressed the eiderdown pillows and Patrick had his answer. Molly's eyes and smile assured him that there would be no barriers preventing either of them from enjoying the pleasure of this wonderful bed.

Tired as she was, Molly couldn't resist completing a tour of their suite. While Patrick made his way to the bathroom for a shower, Molly spun around in the room like a young girl growing more excited by everything she saw.

Below the two steps leading up to their bed, a cream and gold coloured tufted ottoman held two plush bathrobes that Molly found very inviting. An antique writing table, chaise longue and two beige leather chairs sat to the right of the bed and tucked discretely behind a partition on the opposite wall was a tastefully appointed dining area.

Unable to take in any more, Molly lowered herself into one of the soft leather chairs and closed her eyes hoping this wasn't a dream and everything would still be there when she reopened them. But her respite was short lived when Patrick called out from the bathroom, "Oh my God, Mol... you've got to see this!"

Jumping up with a start, Molly proceeded to the only room she had not yet inspected, the bathroom. Rounding the corner in the direction of her husband's voice, Molly stopped in her tracks and gasped. She was sure she must have walked into a museum and not a lavatory.

Black and white mosaic tiles surrounded two brilliant white-marble pedestal sinks. A double claw-foot bathtub occupied the centre of the room, and as with their bed, the tub was also raised on a marble platform. Art deco light fixtures illuminated the room giving it the look of an ice castle. But the most striking feature was in the far corner of the room.

A large walk-in shower created from black and white tiles laid in the pattern of the Shanghai city skyline stood against a bank of white cabinets. And to make the fairy tale complete, Molly eyes rested on the silhouette of her naked husband behind the smoked glass shower doors.

With more energy that she imagined possible after their very long day, Molly peeled off her clothes eagerly. In a matter of seconds, she had joined Patrick in the shower where they stood wrapped in each other's arms while the pulsating shower warmed and massaged their tired bodies. They washed and caressed each other until they were sure they would fall asleep standing up. Patrick reluctantly shut off the water reached for two bath sheets as he guided his wife toward the bed.

"Unpacking and tidying up will just have to wait until tomorrow," said Patrick as he helped Molly throw aside unnecessary pillows and covers from the bed. "The only thing I want to explore tonight is my beautiful wife." Without a word, Molly slid under the silk sheets and opened her arms to her husband.

Molly's first thought the next morning when she awoke was, "Please, please, please, let everything look as amazing as it did last night." One eye opened slowly and then the other. Not only was the room as lovely as she remembered it from their late arrival, but in the morning light it looked even more spectacular.

Not wanting to wake her husband, Molly slipped quietly from the bed and after a quick survey of her surroundings she returned with her laptop. In all of the excitement of the night before they had neglected to email the kids to let them know they had arrived safely. Molly also wanted to send a quick note to Sam. Although she and Patrick would be spending a few days in Shanghai before joining Sam in Dongtan, she promised to touch base with him once they were settled.

Her note to Ava, Cole and Laurie was full of details about the trip and, of course, their magnificent suite at the Fairmount Peace Hotel. Instinctively, she knew that Laurie would want to hear every detail while Ava would see the room as decadent and extravagant. Cole, on the other hand would get a charge out of listening to his wife and sister debate the topic from both perspectives. For two women who genuinely loved each other, they could not be more different. Before signing off, Molly reminded everyone to give Kelly Ann a big kiss from both of them and told Laurie to be sure to let her know how the pregnancy was progressing.

By the time she clicked 'send' on the last email, she noticed Patrick was wide awake and smiling up at her. "Good morning my love," he said softly, while reaching up for a kiss and hug, to which Molly happily obliged. As they lay in the tangled sheets, Molly and Patrick made plans for their first day in Shanghai.

Like everything else thus far in the trip, the weather was also cooperating. At nine o'clock, it was already sunny, and according to the weather report it was going to be lovely all day. Not wanting to miss a moment, the two jumped out of bed and began to get ready. Molly was in and out of the shower in minutes. While Patrick was shaving Molly went through their luggage and unpacked the clothes they would need during their stay in Shanghai.

By ten they were back on the elevator and in search of coffee and breakfast. "We might as well try one of the restaurants here," Molly suggested. "There seem to be plenty to choose from." Patrick agreed as they headed off toward the delectable aromas coming from Victor's Café on the main floor.

Once again, the Fairmount Peace Hotel lived up to its reputation. As they entered the art-deco deli, Molly and Patrick were immediately greeted and taken to a table overlooking the famous Bund. While they sipped their first cup of delicious coffee the happy couple watched in awe as the history of Shanghai appeared before their eyes.

From their window seat in the Persian-style café they could see the charming retail enclaves where local designers were selling their wares—which, according to the brochures, included everything from handmade silk slippers to modern ceramics to freshwater pearls. Mixed among these traditional Chinese venues were many of the top fashion designers from around the world.

Patrick could see that Molly was anxious to finish breakfast and join the throngs of people who were already enjoying the delights of the Bund. For his part, Patrick was more interested in exploring Pudong, known as the new Bund, on the east side of the Huangpu River. Directly across from the historic city centre, Patrick could see the skyline of Pudong. Reminiscent of old Shanghai, Pudong was now considered to be the business, world trade, finance and technological centre of China.

As they dined on fresh fruit and rich French pastry with home-made preserves, Molly and Patrick talked about all the things they wanted to do and see. They were in no immediate hurry to begin their search for the identity of the mystery child and they agreed it would be a shame to waste this glorious day on anything but being a tourist in a new and exciting country.

Chapter 32

Patrick signed the tab for the outrageously expensive breakfast reminding himself that living and eating like this for a month would surely put them in the poor house. As he was leaving a tip for the waitress he saw Molly standing in the doorway of the restaurant bouncing from one foot to the next. God, but he loved to see her happy! He smiled as he added a few extra bills to the tip. "Screw the expense," he muttered under his breath remembering his father's sage advice in these situations. 'My boy,' he would say, "Might as well enjoy it while you can. You're gonna' be dead for a long time.'

"Excusez-moi?" the waitress asked, thinking he was speaking to her.

"Uhhh, nothing," Patrick replied, a bit embarrassed that she heard him talking to himself. "Just wishing you a nice day."

"Merci monsieur." The waitress responded as they walked away from each other… both smiling.

Unable to contain herself any longer, Molly grabbed her husband's hand dragging him out the door and down the steps until their feet were firmly planted on the famous Bund.

The Fairmount Peace Hotel is in the centre of the 1,500-metre-long Bund. Standing together with their hands linked on the busy sidewalk in front of their hotel the two tried to take in all the sights at once. "Oh Pat!" Molly cried with unabridged joy, "I am so happy we did this. Just look at all the buildings and people. The scenery and architecture is beyond amazing. And look over there!" she continued, pointing to a kiosk across from where they were standing. "We can take a cruise on the Huangpu River. Would you like to do that Pat? Please say yes."

When it looked like she was finally going to take a breath Patrick guided Molly to a park bench near the river. "We can do whatever you like," Patrick answered wrapping his arm around Molly. "We just can't do it all at once."

Leaning back against Patrick's broad chest, Molly looked up into her husband's eyes. "I know you must think I've lost my mind," she answered. "But I just love everything about this place. And Pat..." Molly hesitated for a moment, "I really believe that something great is going to come out of this adventure." Taking her hand in his and helping her up he replied. "I don't doubt that for a second. I feel the same way too. Now let's go and see what Shanghai has to offer."

As they started their stroll along the promenade, they quickly learned that the Bund was not only a good place for shopping and sightseeing, but also for exercising and relaxing. Apparently Chinese seniors are very committed to maintaining an active lifestyle. Molly and Patrick stopped to watch large groups of older Chinese men and women practicing Tai Chi and Kung Fu. Others were jogging, or flying kites.

Patrick marvelled at their ability and athleticism as he watched the group – all of whom were considerably older than he and Molly – stretching and moving with the agility of a much younger crowd. "I'd sure like to see something like this happening back home" Patrick commented, referring to the seniors who gathered at Tim Horton's or those who lined the waterfront at Sydney harbour to sit and listen to the musicians who performed there nightly. "We'd all be a hell of a lot better off if we kept this active."

Further along the promenade, Molly noticed a group of tourists stopping to have their pictures taken. Not sure of what the attraction was, Molly made her way to the front of the line, pulling Patrick along with her. A young Chinese man stood behind a table laden with photography equipment.

He introduced himself as Dequan, a student at Shanghai University. Dequan explained that one of the first things travellers like to do when they arrive in Shanghai is head on over to the Bund and get their pictures taken in this spot, with the future of China as the backdrop

He pointed out to Molly how the Bund overlooks the Huangpu River and from the where they stood, he said, you can gaze upon massive and gleaming financial towers in Pudong. The distinctively Western architecture found along the Bund manifests Shanghai's history, while the Pudong side provides a glimpse into the future. With pride in his voice, Dequan proclaimed that this image of the old and the new is representative of Shanghai's modernity and history and, as such, has become a symbol for China itself.

Grinning into the lens of the camera, Patrick and Molly posed for a picture. They also asked Dequan to take a few pictures using their iPhone, so they could send them home to their children and friends. Dequan obliged and as they were leaving, he gave them a booklet that detailed things that they might be interested in seeing while they were in Shanghai. He also suggested an interesting restaurant where they might like to have lunch. Patrick paid the young man and thanked him, promising to try out the restaurant soon.

The couple continued their exploration until mid-afternoon when Patrick finally confessed, he could not walk another step, regardless of how amazing Molly proclaimed the shopping to be. In fact, he was so hungry and his feet so tired that he wasn't sure if he would make it back to the hotel. "I have an idea," Patrick announced in desperation. "Let's grab a cab and find the restaurant Dequan mentioned this morning." Even though she would never admit it herself, Molly was ready for a rest as well, so she happily agreed with Patrick's suggestion.

Finding a cab was easy. Storing all the shopping bags Molly had acquired was another matter. With the driver's assistance, Patrick managed to fit everything into the car's very small trunk and then they were ready to go.

The name of the restaurant was the Rose Garden Café and the cab driver knew exactly where it was. In just a few moments he pulled the car up in front of a quaint little building that could barely be seen from the road. He told the couple to enjoy lunch and said to be sure to eat outdoors.

Walking through the front entrance, Patrick and Molly were delighted to find themselves in an actual working greenhouse. As the employees, who were dressed in gardening clothes, went about their tasks, an exotic blend of fragrances from the flowers and fresh herbs wafted through the air. Molly closed her eyes and breathed in the beautiful combination of aromas.

They took the cab driver's advice and asked to be seated outside where they could enjoy the unusually warm weather. A waitress led them thought the greenhouse and out the back door into the most magnificent garden either had ever seen. As they sat among the lavender, plum and peach blossoms, it was easy to forget they were in a city of nearly twenty-four million people.

Patrick ordered an espresso for both of them in hopes that the strong jolt of coffee would revive them. While she waited for the coffee to arrive, Molly read the pamphlet she had picked up on her way into the restaurant. She flipped to the back page where it listed the names of the flowers they were currently enjoying. From her limited knowledge, Molly was able to pick out Provence Lavender, cosmos, Chinese roses, and lotuses. But for as many flowers as she recognised, there were twice that many that were unfamiliar, and she planned to ask one of the workers what these beautiful plants were.

For lunch, they ordered corn crab soup made with egg whites, corn and of course, fresh crabmeat. Their waitress explained that all of the herbs used in the soup were grown in the garden. The dessert special for the day was shortbread flavoured cake inside a chocolate crust topped with fresh figs. They ordered two because Molly assured her husband that there wasn't a chance in hell she was going to share hers.

The next hour passed in an intoxicating collage of delicious tastes, aromas and scenery as they enjoyed their meal, particularly the dessert. Before leaving, Molly chatted with two of the workers who were able to give her lots of information about the plants and herbs that were grown in working garden and greenhouse of the Rose Garden Café. Promising to come back to this veritable Garden of Eden for another visit, Molly and Patrick strolled around the garden a bit longer while they waited for their cab.

Satisfied but exhausted with their day's adventure, Molly asked Patrick if he still wanted to visit Pudong. The gentle snores that resonated from his side of the cab told Molly that her husband was ready to call it a day. She gave him a nudge as they pulled up in front of the hotel. Patrick smiled lazily as he followed his wife into the elevator and to their room for a quick nap.

Chapter 33

For a few moments after he awoke, Patrick had no idea where he was. He looked around the darkened room to see Molly sound asleep across the bed. Crossing the distance to her side, Patrick wrapped his arms around Molly and woke her with a trail of kisses. "Mmm," she moaned as she came back to consciousness, "Is this heaven?"

"Pretty damn close," Patrick answered as they both squinted to see the time on the clock across from their bed. "Jumped up Jesus, Mol! It's nearly nine o'clock. We slept for four hours!"

By the time Molly returned to the bedroom, showered and wearing the glorious fleecy Fairmount Peace Hotel robe, Patrick had already taken care of their supper plans. "It's room service tonight, my love. I hope that works for you."

"As if you could wrestle me out of this robe," Molly replied laughing and in total agreement.

Taking his wife's lead, Patrick also donned a fluffy white robe and joined Molly just as their meal was arriving. Looking like two happy polar bears Molly and Patrick sat in their little dining area and enjoyed a lite supper and some excellent wine.

Since leaving the room was obviously out of the question, they decided to spend the rest of the evening discussing their plans for the next few days. As promised, Paul Blanchard had sent Patrick an email with the contact information for the investigator who would be handling their file in Shanghai. His name was Tommy Chu and his office was across the Huangpu River in the area of Pudong.

"Bonus!" Patrick exclaimed when he saw the address. "We can take the boat cruise that we didn't get around to today and get off in

Pudong. I'm going to email Mr. Chu right now and hopefully he'll be able to meet with us tomorrow afternoon."

They also sent a note home to the children and made a quick call to Sam. "Hi guys. It's good to hear from you," Sam said when he heard their voice. "I tried to reach you a few times, but you must have been on the go all day." Molly told Sam about all they had seen and how beautiful they found the country to be. "You haven't seen anything yet," Sam boasted. You want beauty... just wait till you get to Chongming Island." Molly and Patrick both knew how proud he and June were of their adopted home and they were looking forward to experiencing it first-hand. "So, when can I expect you? Sam inquired.

Patrick explained that they hoped to be meeting with a private investigator the next day and based on the information he provided, they would be able to determine how much longer they would be staying in Shanghai. Patrick promised to let Sam know when to expect them just as soon as he knew himself.

Although he didn't mention it during the call, Sam had also been doing some investigating on his own. Not certain how much information Molly had, he decided it would be best to wait until they were all together before sharing what he'd found out. Sam thought, and not for the first time, how very difficult this must be for Molly and he vowed to tell her everything he already knew as well as the new information he was able to uncover. "Farewell my dear friends," Sam said as he prepared to sign off. "Can't wait to see you."

"Pat, he knows something," Molly said the second the call was finished. "What do you think it is and why didn't he tell us?" "Hold on Mol," Patrick admonished, "I know our nerves are a little on edge but let's not start reading things into this. We'll see Sam in a few days and I'm sure he'll tell us whatever he knows. And honey, please keep in mind that whatever it is we are hoping to find happened a long time ago. What I'm saying is that Sam might not know any more than we do."

"Of course you're right." Molly said. "We just sprung this on Sam and obviously we caught him off guard. I promise I'll be patient and I won't badger him." Patrick doubted that very much, but he knew Molly would do her best. "Check your email again, Pat. Maybe Tommy Chu got back to you."

"Yep, he did," Patrick answered as he read through the electronic reply. "He said he was expecting our call and he will be happy to meet with us tomorrow at two in the afternoon. That gives us the day to enjoy some more of the Bund. Maybe we'll stay in Pudong after our appointment and have dinner over there. How's that sound?"

"Just perfect." Molly answered promising to try to enjoy everything this amazing city had to offer.

Finding himself wide awake after their four-hour nap, Patrick decided this would be a good time to open the bottle of Fenjui Baijiu that was given to him when he checked into the hotel. *There's nothing like an expensive rice wine with a 40% to 60% alcohol content to make you nice and sleepy*, Patrick mused.

Molly scavenged around the suite to see if she could find some snacks while Patrick poured them each a glass of wine. In a drawer below the little sink in the dining area she came across the motherlode of treats. Chips, crackers, fig candy and an assortment of nuts filled the drawer to overflowing. "This will do." she called out to Patrick who was busy trying to find an English movie, preferably a comedy, for them to watch.

Sitting up on their luxurious bed, wrapped in fluffy robes and surrounded by junk food and very good wine, Patrick and Molly spent the next two hours splitting their sides laughing at a dubbed version of Caddyshack. The movie was thirty-five years old. Between the two of them they must have watched it ten times and yet Chevy Chase, Bill Murray and Rodney Dangerfield cracked them up every time they saw it.

When the screen went to black, Patrick turned to Molly who was sprawled unceremoniously across the bed, bathrobe askew, one leg hanging over the side and apparently sound asleep. Patrick chuckled to himself about what a cheap drunk his wife was. However, his laughter came to an abrupt halt when he stood up and promptly landed on his ass on the floor.

As he crawled to the bathroom and then back to his bed to join his equally inebriated wife. Patrick, a consummate wine drinker knew he had met his match in a bottle of Fenjui Baijiu. His last though before he zonked out was, *Damn, I'll have to bring a bottle of that stuff home to Ryan!* And then everything went black.

Chapter 34

One of the nicest things about being retired is that there is rarely a need to set an alarm clock. Molly and Patrick awoke minutes apart at nine o'clock the next morning. They were thrilled to see the sun streaming in through the window. They were equally pleased that neither of them was suffering any obvious effects of a hangover from the potent wine they consumed the previous night. "Be careful Mol," Patrick advised as his wife swung her legs over the side of the bed. "The damn stuff is kind of sneaky." Not bothering to share his own experience of his ill-fated attempt to stand and walk last night, Patrick still wanted to protect Molly from a similar shock.

"What a wimp I married," Molly chided as she descended the stairs leading down from the platform that their bed sat atop. "I feel just fine… wonderful in fact."

As Patrick threw back the covers and attempted to get up himself, he muttered, "Hum… apparently the devil does take care of his own."

"I heard that!" Molly shot back, laughing.

Knowing that there was no need to rush, Molly put on an extra-large pot of coffee and picked out two bagels from the selection of fresh bread and pastries that was delivered to their room each day. While she waited for the coffee to brew, she opened her email to see if there was any news from home.

The first message was from Laurie telling her she was feeling fine and hoping that they were enjoying their trip. She even attached a picture Kelly Ann, with her little ear pressed up against her mother's belly. The image made Molly smile with joy knowing that Kelly Ann at least partially understood about the little person who was about to invade her world.

Laurie also told Molly that Cole was busier than ever at work. The law firm he worked for had just acquired a large class action suit and Cole was serving as lead counsel. Laurie had insisted he take the opportunity even though he was concerned about spending so much time away from home during this part of her pregnancy.

Molly replied to Laurie's email immediately saying how proud they were of Cole and asked if there was a convenient time when they could arrange to chat on FaceTime. It was so much more personal than email and Molly already found herself missing the baby's sweet face and voice.

The next message was from Marie saying she missed her friend. True Cape Bretoner that she was, Marie wrote about the weather, remarking how cold and snowy it was since they'd left. She assured Molly that she was not missing a thing back home. Ryan included a note at the end of Marie's message notifying Patrick that the house was fine and the guys at Tim Horton's said hello.

"We really are fortunate to have such great friends", Molly told Patrick as he joined her at the desk.

"Yes, we are." Oh, and be sure to tell them we are going to bring home a bottle of Fenjui Baijiu for them," Patrick reminded Molly before she pressed 'send' on Marie's email.

"Still nothing from Ava," Molly said as she deleted the rest of her messages, which were the electronic equivalent of junk mail. "I know she's busy with school, but I wish she would touch base. I'll send her another note and hopefully we'll hear back from her soon."

Patrick knew that when Ava had a bug up her ass there was no dealing with her. He was pretty sure that whatever was keeping her from connecting with them had to do with her initial upset over the trip. Although she seemed OK the last night they'd spent with her, Patrick knew his girl. "Just send a newsy note, Mol. You know if you pressure her, she'll shut down completely. Molly agreed and proceeded to send her daughter news from their travels so far. She described the Rose Garden Café, knowing deep down Ava would love the place despite its decadence. She signed off by saying she missed her and looked forward to hearing her news.

As she clicked 'send', Molly said a silent prayer that she would hear from Ava soon.

While Molly was dealing with the correspondence from home, Patrick had been busy too. He poured two mugs of coffee, which he brought along with the toasted bagels and preserves to their little dining room table. Still dressed in their robes, Molly and Patrick feasted on their homemade breakfast and talked about how they would spend their day.

Patrick reviewed the documents he would be taking to Mr. Chu's office. When he determined everything was in order, he asked Molly to be sure to bring the envelope of pictures she was currently flipping though. In addition to the photograph of Mishi, the lost child, she had also included pictures of her family and Mark's, as Patrick had proposed. With so little to go on in terms of clues, they thought it best to take along anything that might help to solve the mystery.

Patrick could see the fear and uncertainty in his wife's eyes as she handed him the envelope and he hated that there was nothing he could do to assuage her concerns. Getting out of his chair he walked around the small table and knelt down at Molly's side. "Baby, I know this is scary for you, but I want you to remember that we can stop any time you want. All we're going to do today is to listen to what Mr. Chu has to say."

"I'm ready," said Molly, heaving a sigh and sounding much braver than she was actually feeling. "The sooner we get this started, the sooner we'll have our answer." Deep down inside, Molly wasn't sure if she was ready to learn the truth. On the other hand, she knew that whatever the outcome, it would be better than the constant wondering and worrying.

For the rest of the morning until it was time to leave, Patrick and Molly busied themselves getting ready for their day. Both were immersed in their own thoughts and for once, the normally chatty couple remained silent as they went about their respective tasks.

They chose clothes that would be comfortable to spend the day in but that would also be appropriate for dinner in Pudong. Patrick packed his trusty backpack with water, snacks and, of course, the information for Mr. Chu. When there was nothing left for them to do in the suite, they entered the elevator, hand-in-hand.

Stepping out through the main doors of the Fairmont Peace Hotel in the late morning sun, Molly stopped walking and tugged on her husband's hand, indicating that she wanted him to hold up for a minute. "Look around us Pat," Molly said, her voice filled with awe. "We are standing on the freaking Bund in Shanghai China. For the next month we are going to experience things we could never have imagined doing. We have two amazing children and soon we'll have two precious grandchildren." And then as abruptly as she began her impromptu speech, she stopped talking, gave Patrick's arm another tug and resumed walking.

Still somewhat surprised by her behaviour and fully confused by the message, Patrick ambled alongside his wife. Not sure what to say, he went for the obvious. "I agree with everything you said baby, but what the hell was your point?"

Molly burst out laughing. "OK, so maybe I should have started with more of a preamble," she admitted. "It's just that I'm so used to you being on the same page as me in most things we do. My point was that we are so lucky to have each other and this life we were blessed with. Look Pat, I know Mr. Chu, or some other detective, is probably going to tell me something that I don't really want to hear. But I'll deal with it… *we'll* deal with it. I think I just needed to remind myself that our life is very good and whatever happens, happens." Looking up into Patrick's eyes she continued. "Is any of this even making sense?"

Patrick didn't hesitate for a second. "Here is what make sense. I love you Molly and as long as we have our family, friends and each other, we are going to be just fine."

Then with a lighter heart and her husband's hand firmly planted on her back, Molly and Patrick stepped onto the dock where they would leave for their appointment.

Chapter 35

The meeting with Mr. Chu was scheduled for two o'clock, giving them plenty of time to do some sightseeing beforehand. Once again the weather cooperated fully, and the happy tourists decided to begin with the Huangpu River Cruise. Patrick purchased two tickets at a booth along the Bund Promenade. The man who worked there told him this would be an excellent way to acquaint himself with the various attractions on both sides on the river.

For the next hour and a half Molly and Patrick joined a small group of tourists cruising up and down the Huangpu. The boat was much more luxurious than either had imagined and they took full advantage of all the amenities. While Patrick visited the bar and restaurant to pick up a snack, Molly made her way to the upper deck, where she scored the best seats in the house. Patrick found her sitting in a high-backed, upholstered deck chair. Stopping for a moment, Patrick watched as the gentle breeze played with Molly's lustrous auburn curls and thought, not for the first time, what a beautiful woman she was.

As if sensing his presence, Molly turned in her chair, brushing her hair out of her eyes and spotted Patrick. "Over here," she called out, waving her hand. "Were you lost?"

"Nope" he replied, "Just admiring the view."

"Oh I know," Molly echoed. "Isn't it amazing?" Patrick didn't tell Molly that the scenery on the river, lovely as it was, couldn't hold a candle to her. Such compliments only made her uncomfortable. Instead, he leaned over and kissed her cheek before setting down the lunch he just purchased.

As they ate and took in the view, a recording that played in both English and Mandarin described everything they were seeing. They had barely finished their drinks when a horn blew, indicating that the cruise would be ending soon. "Wow, was that really ninety minutes already?" Patrick asked. Molly looked at her watch and she was just as surprised at how quickly the time had passed.

They arranged to disembark on the Pudong side and were glad that they still had plenty of time to find Mr. Chu's office. Correctly assuming that there would be another information centre on that side of the river, Patrick and Molly made their way to the kiosk where a helpful guide drew a map to the building they were looking for. He also suggested they make a visit to the Oriental Pearl TV Tower, Pudong's most famous tourist attraction.

Heading in the direction the guide had pointed them toward, Molly and Patrick truly felt and looked like tourists as they gaped and gawked at the magnificent buildings they passed along the way. Within ten minutes they arrived at their destination. Knowing Molly would be feeling a bit nervous, Patrick took her arm and led her through the front doors and to the bank of elevators. They found Mr. Chu's office suite on the directory that fortunately was written in Mandarin and English. The office was located on the nineteenth floor.

As the elevator climbed, Molly made a futile attempt to tame her windblown hair, a task she quickly gave up on as the elevator doors opened and a throng of people waited to enter. Once in the hallway, all of the bravado she had been feeling the night before disappeared and was replaced by something akin to panic. Seeing the look in her eyes, Patrick took her face in his hands. "Baby, we can get right back on that elevator if you're not ready for this."

To which Molly replied, "Open the door before I change my mind."

The room they entered looked more like a spa than a private investigator's office. In fact, the contrast to Paul Blanchard's dingy little cubbyhole could not have been more marked. A beautiful woman dressed in a trendy business suit greeted them as they walked in. Stiletto heels and expensive jewellery finished off the ensemble. "Jeez," said Patrick in a low whisper. "Am I underdressed?"

Molly's hands flew back to her hair; now wishing she had taken more time to fix it after the cruise.

In an instant, the woman, who introduced herself as Mr. Chu's receptionist, had moved from behind her desk and was standing in front of them. She welcomed them warmly and offered them a beverage, telling the couple that Mr. Chu would be with them shortly.

Declining the drinks, Molly and Patrick took a seat in the waiting room and attempted to let the gentle music and many water features that adorned the office calm them down until it was time for their appointment. Their butts had no sooner hit the lounge-like seats than the door to the inner office opened revealing the oddest little man either of them had even seen.

Tommy Chu stood no more than four-and-a-half feet tall. His hair was dyed bright red and was styled in a pompadour that would have left Elvis Presley feeling envious. Enormous glasses sat atop a Peter Pan-like button nose making Molly wonder what was holding them in place.

Patrick, being the first to recover from the initial shock, got up out of the lounge chair and extended his hand. "Greeting and welcome Mr. and Mrs. O'Neil. I am Tommy Chu. Please come into my office. Elvira will bring us some refreshments."

Patrick looked at his wife and mouthed the name "Elvira," causing Molly to swallow hard to keep from laughing out loud.

If Elvira's office reminded them of a spa then Tommy Chu's could have been lifted right off the Strip in Las Vegas. In one corner of the office sat a large desk in the shape of a craps table. Stools, rather than office chairs, surrounded the monstrosity and proudly displayed on the back wall was a pink flamingo made of neon lights.

Mr. Chu showed off some other features of his unorthodox office, including a working slot machine and a roulette wheel while they waited for Elvira to return with the promised refreshment. While Mr. Chu was explaining to Patrick how he acquired his unique furnishings, Molly was eying the door and wondering if she should be planning their escape route. However, any thoughts of leaving were quickly thwarted as Elvira returned with a tea trolley loaded with a beautiful platter of fresh local fruit and sweets as well as a variety of tea and coffee choices.

Thanking his receptionist after she served the O'Neil's from the tray, Tommy Chu took his seat at the largest stool at the craps table and the meeting began. By the time they were fifteen minutes in, the O'Neil's were certain of two things: Tommy Chu was the most eccentric person they had ever encountered, and he was also a brilliant investigator.

"While you are enjoying your refreshments," Mr. Chu began, in a tone that belied both his diminutive stature and his bizarre hairstyle, "I would like to draw your attention to the presentation screen on your right."

In unison, Molly and Patrick turned their stools in that direction in time to watch a 48-inch flat screen rise, like a phoenix, from the roulette table. As the lights dimmed, the screen came on and Tommy Chu began his presentation. He spoke without interruption for the better part of an hour during which time he outlined his progress to date.

It was obvious that he and Paul Blanchard had communicated at length prior to this meeting. Mr. Chu had utilised every piece of information that Patrick had provided to Paul and had already added to each category. Even at this very early stage of the investigation, Mr. Chu was able to offer some preliminary findings.

Looking directly at Molly, he spoke with compassion telling the O'Neil's that it is typically very difficult to track down missing persons in China. The task becomes especially challenging when there is limited information and the subject was so very young at the time the photograph was taken. "On a more positive note," the investigator continued, "I have begun a dialogue with both the Witness Location and the Missing Person's agencies. They indicated that they are starting to make some headway and will have more information for me in the near future."

Patrick handed over new information he and Molly had brought with them and Mr. Chu reviewed it immediately. "This is most helpful," he said as he focused on the family pictures. "I will send this along to my colleagues today."

Before leaving, Elvira joined the group in the inner office and took the O'Neil's' contact information for when they would be staying in Dongtan. Both Patrick and Molly thanked Tommy Chu and told him they looked forward to talking with him again soon. Tommy, by way of response, bowed and kissed Molly's hand saying that it was a pleasure to meet them. Hard as it was to imagine, Molly found herself growing fonder of the odd little man.

As they stepped out of the building and into the, still warm, afternoon sun, Patrick burst into gales of laughter. "Mother of God, that was a strange encounter!" Getting no reaction from his normally sharp-witted wife, he prodded, "Come on *Mol*, I know you're busting to say it. Go ahead, get it off your chest."

Not able to hold it in any longer, Molly succumbed to the temptation. "OK. If Ronald McDonald and Elvis had a child… well it would be Tommy Chu."

"That's my smart ass girl," Patrick declared, taking her by the hand and walking toward Pudong Park, which was the site of the Oriental Pearl TV Tower.

"Patrick, look over there!" Molly announced as they approached the front of the building.

Patrick looked over and replied, "Well imagine that. We actually have acquaintances in Shanghai." Standing in an information booth outside the Oriental Pearl Tower, camera at his side stood Dequan, the student who took their picture their first day on the Bund promenade.

"Do you think he'll remember us?" asked Molly.

Well, the answer to that question was quickly uncovered. Looking up from the man with whom he was speaking, Dequan broke into a wide smile. "Well hello my new friends from the beautiful island in Canada," he shouted out. "Cape… Cape… Cape something," he said, forgetting the name.

"Cape Breton Island," Patrick reminded him, reaching out to shake Dequan's hand.

The two men fell into an easy conversation. Patrick was interested in learning anything he could about this new piece of China and Dequan was just the man to provide the information.

While they chatted, Molly took the opportunity to scout around the place, which looked to be enormous. Not wanting to venture too far on her own, she looked back frequently to make sure she could still remember where she had left her husband. There was just so much to see, and she wanted to share it with Patrick, so she slowly made her way back to the information booth.

"Time for another important picture for your album, Mrs. Molly," Dequan informed her when he saw her approaching. Strapping his cameras around his neck he directed the couple toward the front of the property where Molly had recently watched others have their picture taken. While she was busy exploring, Dequan had given Patrick some information about the famous landmark they stood before. He explained that the tower, which is surrounded by two bridges, creates a picture of twin dragons, playing with pearls, hence the name. He also told Patrick that the entire structure rests on rich green grassland, which gives the appearance of pearls shining on a jade plate.

As they got into position for the picture, Patrick recounted the rest of the details he learned during his mini lecture. "Dequan told me the Oriental Pearl Tower is 468 meters high and boasts one of the most unique architectural design in all of China." He went on to tell his wife about the eleven steel spheres and three enormous columns that make up the complex. "And Mol, you won't believe this but each one of the spheres houses different attractions. There's a space city and a science fantasy city. Jeez, there's even a five-star hotel and a shopping centre in one of the towers!" Molly had never seen her husband this animated about a building and she thoroughly enjoyed how happy he looked.

Dequan snapped their picture while Molly was listening to Patrick talking about the tower. "Beautiful," he proclaimed as he looked at the proof, and it was clear Dequan was referring to the couple as much as he was to the quality of the picture he had just taken.

Of course, Patrick wanted to take a tour of the tower and Molly was only too happy to oblige. Joining a large group of people, they entered a car on one of the double-decker elevators. Molly felt her stomach rush to her throat as the elevator ascended the quarter mile climb at the rate of seven metres per second. But once they arrived at their destination and stepped out on the top floor all of her nervousness left as she took in her surroundings.

Molly and Patrick were standing inside the magnificent pearl situated at the very apex of the structure. As far as they could see there were exciting places to shop and myriad restaurants, including a rotating restaurant, where they planned to have their dinner. Directly ahead was the sightseeing floor and Patrick quickly guided Molly in that direction.

They held their breath in awe as they tried to take in all the sights at once. The view of Shanghai from this height could only be described as spectacular and Molly was certain she would never be able to capture its splendour in a picture... but she sure as hell was going to give it a try. As they stood spellbound, looking over the amazing city that they had so quickly come to love, the sun began to set, offering yet another delight. The tower's three-dimensional lighting along with the glow from the setting sun painted a portrait of brilliant colour, the likes of which neither had ever seen.

When they finished their tour and, of course some shopping, Molly and Patrick enjoyed a delicious meal in the rotating restaurant as Shanghai and Pudong slowly passed before them. While they ate, they chatted about how they would spend their last days in Shanghai. Although they planned to leave for Dongtan in two days, they knew they would be returning to Shanghai to follow up with Tommy Chu. The thought of coming back made Molly happy. There was something special about this city and she would have been sad to think that she might never see it again.

The evening air had cooled off considerably by the time they took the elevator back to the main floor. Molly was glad they thought to bring along extra clothes in Patrick's trusty old backpack.

Each slipped into a warm sweater as they looked around trying to get their bearings before they started for home. Patrick stopped to ask a guard for directions, and he told them they were only about a ten to fifteen-minute walk to the ferry terminal. He also suggested that the couple considered taking the Bund Sightseeing Tunnel rather than the ferry across the Huangpu River.

He told them that the Bund Sightseeing Tunnel was a popular tourist attraction, and one that they shouldn't miss. "Why not?" said Molly enthusiastically? "We might as well enjoy the full Pudong experience. Patrick had assumed that would be her response and had already gone to purchase two tickets.

At the mouth of the tunnel, Patrick helped his wife into one of the automated cars. Noticing the 360-degree view from the vehicle, they settled themselves in for what they assumed would be another peaceful scenic look at the Huangpu River.

Wrong! Instead of displaying the river itself, the tunnel offered a wild, special-effects light show complete with strobe lights and loud music. Thankfully, the whole trip, which was meant to depict a journey to the Earth's core, was over in less than three minutes, which Molly immediately dubbed the 646.7-meter excursion to hell. Even Patrick, who didn't shock easily, admitted to being happy when they arrived at the Bund Promenade. Although both feeling a bit wobbly after their ride, they were pleased to learn it was only a ten-minute walk we back to the Fairmont Peace Hotel.

Before retiring for the night Patrick called Sam to let him know they would be coming to Dongtan in two days' time and Molly sent a note to Ava and Cole telling them their plans and updating them on the events of the day.

Joining Patrick in the dining room where she found him fixing a much-needed nightcap, Molly tried to hide her disappointment at not yet hearing from Ava. She wished that Ava would call or send a note, so she could stop worrying about her daughter. "Hi gorgeous," Patrick called out to his wife as she approached the wet bar. "Come here often?"

Distracted by her charming husband, Molly set aside her

morose feelings and smiled at Patrick. "Only when my favourite bartender is working." Molly replied. While he prepared their drinks, Patrick told Molly that Sam was looking forward to their visit and he insisted on driving to Shanghai to pick them up. When Patrick tried to protest, his brother-in-law claimed he had business in Shanghai that day. He told Patrick he would be at their hotel around one o'clock and hoped they could have lunch at the Fairmont Peace before leaving for Dongtan.

"He really is a lovely man," Molly said as Patrick carried the drinks to their bed. Both peeled off the clothes they had been in all day, donned the fluffy robes, which by now had become their official uniform and climbed up the platform to their bed. Patrick dimmed the lights as Molly took the first sip of her drink. "Delicious, as always," Molly told her handsome bartender husband. Breathing a contented sigh, they finished the tasty beverages, turned out the lights and, once again, were asleep before the room got dark.

Chapter 36

For their final full day in Shanghai, Molly and Patrick decided to do nothing. That isn't to say that they didn't plan to have a full, rich day but simply that for the next twenty-four hours, they had no set agenda, destinations or time frames. Leaving the hotel after breakfast, the couple turned left and began their exploration of the remaining portion of the Bund that they had not yet visited.

Once again, the quaint shops and markets featuring modern and traditional merchandise mesmerised Molly. She picked up a tiny kimono for their new grandson or granddaughter (although Molly was certain in her heart that this baby would be a boy). She also bought a layette for the baby's crib that she was sure Laurie would love. In the next shop she bought two Cheongsam dresses for Kelly Ann. One was decorated in painted cherry blossoms and the other was adorned in adorable pink dragons. Molly knew this was the traditional dress for little girls in China and Kelly Ann, diva that she was, would be thrilled with her gifts. She added satin pyjamas and slippers to her purchases and left the store, laden with bags and as happy as a clam.

Back on the promenade Patrick took a quick look over his shoulder and realised that they had not moved more than fifty metres from the hotel. Both were already carrying shopping bags and the day had barely begun. Accustomed to his wife's penchant for shopping in unusual places, Patrick figured he'd better at least try to intervene before they exceeded their baggage limit for flying home. "I have a suggestion Mol," he announced as he watched her eyeing the next shop. "What about if I take these parcels to the hotel and meet you back in this area in about fifteen minutes?"

"Sure, that would be great and by the way, I know this is your gentle way of reminding me we have to get all this stuff home." Patrick smiled as he took the parcels from his wife. He didn't want to dampen her spirit and he knew by the wink she gave him that he hadn't.

Patrick jogged back to the hotel, unloaded the treasures and as promised came back in search of his wife. At first he didn't see her and decided to stand in clear view in the area where he left her, hoping she might spot him. His eyes roamed up and down the promenade until they came to rest on a beautiful sight. Sitting on a park bench surrounded by small children and a few adults was his wife. As he neared the happy little group he could hear Molly's melodious voice singing an Irish children song that she use to sing to Cole and Ava when they were young. Approaching quietly so as not to disturb the impromptu concert, Patrick listened as he watched his wife.

Though her voice was happy, her eyes held a glint of sadness. *Was she missing Ava,* Patrick wondered, *or was she thinking about another little girl? A child who was lost to her and whom she called Mishi?*

When she came to the end of the song, the children clapped their little hands as hard as they could and called out, *geng duo xinxi qing,* meaning "more please".

Patrick used this lull in the performance as his opportunity to join Molly on the bench. Looking up, Molly smiled and explained that the children were from a nearby orphanage. She introduced Patrick to Jai, one of the workers who brought the children to the promenade for an outing. Jai told Molly that although the children didn't understand a word of English, they loved listening to any kind of music. Molly, who could remember the joy of singing along with her father from the time she was a young said she would be happy to sing an old Irish tune for the children. And judging from the reaction on the little faces looking up at Molly from their blanket on the grass, she was clearly a rock star in their eyes. Not wanting to disappoint her precious audience, Molly sang one more song, waved goodbye to the children and told Jai that she would see her later this afternoon.

"See her this afternoon?" Patrick repeated with obvious confusion in his voice, "are you doing another concert?"

"No, not a concert," Molly replied. "The orphanage where these children live has been in operation for more than fifty years. I was thinking that if they retained records over the years, it might just prove to be another lead in helping to solve the puzzle."

Patrick agreed that was a great idea. They would finish exploring the Bund, have lunch and then head over to the address Jai had written down for Molly.

Although Molly continued to browse in more shops along the Bund, she didn't do any more shopping. Patrick could tell she was preoccupied and most likely thinking about her upcoming visit to the orphanage. When they stopped for lunch at a lovely little deli, Molly remained distracted as she picked at her meal, scarcely eating a bite. Patrick convinced her to have a cup of coffee as their appointment wasn't until two o'clock and the orphanage was only a short cab ride away. Agreeing, Molly finished her sandwich and enjoyed her coffee although Patrick saw her checking her watch frequently.

At the stroke of two, Molly and Patrick stood on the steps of a large, institutional-looking building and rang the bell. An older, matronly woman answered and invited them into the foyer, which had a surprisingly warm and homely feel to it. Molly relaxed a little as she explained the reason for her visit. "We are expecting you. Please come in," their host invited.

The O'Neil's were led into a large sitting room that was sparsely furnished with an old desk and four wooden chairs. But Molly barely noticed the shabby furniture. The only thing that caught her attention was the row upon row of old metal filing cabinets, which lined three of the walls. Casting a side-glance at her husband, Molly said, "Well, that certainly answers my question about whether or not the orphanage keeps records." Patrick nodded in agreement but inside he was hoping Molly hadn't put too much hope in this particular lead.

Within minutes the door to the office opened again and Jai, along with two ladies and a distinguished-looking younger man entered. When introductions were made, Molly and Patrick learned that the two ladies were social workers who had been employed at this orphanage for thirty-five and forty years, respectively. The man, Mr. Fong, was the administrator of *Xiao Hua* or Little Flower Orphanage.

Once everyone was seated, Molly began to tell her story and the reason for coming here today. Mr. Fong, who spoke and understood English listened intently as Molly talked while Jai did her best to translate for the others. Molly showed them June's letter and the picture of the child. She always carried a copy of this information in her purse now, never knowing when she might need it.

Mr. Fong was first to look at the picture. He glanced at it for just a moment before apologising to the O'Neil's stating that he had only been at Little Flower Orphanage for five years and was not able to help with the identity of the child.

Jai took the photo from Mr. Fong and passed it to the two long-time employees and asked if either of them recognised the young girl. The first lady looked at Molly with sad eyes and shook her head indicating that the child in the picture was not familiar to her. However, when the younger of the two women looked at the photo, she had an entirely different reaction. Speaking rapidly and clutching the picture to her heart, she reached for Molly's hand saying, "*Shi, shi, Wo jide*", which Jai translated as, "Yes, yes, I remember."

Shock, elation and fear hit Molly simultaneously as she looked into the eyes of the social worker who introduced herself as Li. "Thank you," she said when she was finally able to speak. "Please tell us what you know."

With a faraway look in her eyes, Li began to speak in a voice that was both soft and serene. And although Molly could not understand Li's words, she recognized the pain and love in her tone. Jai and Mr. Fong listened intently and took notes, neither uttering a word until Li had finished speaking.

Without hesitation, Jai began to translate for Patrick and Molly. According to Li, this child had been brought to the orphanage late at night on the eve of the Chinese New Year. Li remembered the date specifically because it was her first night working as the shift supervisor, explaining that since most employees are off for the new year's holiday, the orphanage was rather short staffed. Having worked there for nearly fifteen years at the time, Li was the most senior staff member on shift that night.

In her account Li said what she recalled most vividly was when the mother arrived with her infant daughter it was already dark. Li remembered inviting them to come inside because the child was not dressed for the evening weather. She went on to say that the mother refused and abruptly tried to thrust the baby into Li's arms.

Molly, who was looking directly at Li while Jai told the story saw tears in Li's eyes that matched those in her own.

Continuing to speak from her notes, Jai told the O'Neil's how Li tried to encourage the mother to stay at least until she could contact the administrator but once again the woman refused. In fact, the only information the mother provided was that the child was eight months old and that her father was a wealthy man who'd taken advantage of her and then left her with this child. Knowing how hard this was to hear, Jai gently touched Molly's arm and finished the report.

"Molly, when Li asked the baby's name, the mother told her such a wicked child did not deserve a name, and with that she left the orphanage and never returned."

The room fell silent when Jai finished speaking. Both Molly and Patrick need a moment to absorb what they had just heard. When she finally found her voice, Molly looked at each person in the room and said, "I am so sorry for what this dear child must have suffered, but I can't imagine what any of this could possibly have to do with Mark or anyone else in my family. Mark was not a wealthy man and I am certain that he would never abandon a child that he was in any way responsible for." As Molly spoke she was remembering how elated Mark was when he learned they were having a child.

Realising how long they had been there Patrick, who was sitting next to his wife with his arm protectively around her shoulder suggested perhaps they should finish up today's meeting and let the people get back to work.

"Of course," Molly agreed, knowing that they must be very busy. "I really appreciate the information you shared but I still have so many questions". Mr. Fong assured Molly that she could come back or call any time. He also said that he would have Li go through the records for that period and see if they could find anything else that could help.

As the O'Neil's were preparing to leave, Li rushed over to Molly. She grabbed her hand and said in broken English, "*Mei Hui.* I name baby *Mei Hui.* Name mean beautiful wisdom."

"Thank you, Li," Molly replied as she opened the front door, "That is a lovely name."

Chapter 37

Molly was quiet as they made the short walk back to the ferry terminal. Patrick held his wife's hand and, like her, he walked in silence. He always respected Molly's need to work things out on her own and knew she would talk when the time was right for her. In a way Patrick was happy for the solitude. Instinctively, he knew that as a result of this afternoon's events his life with Molly was about to change and he desperately hoped it would not be in a bad way.

In the twenty-two years they'd been together, he'd watched his wife courageously fight off the demons that had haunted her since the death of her first husband, Mark, and her beloved sister, June. But as it was with everything else about Molly, she would deal with her feelings about this new development with grace and dignity... and on her own terms.

As they neared the terminal, Patrick steered Molly toward the ferry rather taking than the tunnel they had travelled through the previous evening. After the day they had just put in, Patrick wisely decided that the bright lights and sounds from the Bund sightseeing tunnel was a bit more drama than either of them needed. Molly followed Patrick as he purchased their tickets and selected seats near the back of the ferry. "You always know exactly what I need Pat," she said as she leaned her head against his broad shoulder and let the soft roll of the ferry sooth her as they crossed the river to their hotel. He answered her with a kiss on her head, which told her all she needed to know.

While Molly changed into some comfortable clothes, Patrick once again took charge, this time ordering dinner from one of the many excellent selections on the room service menu. He was pretty sure Molly would prefer not to go out to dinner tonight.

"See, this is why I love you," Molly announced when Patrick told her dinner would arrive in about an hour. Noticing how much more relaxed Molly looked already made him feel better. "Here kiddo," he said passing her a drink of wine. "Start without me. I'm going to have a quick shower and get out of these clothes."

"Hell of a plan," Molly replied, accepting the glass he handed her.

One of the things Molly missed about not being at home was listening to the great music stations they both enjoyed so much. As she sipped her wine, she fumbled through the box in which they had packed their electronics until she found her iPad. She barley gave the more than two thousand songs stored in iTunes a second look before selecting Matt Anderson's latest album.

Matt was a young entertainer from the Atlantic Provinces who won her and Patrick's heart the first time they heard him play. Matt had a jazzy, bluesy, soulful sound that kept his audience mesmerised from the first note. And as if that wasn't enough… he had a voice that could make an angel cry.

Although far from an angel herself, the music apparently was having the same effect on Molly. Perhaps it was the events of the day, or maybe combination of good wine and the tender words of Matt singing *My Old Friend the Blues.* Whatever the reason, Patrick returned from his shower to find Molly curled up in an armchair, crying as though her heart was breaking.

"Privacy be damned," Patrick swore quietly as he knelt beside his wife and kissed away her tears. Looking almost embarrassed to have been caught, Molly put on a brave face and assured her husband she was just feeling a bit melancholy.

"Not this time, baby," Patrick announced in a tone that surprise her. Leading her over to the sofa where they could sit together, Patrick turned the music down and the lights up. He topped up Molly's drink and poured one for himself. This unexpected change of behaviour had Molly's total attention and she looked at her husband not at all sure what was coming next.

"So here's what's going to happen," Patrick began without preamble. "First of all, you are going to tell me exactly how you're feeling about everything that happened today. Then I'm going to do the same. Mol, one of the things I love about us is that we have always been honest with each other and we don't play head games. I know the information we heard this afternoon must have scared the hell out of you. I also know that very soon you are going to learn some things that will most likely have an impact on all of our lives. What I need for you to understand is that Ava, Cole and I are going to be here for you, no matter what happens. But honey, we're a little scared too. So please Molly, talk to me. You don't have to do this on your own... so please don't shut us out."

When Patrick finished speaking, neither said a word. For the next few minutes the only sound was the music that emanated quietly from the speakers. Perhaps that was why Patrick got such a fright when Molly bounded out of her seat and stood before him, arms planted on her hips.

"You're damn right I'm scared. I'm scared that Ava is going to hate me more than she already does for not letting this go. And I'm very afraid that you've had enough of it too. Pat, we've made an amazing life together, you, me and our children and that should have been more than enough for me." Molly took a long drink from her glass before she continued. "I mean, you and Cole had a shitty thing happen to you during your first marriage... but you let it go and allowed me and Ava to become your family. I didn't do that for *you* Pat. I held onto the insecurities from my marriage to Mark and my anger over June's death and now..." she looked up at Pat with shame and terror in her eyes. "... and now I'm bringing something huge into our life. Something I know I can't walk away from."

No one had to tell Molly what the connection between her family and Mei Hui was. God knows she tried to pretend the child she only knew from a photograph was a stranger, but deep inside Molly knew she was only fooling herself. And clearly, she wasn't even doing a good job of that.

One look at Mei Hui's mouth and Molly knew she was looking at an exact replica of Ava's. She was pretty sure Patrick saw it too, even though he couldn't put his finger on what was familiar about her. The first time she saw the picture attached to June's letter she recognised the same distinctive scowl that baby Ava had perfected whenever she gave Patrick one of her infamous stink eyes. There was not another iota of similarity between the two girls but there was no doubt in Molly's mind that in the very near future she was going to meet Mark's first child. The time for silence was over and she told her husband what she should have said a month before.

"Oh my God!" exclaimed Patrick. "How the hell could I have missed that?" Patrick immediately grabbed the picture from the file they had brought along to China. He placed the tiny photo on the table and next to it he laid a picture of Ava and Cole holding their teddy bears. Although Ava was smiling in that particular picture, the bow of her lip and the slight droop on the right side was unquestionably exactly the same.

"Molly. Why did you not mention this before?" He sounded truly angry with her and that made Molly all the more afraid.

"I'm so sorry Pat. I don't know why I didn't tell you. At first I thought it was my imagination and then when you didn't seem to notice, well I guess I just hoped I was wrong. Before she had a chance to continue with her explanation Patrick interrupted her by asking if there was anything else she was not telling him.

"No Patrick," she answered through her tears. "There is nothing else. Please say that you believe me." Just looking at her husband as he stared into her eyes, Molly knew that she had hurt him, and she prayed that there was something she could do to make it right.

Getting up from the sofa and standing next to her, Patrick took Molly's hands in his.

"I just need a few minutes," he told her. I'm going to take a little walk and clear my head. I'll be back within an hour and I promise we'll straighten this out. I just need to be alone right now."

Molly stepped aside as she watched Patrick walk out the door. She understood completely why he would need some time to himself, but she couldn't control the pounding of her heart as the door closed behind him.

Chapter 38

For what seemed like an eternity, Molly sat on the sofa, where Patrick had so recently sat beside her and kissed away her tears. Too sad to cry anymore and too afraid to move, Molly sat motionless staring at the door of their suite feeling miserable and conflicted. For as much as she wanted to see him walk back into the room, she was overcome with anxiety about what he might say to her when he eventually returned.

When she was able to, she stood and walked into the washroom where splashed her face with cold water, hoping the icy spray would bring some colour back to her cheeks and some semblance of life to her eyes.

Feeling like a woman twenty years her senior, Molly slowly straightened up and looked at her reflection in the mirror. But rather than her own sad face, the image she saw took her breath away. Standing in the hallway behind her with outstretched arms was Patrick.

Afraid to blink for fear the image would disappear, Molly spun around to face him. Within a heartbeat they were wrapped in each other's arms, both talking at the same time. Between passionate kisses and hot tears, neither could make out what the other was saying... but at that moment, words really didn't matter.

Without breaking the embrace, they made their way back to the sofa where they continued to hold tightly to each other. There would be time for talking later. Right now, each was content to touch and feel and be reassured that regardless of life's trials and tribulations, their place would always be right here...together.

When the door chimes to their suite sounded announcing the arrival of the meal Patrick had ordered earlier, they jumped up and pulled apart as if they were children who had been caught misbehaving. Laughing with a light-heartedness neither of them could have imagined a mere hour before. Patrick planted a quick kiss on his wife's cheek and opened the door to the waiter.

As with every meal they ordered since arriving at the Fairmount Peace Hotel, tonight's was equally delicious. Patrick poured wine into two glasses as Molly uncovered and set out the feast that was to be their dinner. Seated side by side at their little dining room table, so as not to break physical contact entirely, they began to eat and to talk.

Patrick went first. He started by apologising for having walked out on Molly, especially knowing how upset she was. Twenty-two years ago, Patrick had made a promise to his new wife that he would always be there for her. This was the first time in their marriage that he had broken that vow and he felt ashamed that he had walked away in anger.

When it was her turn, Molly told Patrick that she was truly sorry for not sharing her suspicions about Mark having fathered Mei Hui. Looking deeply into his eyes Molly asked her husband to forgive her for not trusting him with the information that had as much to do with him as it did her. "I don't even know why I didn't tell you right away. Pat, you have been so wonderful to Ava and me, even through all the baggage I carried around from my first marriage. I guess I just wanted to spare you from having to deal with any more."

When dinner was finished, and the dishes were cleared from their room, Molly and Patrick continued to talk. The venue changed from the dining room table to their bed, but the dialogue between went on late into the night, with both admitting they were a little nervous about the impact of finding out Ava had a half-sister... if that turned out to be the case.

Of the whole family Ava had expressed the most concern about this trip and Molly felt certain that her daughter was not going to take the news about a possible new addition to her family very well.

"Let's not get too far ahead of ourselves," Patrick cautioned, taking Molly's hand in his and tenderly kissing her fingers. "If it comes to pass that Mei Hui turns out to be Mark's child—and Mol that's still a *big* if, we will tell Ava together. For now, let's focus on getting as much information as we can."

They continued talking much later into the night until. Unable to form another coherent sentence, they fell asleep in each other's arms. When the sun streamed through the window the next morning, it was Molly who woke first. Before she turned toward her still sleeping husband, she took a quick inventory of her feelings. She shuddered when she remembered how terrified she'd felt the night before when Patrick left, but in the light of day, and particularly following the wonderful talk they had the night before, in a strange way, Molly was almost glad that it happened. Not the crying and yelling or the fight, but the chance to bring everything out in the open and start afresh.

Turning her head to the side, she smiled as she saw Patrick, now awake and grinning back at her. "Good morning beautiful," he greeted her. "You know, in a crazy kind of way, I think I'm glad we were forced into the discussion we had last night. I feel better about a whole lot of things... even more focused. Does that sound odd to you?"

"Not in the least," Molly replied. "That is exactly what I was lying here thinking about. That... and how much I love you."

"Yeah, well right back at you," Patrick replied giving her a little pat on her butt and reminding her it was time to get up and prepare to check out of this magnificent hotel. Sam would be coming by to collect them at one o'clock and they still had to have breakfast and pack for the next leg of their journey.

Indulging in one more hug, Molly kicked back the duvet and headed off to the shower. She wanted to have enough time to send a note to the children and one to Marie. Although she planned to heed Patrick's advice about not sharing unconfirmed information about Mark's possible connection to Mei Hui, she did think it would be prudent to at least mention their trip to the orphanage. Patrick agreed that it was a good idea to let the family know they were making some progress with piecing together the puzzle that had brought them to China. Introducing it now would also lessen the shock if and when it came.

It didn't take long to pack their bags. Molly spent a few minutes looking at the precious clothes they picked up for Kelly Ann and their new grandchild. She felt her throat tighten as she ran her fingers over the silky kimono and dresses wondering for the hundredth time how she was ever going to get through a month without seeing her precious baby girl. Laurie had been great to send photos and updates, but it wasn't the same as being able to touch her.

Molly shook off her lethargy as she watched Patrick emerge from the bathroom shaved, showered and smelling wonderful. His toiletries were the last things to be packed and Molly had made room in the valise for them.

"Ready for breakfast? I'm starving," he announced as he made a final search of the suite to make sure they weren't leaving anything behind. "Damn, I'm gonna miss this place!" And with one last look over their shoulder they closed the door to their room and on the first leg of their journey.

Chapter 39

"When you get to a mountain, there will always be a way through"
(Chinese Proverb)

No sooner had they put down their coffee cups after a delightfully decadent breakfast when Molly jumped to her feet and tore out of the hotel without a word to her husband. Not sure whether to chase after her or call 911, Patrick decided to wait it out and see what transpired.

Patrick craned his neck as he watched his wife disappear from view. Rounding the corner of the building at breakneck speed she reappeared, eyes firmly fixed on her target. With one final burst of energy Molly's feet left the ground as she landed in the arms of a man Patrick knew only from photographs and telephone conversations. He watched in silence for a moment longer while giving them time for their private reunion. When their embrace gave way to laughter Patrick signed the breakfast bill to their room and made his way-out side to meet Sam Friedman.

"OK. Break it up you two. That's my wife you're molesting" he called out in mock horror as he approached the still entwined couple. Sam jumped back with a start, releasing Molly and at the same time, adjusting his glasses, which, by now were perched precariously at the end of his nose.

"As I live and breathe Pat, is this really you?" Unprepared for such an exuberant welcome, Patrick found himself wrapped in the same warm embrace he had just rescued his wife from.

"Sam Friedman, I presume?" Patrick jokingly inquired as he hugged Molly's brother-in-law.

When the two men pulled apart they continued to stare at one another, each with a look on their face that Molly couldn't quite discern. "God it's good to finally meet you," they said in perfect unison and Molly knew at that moment that she was in the presence of two men who truly loved her as much as she did them.

Arm in arm, the three headed back into the restaurant. The O'Neil's still had to collect their belongings, which had been stored with the concierge. Patrick volunteered to complete the checkout process, suggesting Molly and Sam go inside and order up some coffee. Molly, who had never in her adult life turned down a cup of coffee, was happy to comply. She took Sam's arm and led him toward the seats by the window that she and Patrick had recently vacated.

After completing his business at the front desk, Patrick stopped at the entrance to the dining room and took a few minutes to observe Molly and Sam. He couldn't help but smile as he watched his wife. With her arms flying as she spoke, and her beautiful russet curls thrown back in laughter, Patrick imagined that poor Sam probably hadn't had a chance to utter a word since he arrived.

Having said that, the look of sheer pleasure on Sam's face told Patrick with certainty that he didn't mind his role of passive listener in the least. As he took his own seat at the table and joined the little group, Patrick found himself immediately caught up in the whirlwind that was Molly. "Oh, Hi Pat," she said looking somewhat surprised to see that he had returned, "Isn't it wonderful to be here together, at last?"

"It certainly is, baby," he replied.

When the waiter arrived with a carafe of coffee, Patrick took over the host duties, filling the three cups while Molly continued to regale Sam with stories from home and anecdotes about the children. She spoke with such pride about Cole and Ava that Patrick felt his throat catch as he was reminded again what an amazing mother Molly had been to his son.

Not wanting to interrupt the conversation but realising they probably had a bit of drive ahead of them, Patrick waited for a break in the conversation before asking Sam what time he would like to leave for Dongtan. Sam replied that he could sit here all night and listen to Molly, but he agreed with Patrick that they probably should be heading out soon.

The two men collected the luggage, stowing it in Sam's Jeep while Molly bought a few souvenirs from the hotel gift shop. Not that she could ever forget this magnificent hotel, but it would be nice to bring home a trinket for their family and friends.

When they were ready to roll, Molly hopped into the cluttered back seat of the jeep. Although her husband objected saying Molly should ride shotgun, she knew Patrick would never have been able to fold his long legs into the rear of the vehicle. She also wanted to give the guys a chance to talk during the drive. For her part, Molly was happy to sit and listen, knowing there would be plenty of time for conversation over the next few weeks.

Dongtan was about 250 kilometres from the Fairmount Peace Hotel and both Molly and Patrick were happy to play the role of sightseers as Sam gave them a guided tour. As they neared the city, Patrick's head whipped from side to side as Sam rapidly pointed out the many amazing sight along the road. Listening from the back seat, Molly joined in the conversation, expressing her own surprise as they drove through what seemed to her to be a vibrant new city. Patrick was equally taken aback to see such progress, but Sam reminded them both that Dongtan had recently gone through a complete transformation.

Where once sat an aging rural island nestled in the Yangtze River near Shanghai, today's Dongtan was well on its way to becoming a fully sustainable city.

With unmistakable pride in his voice, Sam talked about how the entire region had worked together to develop and implement state-of-the-art green technology solutions and infrastructures. "You want to know the best part?" Sam asked and without even waiting for their response he answered his own question. "By continuing to follow the design we have already put in place, we will soon be able to generate all the energy we could ever need solely from renewable resources. And not only that, but the same sustainability plan will allow residents to grow their own food and recycle waste!"

"Congratulations old boy," Patrick said when Sam finished. "That's is an amazing accomplishment and while I certainly don't have the background that you do, I know how tirelessly you have worked on this project over the years. Sam nodded to acknowledge the compliment and told his brother-in-law that he was just one person on a very large team.

From her spot in the back seat, Molly smiled, knowing full well that Sam had been instrumental in overseeing much of the work that had already been accomplished. She also knew that both Sam and June would never accept the accolades for their efforts, choosing instead to share such praise among their colleagues.

Patrick was intrigued with what he was hearing, and he continued to ask questions, which Sam was only too glad to answer. While the boys chatted, Molly closed her eyes and turned her thoughts to June.

In the two decades since her sister's untimely death, the city of Dongtan had continued to move forward with its ecological agenda. June had often talked about the city's enormous potential and now Dongtan was well on its way to becoming entirely self-sufficient and an exemplary model for how cities should be built.

Damn it all, Molly thought angrily, *why couldn't she have lived to see this?*

"You still with us Mol?" Sam called over his shoulder realising Molly hadn't said a word in the past half hour. "I'm here all right," she answered. "I just couldn't get a word in edgewise with you two guys yakking your heads off."

Shaking off her melancholy, Molly leaned over the front seat of the jeep and draped one arm over each man. "Did I mention how glad I am that we are together at last?"

"Me too kiddo," Sam replied. "More that you can even imagine."

Chongming Island was where June had conducted much of her

research and Sam had selected a hotel for the couple very near the site of June's first office. Initially, Sam worried that Molly might not want to stay in a place that held so many memories of her sister, but his fears were soon put to rest when they passed the first sign indicating that Chongming Island was fifty kilometres away.

"Sam, Pat, look!" Molly shouted when she read the sign. "Chongming Island. June told me so much about this place, I feel like I've been here before. Oh Sam, please tell me we are going to staying somewhere near this magnificent island."

Sam laughed telling Molly that she was indeed going to be staying near Chongming. "I'd say you'll be within spittin' distance," he replied, using one of the wonderfully colourful phrases he picked up during his visit to Cape Breton Island. "In fact, you should be able to see your sister's old office from your hotel window."

For the remainder of the drive Molly could hardly contain herself. She felt like a child waiting for Christmas morning. When Sam pulled up in front of the hotel, she leapt from the car before it was even fully stopped.

"Let her be," Patrick told Sam as he hollered for her to wait until he found a parking spot near the lobby. "She has been waiting most of her adult life to walk where June walked and to breath the same air June breathed. Sam, I know my wife as well as I know myself, so believe me when I tell you what she needs right now is for us to go and register and to leave her on her own. And don't worry, she'll find us when she's ready."

"You got it, my friend," Sam answered. "Let's go and get you checked in."

With registration out of the way, the two men proceeded to a lobby café where Patrick ordered two large coffees, one for himself and one for Molly. Upon hearing his order, Sam quickly intervened in both English for Patrick and Chinese for the waitress. "You might want to rethink that. Remember you are in the tea capital of the world. Unless otherwise specified, you're gonna find yourself in procession of two big old cups of instant coffee."

Seeing the look of absolute horror on Patrick's face, Sam

continued. "Not to worry, there's a Starbucks around the corner. It's not Tim Horton's… but it's not half bad." Satisfied that he wasn't going to be suffering from caffeine withdrawal while he was on the Island, Patrick settled for a cup of tea and joined Sam in the lobby where they waited for Molly's return.

Settled in their seats, Sam checked over his shoulder to make sure his sister-in-law had not yet arrived, Leaning close to Patrick he asked in a voice barely above a whisper, "Can you help me out here, buddy. I'm beyond delighted that you are both here, but I also know the real reason for your trip. Do you think Molly wants to get into it right away or would she rather wait until she's had a chance to visit the island and have a bit of a rest?"

"Sam Friedman!" came a bellow from behind then, startling both men and making them leap from their chairs.

"Jesus, Mary and Joseph, Mol! What's the matter? You nearly gave us a heart attack."

"I'll tell you what the matter is Sam… and Patrick, you should hear this too." Like two petulant children, the men took their seats and stared at Molly waiting for their admonishment, or at least an explanation for what had made her so angry.

She addressed Sam first. "Sam, we are also thrilled to be here with you. And yes, there is another reason for the trip, which I told you about on the phone. But you are my only brother-in-law and I love that we are going to get to spend time together, so don't you dare think, even for a second, that you are not an important part of this visit."

"I love you too Molly and I'm sorry for—" That was as far as Sam got with his apology before Molly held up her hand with the same annoyed look on her face.

"Not finished yet," she announced. "The second thing I want to say, and this one is for both of you. *Do not* exclude me, or even try to shelter me from any information that could help to solve this puzzle. If you two guys want to bond over a bottle of rum, well that's fine, great in fact. But I have spent nearly twenty-five years feeling like I failed my sister for not having made this trip." Molly stopped for a moment as unchecked emotions welled inside her and fresh tears filled her eyes.

Springing to his feet, Patrick approached his wife and wrapped his arms around her. "Baby, you are absolutely right," he confirmed. "It was never anyone's intention to exclude you from anything. Sam here just wanted to know if you wanted a little break before we got into it."

From where he stood, Sam nodded his head, still not entirely sure if he should attempt to come any closer. When Molly saw the look of terror on his face, she burst into gales of laughter. "Oh Sam, you poor soul. I'm sorry I was such a bitch. It's just that I finally get to come to Dongtan and now I have to deal with finding the identity of Mei Hui. I guess I'm just overwhelmed with everything. I promise I'll be in a better mood in the morning."

No longer afraid of his loveable, albeit eccentric, sister-in-law, Sam leaned in and gave her a kiss on the cheek. "Good night, Sam."

"Good night, my little nutcase. I'm going to leave you on your own for the evening and I'll be by to pick you up around ten tomorrow morning. I have a full day planned for all of us. As for tomorrow night, I already booked another room at the hotel. If it works for both of you, we'll have dinner and then retire to one of the rooms with a big bottle of rum and get this thing started."

Sam shook Pat's hand and kissed Molly one more time. As Pat led his wife to the elevator, Sam could hear her say, "He called me a nutcase! Imagine... *me*! A nutcase!"

Sam shook his head slowly from side to side as he walked back to his Jeep.

God, how he missed June tonight.

Chapter 40

The next morning dawned sunny and bright as Molly stretched luxuriously in their oh-so-comfortable bed.

Last night after dinner and a call home to the kids, Molly and Patrick had opted for an early night. Both were more tired than either had realised. They slept soundly for over ten hours and awoke feeling refreshed and ready to go.

Anxious to start her day, Molly slipped out of bed and watched the sunrise over the Yangtze River. She thought about her conversation with Cole and Ava last night and although nothing overtly wrong had happened during the conversation, her motherly intuition was telling her that Ava was withdrawing more and more, each time she updated her on the progress of their trip and especially their search for answers about Mei Hui's identity. This became particularly evident when Molly told them about her chance meeting with the children on the Pudong and how she ended up at the orphanage where she learned Mei Hui had spent at least part of her life.

Both Cole and Laurie could barely contain their excitement. They were amazed at the irony of Molly's little impromptu concert leading them to such a significant clue so early in the search. Ava, on the other hand, had nothing to say on the topic of Mei Hui, even though her brother prompted her to participate in the conversation. In fact, as soon as she learned that the 'mystery child' now had a name, Ava immediately made an excuse to leave the conversation, claiming she had an errand to run. And although she tried to sound cheerful, it was a weak attempt and didn't fool anyone.

"Don't fret Mom," Cole gently consoled his mother when he caught the change in her voice. "Ava is all strung out between waiting on her grades and finalising her work placement to Tanzania. Apparently, there was a problem with getting her visa."

Laurie, who had also picked up on her mother-in-law's concern, was quick to jump in. "Well, Cole and I think this is *wonderful* news and we want to hear about your progress, every step of the way. Ava will come around," Laurie promised, trying hard to sound more confident than she felt. "Just wait and see."

"Thanks guys," Molly said before she and Patrick signed off. She actually felt somewhat better after talking to Cole and Laurie. She had no illusions about her younger child's reaction changing anytime soon. But she was very thankful for the supportive phone call.

As she sat in the hotel watching as the brilliant sun made its appearance, Molly was able to think about Ava's behaviour more clearly and with less emotion. *Of course, Ava would be feeling stressed*, Molly rationalised. She vowed to call her at her apartment in a few days and not even bring up the trip or Mei Hui. In fact, Molly would make sure that she and Patrick would focus solely on Ava and her own exciting plans.

"You are muttering to yourself... what's up?" came a sleepy voice from across the room.

"Sorry sweetheart" Molly apologised, getting back into bed with Patrick. "I didn't realise I was talking out loud."

Patrick scooped his still bed warm wife into his arms and buried his face in her gorgeous hair. "Look, I know Ava was being... well she was being Ava, when we talked to her last night. Did her behaviour upset you?"

"Yeah, it did." Molly confessed. "But we both knew that Ava had reservations about the whole idea from the beginning. I decided I'm just going to back off on discussing Mei Hui when I talk to Ava next time. If she wants to know anything, she'll ask." Patrick agreed that was a good plan and promised he would do the same.

Checking the clock beside the bed, Patrick saw that it was only seven o'clock. "We still have a few hours before Sam gets here. Any idea of how we could kill some time?" Without further invitation, Molly snuggled back under the covers where they spent the next hour 'killing time' in the most delightful way.

Sam arrived at ten sharp and Molly and Patrick were in the lobby waiting when he arrived. With a knapsack packed for whatever the day might bring, they climbed into the Jeep. This time Molly got to ride up front. Leaning over, she kissed Sam on the cheek and told him she'd had a great sleep and they were ready for anything.

True to his word, Sam had indeed planned a rich, full day for his guests.

For starters, Molly and Patrick were treated to private tour of some seldom seen locations around Chongming Island. Prior to their visit, Sam had arranged with his government counterparts to gain access to some of the most beautiful and protected areas on the island.

A short time later, Sam drove his Jeep over a curb and proceeded to travel through what seemed to be an empty field. Stopping at a lone picnic table under a rustic enclosure, he announced, "We're here."

Happy to follow Sam's lead, Molly and Pat took their seat at the table. Having checked for sizes the night before, Sam handed each a pair of government-issue hiking boots, which they promptly donned. Street shoes stored back in the Jeep, Molly and Patrick waited for their next instruction.

"If you are going to be needing a washroom for the next few hours, I strongly suggest you find a tree before we set out," Sam announced.

"On my way," Patrick replied as he headed for the woods behind them. Molly, who had no intention of discovering what might be lurking beyond the tree line opted to wait it out.

As they sat at the picnic table waiting for Patrick's return, Sam put his arm around Molly's shoulder. Taking her hands in his own, he looked into her eyes and said, "Mol, today I'm finally going to get to show you some of the amazing work your sister did." He went on to explain how Chongming Island was under constant risk for exploitation of its habitats and natural resources. "You know the spot where we are sitting is geographically located less than fifty kilometres from Shanghai, which is the world's fastest growing city. "June's early work played a very big role in preventing this island from becoming a victim of the unrelenting urban sprawl."

When he saw her eyes fill with tears Sam continued. "I hope those are tears of pride I'm seeing. Because of June's research, instead of certain destruction, Chongming is now a green island and a national model for environmentally sustainable development."

Molly smiled and wiped away her tears. "Thank you for taking us here Sam. I know this is still as hard for you as it is for me. I could see the pain in your eyes when you saw me for the first time yesterday. And I do understand exactly what it feels like because I still feel her loss every day."

Patrick, who walked into the end of the conversation, paused for a moment again to allow these two beautiful people to share their long-overdue expression of grief in privacy. When he saw them pull away from each other he joined them and took the opportunity to lighten the mood.

"OK, old man," he said, "let's get this show on the road."

"You got it, my friend," Sam replied as they set off on their adventure.

In his best tour guide voice, Sam began. "Ladies and Gentlemen, welcome to my island. Encompassing 750 square miles, Chongming is the world's largest alluvial island. Situated at the mouth of the Yangtze River, its rich soils and extensive wetlands are abundant with fresh and saltwater marshes as well as tidal creeks and mudflats."

Patrick laughed at his brother-in-law's theatrical efforts, but he and Molly were both interested to learn more about this beautiful island. Reverting to his own voice, Sam pointed out that the condition of its environment was so important because it creates a veritable haven for a wide assortment of birds and fish.

Leading them carefully along the riverbank, Sam showed his guests aquatic species such as Japanese eel and Chinese sturgeon.

Molly was delighted with the chance to observe these magnificent fish as they lingered in the moist, muddy everglades. Sam told them the creatures travelled upriver to their spawning sites.

The group walked for over an hour when Patrick announced he was getting hungry. "Jeez, the guy must be psychic!" Sam told Molly. "About half a mile upstream we are going to reach one of the camps. Jin is expecting us and I'm sure she'll have something to fill the hole."

"Don't know who Jin is but it sounds good to me" Pat responded. "I think I can last a few more minutes."

Jin, as it turned out, was the camp's cook. When Sam introduced his guests and told Jin how hungry Pat was, she sprang into action. "Come eat. I make lots of food." Not needing any further invitation, Patrick took Jin by the arm and let her lead him to a table laden with unfamiliar but wonderfully smelling treats.

After enjoying a tasty and very filling lunch that consisted of delectable slow-cooked pork with dried sautéed string beans, Patrick said he felt like he was going to burst at the seams. "I have just the cure for that" Sam announced as he led the way to where they would begin their bird-watching tour.

The group thanked Jin for her hospitality and with full bellies prepared to set out on the next leg of their adventure.

The camp had a restroom, which Molly was very happy to see. Sam also checked Molly's backpack to make sure she had all of the essential gear and provisions they would need for what turned out to be a three-hour trek.

With over 150 known species on the island, Molly and Patrick took turns pointing and asking questions as they observed swans, geese, and shorebirds like the dunlin, great knot and whimbrels. With patience and pride, Sam recounted how many of the species of birds they saw had travelled along Asia's north-south migratory route from as far away as Alaska and New Zealand. Chongming, he told them, had become a destination for staging and wintering.

Between the sights and sounds, and the beautiful weather, the time passed quickly, and Molly could barely believe three hours had passed. As they walked back to the Jeep, Patrick said he'd taken so many pictures that his fingers were as sore as his feet.

The drive back to the hotel was a silent trip as the trio quietly reflected on their day. In the two decades since her sister's death, Chongming Island had become a national model for environmentally sustainable development and even received international recognition for the design and improvement of conversation strategies.

Oh, how proud June would have been to know that she had played a role in the preservation of this land that she so loved, and how sorry Molly felt knowing her sister had been deprived of so much of what should have been a long and productive life.

Chapter 41

Back at the hotel the group said goodbye and went their separate ways. Sam to check in and Molly and Patrick to their room for a nap. The plan was to meet back at the dining room where they would have dinner together and then on to Sam's room to for drinks and 'the talk'.

While Molly showered and attempted to wash the sand and twigs from her hair, she found herself humming a Celtic tune, as she often did in the shower. *How strange to feel so normal*, she thought, *knowing in a few hours I am probably going to add new pieces to the puzzle I came here to solve.* Although Molly knew there was nothing she could do to change the past, she fervently hoped that whatever came out of tonight's conversation wouldn't damage her family's future.

Regardless of the outcome she was truly glad that she and Pat had got to spend the whole day with Sam before they got down to business. For Molly it was a great way to reconnect with her much loved brother-in-law and for Patrick, it was an opportunity to finally get to know him.

Towelling off and drying her hair Molly felt surprisingly calm. Maybe she was ready for the next step. She called out to Patrick to tell him she was finished in the shower but the only answer she received was the sound of even breathing coming from her sleeping husband. Molly took her place beside Patrick and was asleep in a matter of minutes.

The next thing she remembered was the sound of the bureau drawer banging shut and the smell of her squeaky clean man wafting through the room. "Wow, I must have fallen asleep," she said blearily.

"Judging from the noise coming from your side of the bed, I'd say you nodded off." Patrick cajoled, knowing Molly would argue vehemently that she did not snore.

"Well, I sure feel refreshed and hungry. How about you?"

Not missing a beat, he answered, "I could eat the leg off the Lamb of God."

"No surprise there," Molly shot back.

Sam was already seated when the O'Neil's arrived at the restaurant and he stood up to wave, so they could see him. "I took the liberty of ordering some wine. I hope you'll like it," he said after greeting them both with a hug.

"Hell yeah," they replied in unison as they noticed his selections.

They had no sooner taken their seats and toasted each other over the exquisite wine than a waiter appeared at Patrick's side carrying a tray overflowing with delicious-smelling appetisers. "World famous Shanghai dumplings," Sam announced. I also took the liberty of ordering your meals."

"I *love* this guy!" Patrick declared kissing Sam on the cheek and actually making him blush. Regaining his composure, Sam admitted that he kind of liked Patrick too…but there was no way in hell he was kissing him. The group laughed and joked throughout the appetisers, the main course, which consisted of pork and lamb *roujiamo* accompanied by spiced vegetables and hot flat bread. Two more bottles of wine topped off the feast.

Full and contented, Sam ordered a large pot of coffee to be sent to his room and invited Patrick and Molly to join him. "See you soon," he said as he left the table headed for the elevator.

Molly made a quick trip to the facilities while Patrick took care of the bill. Or at least that's what he had planned to do. When Molly joined him at the counter she could see that there was a problem. Patrick was trying to give his credit card to the waiter while the waiter frantically shook his head and repeated, "No sir. I can't take your money." Bewildered, Patrick asked to see the manager who explained that Mr. Friedman had already taken care of the bill as well as any other expenses they should incur while they were guests at this hotel.

When it became apparent that further discussion on the matter would be futile, Patrick lead Molly to the elevator making it known that he was going to insist on paying their own expenses. "Yeah, that's not going to happen," she told her husband. Molly understood how important their visit was to Sam because she knew how much it would have meant to June. She also knew that once Sam made his mind up, there was no changing it. "But be my guest and knock yourself out trying."

When they reached Sam's room, they found his door ajar. "Come in, sit down and let me pour you a coffee. And by the way Pat, don't even bring it up. I already waited way too long for this and you *are* my guests. So suck it up. Coffee?" Sam asked with a face as innocent as a child's.

With the feeling that he just had the rug pulled soundly out from under him, Patrick relented. He reached for his cup, said thank you and not another word.

With that matter settled, Molly, who was already drinking a cup of steaming hot coffee, decided it was time to take the bull by the horns. "OK, I can't think of any way to approach this part of the evening other than by being very direct. So, if there aren't any objections, I'll get the ball rolling.

When she saw both men nodding, and looking happy that she had volunteered, Molly began with a recap of the events that had taken place so far. She started by talking about how she came to find June's letter and the picture of a small child as she and Pat were cleaning out their basement. From the date on the letter, Molly knew that the note had been written prior to Sam and June's wedding.

Although there was no date on the photo, Molly remarked that the child looked to be about two or three years old. She held off on mentioning that both she and Patrick thought there was something familiar about the child's face, choosing to wait and see what, if anything, Sam had to add to the story.

When she stopped talking, Patrick picked up where Molly had left off. "Once Mol decided she wanted to pursue the search, I contacted a friend of mine, as ex-RCMP officer, who now works as a PI." He explained how Paul Blanchard was able to confirm that the photograph was taken and developed in the mid-seventies, but that he could determine little else. "He did, however put us in contact with a colleague in Dongtan, who turned out to be very helpful. Odd little dude, but helpful," Patrick concluded remembering the eccentric Mr. Tommy Chu.

Sam sipped his coffee, still not saying a word, so Molly went on with the story. "Then there was the visit to the orphanage. Sam, I couldn't believe it. We weren't even looking for clues at that point and we wound up in the orphanage where our mystery child was dropped off as an infant. We even met the woman who did her admission. And oh, by the way, her name is Mie Hui." With nothing else significant to add, Molly ended her story by telling Sam that they were currently waiting on a report from the administrator of the orphanage and from Mr. Chu.

Sam remained silent for a few more moments. It looked as though he struggling with how and where to start. Patrick could see the concern in Molly's eyes and he reached for her hand, hoping to provide some comfort while they waited for Sam to talk.

"OK then," Sam blurted out, startling his guests when he finally spoke. "The first thing I need for both of you to know is the only reason I never brought up this topic with you in the past is because I thought you already knew about it."

Sensing his profound discomfort, Patrick crossed the room and took the seat next to Sam. Looking him square in the eyes he said, "My God, Sam, none of this is your fault. We would never think that you would intentionally withhold information. And anyway, as I'm sure you can tell from the brief recap we just gave you, anything new you can add to help solve the puzzle would be helpful and very much appreciated."

When Molly confirmed that she felt the same way, Sam continued. "Mol, a long time ago, June told me that she did see

Mark with a young child. She had been in the city doing some shopping and she spotted a man who looked very much like Mark. June said she called out to him and even tried to catch up with him, but he wouldn't stop. She said she followed him for as long as she could, but it was obvious that he was avoiding her and eventually she lost track of him."

Sam stopped talking and tried to gauge his sister-in-law's reaction to what she had just heard. "When was that, Sam? When did June see him?" Molly's question sounded more like a plea and it tore at Sam's heart to think he had already hurt her.

"It was before you were married," he answered. "Honey, I didn't know you then, except for the pictures and stories that June loved to share. And if there was some kind of connection between Mark and the child, June never mentioned it. I do remember how angry she was about it and Mol, it was no secret that there was always tension between June and Mark."

"But how can that be?" Molly exclaimed. "Mark was working in the Sudan during that time. What in the hell was he doing in Dongtan and why would he run away from June?"

Sam understood Molly's angst and reminded her that according to June, throughout Mark's residency at McGill University and even during the time he worked with Doctors Without Borders in the Sudan, Mark's research often brought him to various locations in China.

"Of course. How could I have forgotten?" Molly mused, remembering how, even early in his career, Mark had already become well known and respected in the field of autoimmune diseases. She knew he'd been invited all over the world to lecture.

In fact, stored away in a trunk at home, Molly still had copies of many of Mark's articles on combining traditional Chinese approaches for treatment of autoimmune disease into modern practice. She had intended to save them for Ava, but for some reason she'd never got around to giving them to her.

"No wonder Ava is so confused and angry about all of this." Molly said, feeling and sounding like she was on the verge of tears.

"She never even had the opportunity to meet her biological father and what do I do? I don't even share the little bit of him that still exists. And to make matters worse, I'm traipsing halfway around the world looking for another child Mark may or may not have had a connection to. Pat, what I am even *doing* here?" The last comment was spoken in barely a whisper.

Sam quietly stepped away to give Patrick and Molly a moment of privacy. When he returned to the sitting room, he did so carrying a tray of vodka and black rum.

"If no one objects, I think this might be a good time to move from coffee to a more potent potable," he announced, setting the glasses and ice bucket on the side table.

Nobody objected.

For the next few hours the trio discussed what their next course of action might be. But in the end, other than sharing old memories and too much vodka and rum, it was clear that the only practical thing left to do was to wait.

Chapter 42

Patrick and Molly were happy to be able to spend more time in Dongtan. Although Sam had to go back to work, he had arranged a full schedule of events for his guests, for as long as they chose to stay. Sam was enjoying their visit so much and he hoped their stay would be an extended one.

Each morning Molly and Patrick were excited to see what new adventure Sam had planned for them. Sometimes they would browse through the busy markets where vendors in less than clean aprons displayed freshly slaughtered chickens, while others tempted the always willing couple to purchase fresh figs and warm chestnuts.

Patrick, who was never one to pass up a new gastronomic delight tried, and then immediately fell in love with *youtiao,* which turned out to be a fried breadstick that some genius had the foresight to wrap in large warm pancake-like crepe.

The first time he tasted one, Molly burst into fits of laughter as she watched her husband struggle to fit the entire breakfast pastry in his mouth. She took countless pictures to send home to the family and especially their friends Ryan and Marie who would never believe a food existed that was too big for Pat to eat.

"Don't be too quick to mock me, my love," Patrick quipped when he heard her laughing. "You have probably eaten your body weight in dumplings since we arrived." It was true. Molly couldn't seem to get enough of that particular delicacy. More than once, as they both struggled with the tightening waistband of their jeans, Molly couldn't help but comment on the unfairness of the Western metabolism. The local people seemed to be able to wolf down these delectable carbohydrate-filled treats as though they were drinking water and remain lithe and slim.

One evening after bemoaning the consequences of their new eating addiction, Patrick announced that they had to start getting more exercise. Sam quickly solved that dilemma by scheduling a walking tour for the following morning. He provided them with a map to guide them through a small village he knew they would enjoy seeing and then on to a bird sanctuary.

Everything about the day was terrific, even the weather and although it didn't stop them from eating every two hours, Pat felt like he had a great and much-needed workout.

Once again, the O'Neil's returned to their hotel happy and tired. With each passing day they found themselves more and more captivated by the wondrous sights, sounds and smells of this land.

Because they were a bit later getting home from their outing, Molly decided to forego her mid afternoon nap, which by now had become a favourite part of her routine. While Patrick caught a quick snooze, Molly opted for a luxurious bath. With the intoxicating aroma of the lavender bath salts provided by the hotel filling her nostrils, Molly closed her eyes and, once more, let her thoughts wander to June.

It seemed so simple to conjure up wonderful and happy memories of her sister while she was staying in Dongtan. Of course she thought about June when she was at home in Cape Breton, but this feeling somehow seemed more real, more personal, here. Molly decided she really didn't care what the reason was. She was content just to experience the feeling of being connected to June once again.

That evening they met up with Sam for dinner and filled him in on all they had seen and done. Patrick thanked Sam repeatedly for being such a wonderful host, but he could tell that Sam was just as happy to have them in Dongtan, as they were to be with him. It was obvious to Molly that Sam and Patrick were becoming good friends, which made her very happy. She enjoyed watching the two men tease and cajole each other like kids but she couldn't help but wish that she and June could have been part of the fun.

That night as they prepared for bed, Molly told Patrick that she was beginning to understand why June loved Dongtan as she did. Patrick agreed saying that after only one week he already felt like he was fitting into life on the streets and in the markets. Everywhere they went they were warmly welcomed into this strange but exciting new culture.

Early the next morning while eating breakfast in their room, Molly's phone rang. Seeing that the call was from China, she crossed her fingers, said a quick prayer and answered the call.

"Good morning, Mrs. O'Neil, this is Mr. Fong from *Xiao Hua* Orphanage. Am I calling at a good time?" Molly assured him this was an excellent time and she called out to Patrick to join her in the conversation.

"I don't have a lot of information yet," he began, sounding almost apologetic. "But with the help of Jai, Li and others here at *Xiao Hua* Orphanage, I am now able to add a few more pieces to your puzzle, as you referred to it. Is there a time that would be convenient for you and your husband to come to my office?"

"Yes, of course," Molly and Patrick answered at the same time. Molly explained that they were visiting with her brother-in-law in Dongtan but were able to come to Shanghai at any time. "Excellent!" Mr. Fong replied and scheduled an appointment for the following afternoon.

The first thing Molly did when she hung up was to place a call home to Ava. "Are you sure you want to do that right now?" Patrick asked, remembering the unfortunate circumstances surrounding their last telephone conversation with their daughter. "Absolutely," Molly replied. "I want to talk to Ava before I have any new information about Mei Hui. That way, I won't be tempted to say something that Ava is not ready to hear."

Completing the time calculation in her head and referring to Ava's work schedule, they realised this would be a good time to reach their daughter. Although feeling somewhat apprehensive, Molly dialled the number and within seconds was listening to the phone ringing in Ava's Nova Scotia home.

"Good morning parental units," Ava sang into the phone by way of greeting. Ever since she had watched *The Cone Heads* as a child, she thought the term was hysterical and suited her patents to a tee. Molly and Patrick smiled at the pleasant reminiscence and then breathed a collective sigh of relief as they heard the happy sound of their daughter's voice.

In fact, everything about the call was positive. This time Ava was completely engaged in the stories about her parents' adventures. When Molly and Patrick finished talking, Ava continued to inundate them with questions about Dongtan, its people, the climate and food. It was like she couldn't get enough information. Whatever the reason for the change in her demeanour, Patrick was relieved to hear Ava sounding so much more relaxed and, more importantly, less angry.

When the conversation finally moved from their travels to the family, Molly asked how Laurie was getting on with her pregnancy. Ava assured them she was doing great and went on to regale her parents with stories about Kelly Ann's newly found obsession with reproduction, specifically how the baby got into mommy's belly. Molly laughed until she cried imagining Cole's absolute horror at having to address such enquiries from his precious little girl.

When they signed off Patrick and Molly told Ava they loved and missed her and promised to FaceTime in a few days when the whole family was together. "That girl has kept my head spinning since the second I met her," Patrick declared lovingly as he made his way to the shower before they headed out to see Sam and tell him about the new development.

Chapter 43

The return trip to Shanghai turned out to be another new experience for Molly and Patrick. Against Sam's advice, Patrick rented a car. He insisted that he would not inconvenience Sam by making him drive them back and forth from Shanghai for their meeting with Mr. Fong. Both Molly and Sam knew that Patrick was itching to drive in these new and exciting streets and handle the traffic on his own.

Equipped with a GPS and a firm lecture from Sam about the crazy drivers in this country, the O'Neil's set out early the following morning. Before leaving, they solemnly swore to let Sam know the moment they arrived.

Patrick was as visibly excited as he pulled away from the hotel in his rented, decade-old Land Rover. Molly cringed when she thought what her friend Marie would think of this vehicle. Marie, who couldn't fathom why anyone would want to drive such a monstrosity when there were so many wonderful sports cars to choose from would probably just shake her head and laugh at Patrick.

Molly found herself thinking about Marie, her kids, in fact, all things Cape Breton more often over the last few days. Not because she wasn't enjoying her adventure. She loved everything they had seen and experienced since they arrived. She assumed her melancholy was more about the uncertainty of what she was going to find out as a result of her search and, more importantly, what impact the information was going to have on her life, particularly her family.

Her thoughts were soon interrupted, however, as their car made a sharp, unexpected jolting turn to the right hand side of the road. Molly grabbed for the arm rest and held her breath as she watched the string of oncoming traffic seemingly trying to pass each other on a road that was barely wide enough to accommodate two small cars.

"For the love of God!" Molly swore once Patrick had the Land Rover under control. "What the hell was that about? This is exactly what Sam warned us about and we haven't even been gone for more than fifteen minutes!"

"Sorry Mol. I didn't mean to scare you." Patrick answered, promising to reduce his speed and be more alert. Although Molly accepted his apology, Patrick couldn't hide the excitement he still felt about driving in China.

Damn fool is probably thinking about all the stories he is going to have to tell at Tim Horton's, when we get home, Molly thought snugging her seat belt a little tighter.

Thankfully, the rest of the drive was uneventful and by the time they reached the *Xiao Hua* Orphanage, even Patrick looked as though he was happy the trip was over.

It had been prearranged that the O'Neil's could use the limited staff parking, which saved them a lot of time. Neither Molly nor Patrick had ever experienced traffic like they did in Shanghai and they were certain that parking would be another challenge.

Once again Li greeted them at the door when they rang the bell. From the speed in which the door was opened, Molly thought Li must have been standing in the foyer waiting for them. She welcomed them politely and invited them to come into the small office they used during their first visit. Once they were seated, Li excused herself to retrieve the tea and sweets that had been prepared for the meeting.

Jai was already waiting in the office and Molly was so happy to see her again. The women greeted each other with a warm hug, while Patrick shook the hand that Jai offered. "Will Li be joining us in the meeting?" Molly inquired. When Jai assured her Li would be staying, Molly was relieved. After all Li was the one who met and named Mie Hui. She was also the only one who'd seen the child's mother.

Li returned and as they waited for Mr. Fong to join them Molly sipped her tea and thought how odd it was that not once during this entire process did she even give a moment's thought to the woman who gave birth to, and then deserted, the child that they were searching for. Stranger still was the fact that her then fiancé may have had an affair with this unknown woman and fathered a child. From the second she found June's letter and the picture, Molly's only interest was uncovering the identity of the child and whether or not there was a family connection between Mie Hui and Ava.

Only now, as she sat in this tiny office in a foreign country, did she consider the ramifications of the bigger picture. She knew it should have made her sad, or at the very least angry that her husband hadn't bothered to share this information with her. But instead, all she felt was disgust. *What kind of man was he?* Molly wondered. *And how could I have fallen in love with and married a person I apparently didn't even know?*

Her thoughts were interrupted by the arrival of Mr. Fong. "Please accept my apologies for keeping you waiting. I had a matter that I had to attend to. I see you already have tea. Is there anything else I can get for you?"

"No thank you," Patrick answered. It was obvious that Mr. Fong was quite busy. "My wife and I appreciate all that you are doing to help us, and we don't want to take any more of your time than necessary."

Mr. Fong nodded and began talking immediately. "As we suspected, because of the timing of this case, the file was closed and therefore not transferred to our computer system. However, Li volunteered to go through the archived files that were in cardboard cartons in the basement. And I am happy to report that as a result of her diligence, we now have some information to share with you." Li blushed as Mr. Fong's compliment was translated never once taking her eyes from Molly. It was clear to both women they had already formed a bond that only a mother could understand.

Mr. Fong continued by providing a brief summary of the information included in the file. He told them that a person saying she was the child's mother left the child there, as Li had described during their previous visit. He confirmed that they did not have any other information about the mother and for the short while the child had been in their care, the mother had made no further contact with her or the orphanage.

Molly interrupted asking how long Mei Hui had actually been with them. Mr. Fong once again referred to his notes and said she was at *Xiao Hua* Orphanage for less than six months.

"You will be pleased to know," he continued, "that the little girl was adopted by what is described in this file as an 'excellent family'. There is only one follow-up report, which states that the child had adjusted quickly to her new home. I must tell you, however, that the adoption was not conducted in the traditional fashion."

"May I ask what was different about the process?" Patrick asked, speaking for the first time. Clearing his throat and without looking at the papers he was holding, Mr. Fong explained that a couple from Hangzhou contacted the orphanage and asked to meet with the staff about the adoption of a specific child. He said the child they sought to meet fit the description of the child named Mei Hui. Mr. Fong told Molly and Patrick that the couple were very knowledgeable about the child's background and were even aware of the circumstances under which she came into care.

Both talking at the same time, Molly and Patrick began asking questions in rapid succession. "Do you know the name and whereabouts of the family that Mei Hui went to live with?" Molly inquired. Patrick's questions were more focused on who the administrator of the orphanage was at that time and if there was any way they could speak with him or her.

Mr. Fong stood and raised his hand in an effort to regain control over the meeting. "I am sorry to report that the former administrator died several years ago. The only current staff member who has any knowledge of this case is Li. You may direct questions to her very soon."

Turning away from Patrick, Mr. Fong faced Molly and with compassion in his voice and eyes he addressed her query. "Mrs. O'Neil, please try to understand that for obvious reasons, the identity of the adoptive parents is protected. I do have a telephone number and address. If you would like, I can attempt to reach them and provide them with information on how to contact you. But Mr. and Mrs. O'Neil, I must stress that it is entirely up to the adoptive parents as to whether or not they wish to do so."

"Yes please," Molly said without even looking to see if Patrick agreed. She gave Mr. Fong her cell phone number, the number of the hotel they would be staying at in Dongtan and also Sam's number. She felt certain Sam wouldn't mind.

"Very well, "Mr. Fong agreed. "I will attempt to contact them this week."

Thinking that Mr. Fong had finished sharing all of the information he had, Molly turned her attention to Li. Using Jai as their translator, the two women talked about Li's memories of Mei Hui.

Because Li was the person who gave Mei Hui her name Molly understood why she felt a special connection to the child. Although she was not able to provide any new information that would be useful in helping them solve the puzzle, it was nice to learn that the child was well loved while she'd been at the orphanage. Li also told Molly that she met the adoptive parents and they had agreed to keep the name Li had given her.

Molly thanked Li. She saw that Patrick was preparing to leave and she also began to gather up her notes. As they stood to shake hands with the others, Jai told Molly and Patrick that there was one additional entry in the file that they should be aware of.

Clutching each other's hand for support, the O'Neil's took their seats again. Jai told the anxious couple that prior to Mei Hui's adoption, a man came to the orphanage and provided documentation regarding a trust fund that had been established for the child's wellbeing and education through university, if in fact she chose to go. He indicated that the remaining funds would have been made available for Mei Hui to use as she wished, once she had turned twenty years old.

Picking up the conversation, Mr. Fong added that the trust fund had been given to the adoptive parents to manage. Speaking directly to Molly, he said, "I have that letter, if you wish to see it." Gingerly extending her hand, Molly accepted the yellowed sheet of paper from. For a moment, she kept the paper folded in her lap as she prepared herself to see her first husband's signature on the letter.

To Molly shock the name on the document was not her husband's but rather Dr. Kent Granton, Mark's friend and mentor!

Chapter 44

Instead of returning immediately to Dongtan as they had planned, Patrick proposed taking a hotel nearby for a few days. "It will give us some time to digest this new information in privacy," he suggested. "We can also try to get an appointment with Tommy Chu and see if he has any news."

Molly nodded in agreement, not saying a word and Patrick didn't push. He couldn't even imagine what was going through her mind after their visit to *Xiao Hua* Orphanage.

Consulting the GPS, Patrick searched for hotels in Pudong. He recognised many of the names from their earlier visit. Wasting no time, he selected one that he recalled seeing during their many walks along the Bund. While this hotel wasn't as lavish as the Fairmount Peace, He remembered how they had both commented on what a lovely building it was, the first time they saw it.

The GPS guided them directly to the front entrance of the hotel in a matter of minutes. Patrick left the car running and went inside to check on the availability of a room for the next three days. As soon as he entered the lobby a receptionist welcomed him telling him there was a lovely room overlooking the Bund and assured him they could have it for as long as they needed it.

Then, in true Shanghai service fashion, a valet followed Patrick to his car while a concierge and porter appeared at the door to collect their luggage and transport it to their room.

Molly was thrilled with Patrick's choice of hotel and by the time he escorted her to their room Molly was already looking and feeling better.

"Come and sit with me, my love," Patrick crooned, as he patted the cushion beside him on the love seat. Draping his arm around her shoulder he brought her closer to him and whispered loving endearments while he gently massaged her neck.

Molly sighed in utter contentment and let herself enjoy this beautiful moment between them. *How well he knows me*, Molly thought as she basked in the glorious feeling of his gentle touch, *never pushing, never demanding and never asking more of me than I'm able to give.*

When she was finally ready to speak, she turned her head slightly, so she could look into her husband's kind eyes. She murmured the words, "I love you, Pat." She was rewarded with a look that let her know he shared her feelings.

For the rest of the evening and into the night they rehashed the new information they had acquired during their visit to the orphanage. It was obvious that the puzzle was becoming more complex with each bit of information they received. But clearly the most perplexing piece now was how Kent Granton fitted into the picture.

Kent, the man who was Mark's closest friend, Kent, the kind person who'd contacted Molly to tell her that her husband had been killed… these things she could wrap her head around. But Kent, the benefactor to the child she had travelled halfway around the world to find, well that just didn't make any sense at all.

They continued talking until they reached the point where neither of them could complete a thought without yawning. Rubbing his eyes and shaking the cobwebs out of his groggy brain, Patrick finally suggested they try to get some sleep and start fresh in the morning. "Good plan," said Molly, leading the way.

As she drifted into blissful slumber in her husband's arms, Molly reminded herself again what a lucky woman she was. Mark was her past. Pat, Ava, Cole, Laurie, Kelly Ann and their soon-to-be-new grandchild were her life now. Instinctively she knew that with their love and support she would be able to deal with whatever this puzzle uncovered.

By the time Molly awoke, Patrick's day was already well underway. Up, showered and dressed, he busied himself arranging a breakfast tray. "Damn, you're good!" Molly called out, startling Patrick to the point where he nearly dropped the tray on his way to the bed.

"Jeez Mol, you scared the crap out of me! I thought you were still asleep. I was going to wake you with a kiss and then surprise you with breakfast in bed. Instead, you almost ended up with breakfast *on* bed."

Laughing at his dramatic little scene, Molly quickly propped up two fluffy pillows and sat up in the bed. "You know I realise that you are spoiling me... but honey, I'm lovin' it," Molly responded, with an Irish glint in her eyes.

No longer even pretending to be angry with her, Patrick poured two cups of coffee, placed the tray in the middle of the bed and climbed back into his own spot in the bed where he joined his wife for breakfast.

The two tasks on Molly's to-do list once she was fed and mobile were to make an appointment with Tommy Chu and to try to track down Kent. The former turned out to be quite simple. Mr. Chu was available to see them the following afternoon. The latter took a bit more work.

It had been a few years since Molly heard from Kent and she did not have his contact information with her. A quick check of the time told Molly that if was nine-thirty a.m. on Thursday it would be nine-thirty p.m. on Wednesday night in Cape Breton. Figuring it wouldn't be too late to call her friend, Molly quickly dialled Marie's number.

Ryan answered on the first ring. "Is everything OK?" he blurted out as soon as he recognised the international number on his call display. "Yes Ryan, we're fine. I just have a favour to ask."

By now, Marie had joined the conversation. "Hello, dear friend. I miss you so much!"

"I miss you too," Molly answered, and then told her friends what she needed. Marie immediately dispatched Ryan to run over to the O'Neil's' house and get Molly's address book.

Happy to utilise the time to have a quick catch up, Molly provided Marie with a very abridged version of the recent events that had transpired, promising to call her when they had more information. "My God, he's back already," Marie announced as Ryan arrived in the kitchen out of breath and clutching the book. Knowing that her friend was anxious to make the next call, Marie gave Molly the number, told her that she loved her and signed off.

Patrick refilled his wife's coffee cup as she dialled the next number. "It is two-thirty in Nuba; I hope he answers." Molly said this as much for her own benefit as for Patrick's. She stared at her husband for moral support while the phone rang four times, each ring seemingly longer than the previous. When she was certain that the phone was about to go to an answering service, Molly heard Kent's voice.

"Kent, it's Molly. Is this a good time to talk?"

"Oh sweetheart, there could never be a bad time to hear from you. Mol, where are you? I don't recognise the number."

Molly took a deep breath and answered, "Shanghai, China." The silence on the other end of the line told her everything she needed to know and much of what she already suspected.

"What do you know and what do you need?" Never being one to waste words, Kent came right to the point. Molly told him about June's letter and the attached picture. She also shared the information she learned from the orphanage, including the document that bore Kent's name.

"Mol, the child is Mark's." Molly blew out the breath that she had been holding and told Kent that she was going to put the call on speaker, so her husband could listen in. "Of course," Kent replied and continued with the story.

In the course of the next half hour Molly learned that the pregnancy was the result of a one-time affair Mark had with a nurse who worked in a clinic in Shanghai. It happened before he and Molly were married, and Mark was not even aware that he had fathered this child until nearly two years after her birth.

When Molly questioned Kent further, he did not hesitate to tell her everything he could. She knew Kent loved Mark like a son and how it must have pained him to have to tell her this story. "The woman's name is Ai Syun. Molly, I knew her as well. She started out as a great nurse and we often hired her when we held clinics in various parts of China. She was efficient and always professional. After she worked with us for about a year and a half, we noticed a change in her attitude and behaviour. We assumed it stemmed from difficulties she was having in her personal life, so we didn't pry. As time passed things became much worse. Molly, it turned out that Ai had been stealing narcotics from the clinic. She had been both selling and using the drugs she stole."

"I don't understand, Kent!" Molly sobbed, her voice filled with anguish. "Why would Mark have anything to do with a woman like that?" Sounding every bit as distraught as the woman on the other end of the line, Kent relayed the part of the story that he most wished he would never have to tell.

"It happened just before Mark's graduation from med school. The clinic hosted a party to congratulate him and thank him for all his hard work. Ai was there that night and although most of the staff already suspected she had a problem with drugs or alcohol, she was the only one on staff who didn't have a drink. In fact, for most of the night she acted as the hostess, making sure everyone's glass was full. When it was time to leave, Ai offered to drive both Mark and I home, and given our condition, we accepted."

When Molly didn't say anything, Kent continued. His heart ached as he told his best friend's wife that Ai dropped him off first and then took Mark to his apartment. Kent said that the following day when he collected Mark to take him to the airport, he confessed that Ai helped him into his apartment and that something had happened between them. "Mol, Mark was already quite drunk. He said Ai offered him a nightcap and he swore that was the last thing he remembered until he awoke the next morning. "Honey, he knew that what he did was wrong, and he was riddled with guilt and terrified that you would leave him if you found out."

Patrick, who had held his tongue up to this point, finally spoke. "Kent, Molly doesn't need anyone making excuses for Mark. What she needs right now is the truth."

"Of course she does. I apologise if you thought I was condoning Mark's actions. I most certainly was not." Quickly finishing the story, Kent told the anxious couple that Ai had been fired about one month later when she was caught red-handed stealing drugs from the dispensary. She'd obtained access to the drugs by using Mark's key. When questioned, Ai admitted that she stole the key the night she spent in Mark's apartment.

Still not understanding how any of this had a connection to Mei Hui, Molly asked Mark to tell her what he knew about the child. Sitting at his desk at the hospital in Nuba, Kent rubbed his temples as if the massaging motion could take away the pain in his head. He knew the worst part of the story was yet to be told and he also knew there was no way to protect Molly from the hurt it would cause.

Taking a drink of the cold, bitter coffee that had been sitting on his desk since the morning, Kent took one last deep breath and finished the saga. "Mark returned home and for the next year we worked in different locations. Because of our research projects, we stayed in close touch electronically or by phone. Mol, every time we talked, most of the conversation was about you. When you agreed to marry him, you made Mark the happiest man in the world."

"Apparently not," snapped Molly. "Otherwise he might have seen fit to tell me he had fathered and then deserted a child halfway around the world!"

"Oh Molly, I hate that on top of everything else, I am telling you this news over the phone. Would you like me to come to China or to Nova Scotia to talk to you in person"

Assuring Kent that geography was not going to change the situation, Molly said she just had a few more questions.

By the time the call ended Molly and Patrick had lots of information to take to their meeting with Tommy Chu the next day. She regretted the way she had fired the last questions at Kent, but at that point she was so numb she just wanted the conversation to be over. Now, in addition to knowing conclusively that Mark was Mie Hui's father, they also had the mother's name and the extent of Kent's involvement.

According to Kent, it was well publicised among the medical community that Mark would be returning to China to give a lecture.

"Molly, I expect it wouldn't be too difficult for Ai to track him down. She probably used her credentials to get into the lecture". Kent continued with the story recounting that Ai was waiting outside the conference room when the lecture ended.

Filthy and with eyes that registered no life, Ai lunged for Marks's arm as he passed her. In a rage she shouted obscenities at Mark until a security guard escorted her unceremoniously from the building. As they reached the door, Ai, in a final desperate attempt told Mark she had left his bastard daughter at an orphanage and demanded money from him.

As Kent relayed this part of the story Molly heard the anguish in his voice. He described Mark's shock at hearing about the baby. Mark managed to track down information from the orphanage where Ai had left her. Through DNA testing – that Kent admitted to arranging – it was confirmed that Mark was indeed the child's father. He immediately assumed responsibility for child support. Working through the Sacred Heart Hospital, he arranged for a private adoption and set up a trust fund for her care and education.

Once the adoption was complete, Mark returned one last time to China, this time to meet the child and to thank her adoptive parents. Molly didn't have to do the math to know that the timing of this visit coincided with the timing of her pregnancy. She still didn't know – or even care – how June came to have the picture she had attached to her letter... but at least now Molly understood why June had wanted her little sister to have this information.

Chapter 45

Patrick called Sam to let him know they would probably be staying at their hotel in Shanghai longer than they'd expected. Sam wished them both good luck with their meetings and said he looked forward to getting together with them whenever they were ready for a visit. "Thanks buddy," Patrick told his brother-in-law. "We'll look forward to sharing a drink and meal with you soon. You know Sam, being with you this past week was the best thing that could have happened to Molly."

"Right back at you," Sam replied.

Returning to their bedroom Patrick was surprised to find Molly showered, dressed and ready for their meeting with Tommy Chu. He sensed her anxiety and not wanting to make her wait any longer, suggested they leave right away and take the ferry across the Huangpu River. Even if they were a bit early, Patrick was sure he could keep Molly distracted by strolling through Pudong Park until it was time to meet with Mr. Chu.

Apparently, that was the right decision, because Molly got so caught up in sightseeing at the Oriental Pearl TV Tower they had to rush back so as not to be late.

As with their last visit, the same model-like receptionist welcomed them. This time there was no waiting, as Elvira immediately ushered the couple into Mr. Chu's opulent office. Tommy stood and extended his hand. He greeted the O'Neil's, inviting them to take a seat at the strange boardroom table.

Maybe it was because of the nature of the business they were about to discuss, but whatever the reason, today despite his diminutive stature and flaming red pompadour, Tommy Chu came across as the consummate professional.

He listened to the information the O'Neil's had collected since their last conversation, making copious notations and asking lots of follow-up questions. He was especially interested in finding out if Dr. Kent Granton would be willing to sign a release form allowing his firm to access to the trust fund information. Molly said she was sure he would and promised to contact him that evening.

Next Mr. Chu brought the couple up to date on his progress, informing them that the investigation was continuing to focus on locating Mei Hui and perhaps her birth mother. "Then again," Mr. Chu said shaking his head in disgust, "Given what you just told me about the woman, I am not certain the whereabouts of Ai Syun would be of any real use to us."

Patrick and Molly readily agreed that they wanted nothing to do with Mei Hui's biological mother. Tommy Chu told them he was pleased the orphanage had agreed to contact the child's adoptive parents. "This is not information I could have easily obtained. Please be certain to let me know if you hear from the parents. It would be useful to have a release of information from them as well." Patrick assured him they would forward any new information and asked him to do the same.

The meeting turned out to be brief, lasting no more than half an hour. Molly left feeling that she had provided more information than she had received. *Oh well, she thought, I guess it's all part of the process.*

Back in the elevator Patrick asked Molly if she would like to spend the rest of the day in Pudong and maybe even have dinner at one of the many fabulous restaurants on this side of the Bund. "I would love to," Molly answered, brightening up a bit. "I know there is nothing else we can do at this point but wait… so we might as well enjoy the city while we can."

"That's my girl," Patrick said, leaning forward to kiss her.

The waiting continued for another three days without them hearing back from anyone. On the third night Molly decided to call home. It was Cole's birthday and she was pretty sure the family would be together.

Patrick sent Cole a text message to ask what a good time would be for a FaceTime chat. Their answer came seconds later when their own computer chimed, signalling that Cole was trying to reach them.

Not unlike Pavlov's dog, at the sound of the first ring Patrick sprang into action. Again, frantically pushing random buttons and yelling 'hello' at the blank screen, Patrick tried to make the connection (or as he referred to it, 'answer the computer'). Molly let the mayhem continue for a moment longer before reaching over and pressing the 'accept' icon.

"I hate this damn thing," Patrick grumbled but his mood changed instantly when the faces of their family appeared on the screen, blowing air kisses.

With everyone talking and waving at once, it was Kelly Ann who stepped up to restore order. Raising her chubby little arms in victory she threw back her head and announced: "It's my birthday!" This sent the whole family into gales of laughter. When Molly and Patrick broke into singing Happy Birthday to their son, Kelly Ann was delighted to join in, as long as everyone sang 'Happy Birthday to Daddy *and Kelly Ann*'.

With the online celebrations complete, Molly was excited to hear all the news from home, beginning of course with Laurie's pregnancy. "Mom, I'm doing great. I think this one is going to be a football player though. I swear I'm nearly as big right now as I was when I was six months pregnant with Kelly Ann."

Cole smiled at his wife as she protectively patted her belly. "Not true!" he interjected, saying that his wife looked beautiful and, according to her doctor, she was the picture of health.

They talked about the weather home and in China, Cole's work and Ava's pending trip to Tanzania. Cole told his parents he was much busier than he wanted to be and that he hated spending time away from his family. He said he was working hard now to get everything in place, so he could be close to home for the last month of Laurie's pregnancy.

When it was her turn, Ava told her parents that her work placement was not confirmed. "Don't worry," she told them. "I'll let you know as soon as I know myself. But enough about me; tell me how you are making out. Do you still love China? Are you getting any closer to solving the puzzle?"

As Ava continued to fire questions, Cole, Laurie and Kelly Ann said their good byes. "We'll talk soon." Cole promised. "Right now this little one needs a nap."

Molly assumed Cole and Laurie were giving Ava some privacy to talk with her parents and she was delighted to have some time alone with her daughter. As with their last conversation, Ava was totally animated and very interested in everything that her parents were doing. Feeling like they had at last turned a corner, Molly decided to take a risk and share a bit more about what had transpired in the last few days. She began by telling Ava about Mark's academic papers.

"Honey, I know you've read a number of articles your father published but what you don't know is that I have the originals of all of Mark's work." Molly paused waiting for a reaction, when none came, she continued. "I'm not even sure why I didn't give them to you earlier but if you want them, they are in a chest in the closet in your old room at home."

"That's awesome Mom, I'd love to have them." Ava answered enthusiastically. "I was planning to visit Marie and Ryan in the next few weeks anyway, so maybe I'll stay at the house and pick up the papers while I'm there. Do you mind if I take them back to Halifax with me?" Relived that they were able to have this conversation without drama, Molly told her daughter that the papers were always meant for her and of course she should take them.

Molly also told her daughter about her conversation with Kent and although she listened, she didn't react other than to say how very difficult it must have been to hear those words. Before they signed off, Ava told her mother she was glad they had this talk. "Mom, I acted like a total ass about your trip. I know it's important that you find some answers about the 'mystery kid'. I've been thinking about this a lot in the past few weeks and I'm really sorry I behaved like a selfish, spoiled brat. You and Dad are my parents. Mark was my biological father, but he was never really part of my life."

As Molly listened, she held tightly to her husband's hand. Their daughter just used the exact words that she said to Patrick only a few days earlier. They truly were a family, and nothing was going to change that. "I love you, baby girl," Patrick and Molly said as they prepared to sign off.

"You too," Ava responded, "but I think it might be time to drop the 'baby girl' thing."

"Never!" her parents said together before the computer screen faded to black.

Molly and Patrick enjoyed every minute of being a tourist in China for the next few days. Even though she was anxious to hear some news about Mei Hui, it didn't prevent her from appreciating the beauty and excitement of the Bund.

Molly admitted she felt lighter than she had in months and Patrick couldn't be happier. He enjoyed these wonderful days and exotic nights with his wife.

Exactly one week after their meeting with Tommy Chu, the telephone rang at nine o'clock. Still asleep, Patrick fumbled for the phone and said hello.

"Good morning. My name is Brenda Luo. May I please speak with Mrs. Molly O'Neil?"

"Yes, of course. One moment please." Patrick covered the speaker with his hand as he woke his wife and mouthed the words, "I think this is the call we've been waiting for."

Sitting up in the bed and trying not to sound as sleepy as she felt, Molly cleared her throat, took the handset from Patrick and spoke to the woman. "Good morning. Yes, this is Molly O'Neil. How may I help you?"

"As I mentioned to your husband, my name is Brenda Luo. Twenty-three years ago my husband and I adopted a child. Mr. Fong, the administrator of *Xiao Hua* orphanage, contacted me recently. He told me of your visit and inquiry and he gave me your contact information. So I guess the real question is 'how may *I* help *you*'?

Wide awake now, Molly explained why she was trying to track down information about Mei Hui. Although Brenda expressed empathy for her situation, she remained guarded throughout the conversation, careful not to divulge too much to the stranger with whom she was speaking. However, when Molly told her she also had a daughter from Mark Connor and that she'd been pregnant with her own child when Mark was killed, the conversation took a noticeable change.

Brenda surprised Molly by suggesting, "Perhaps we should meet for a cup of tea and talk a little more."

"Yes, I would love that. Thank you so much!" Molly could barely contain her excitement. "Where and when would you like to meet?"

They decided that the two couples would meet at Molly and Patrick's hotel. Brenda was familiar with the area and said she remembered a lovely coffee shop in the lobby area. The date was scheduled for Saturday, giving Molly two full days to prepare what she would ask of Brenda Luo and her husband.

She had no sooner hung up than the phone rang again. "Figures," Patrick said reaching for the handset Molly had just replaced. Taking this call himself, Patrick was not at all surprised to hear Tommy Chu's voice.

"Mr. O'Neil, is it possible for you and your wife to come to my office today? I have some information that I would like to share with you." When Patrick asked if this was something they could discuss over the phone, Mr. Chu insisted that it would be better if they spoke in person.

Molly and Patrick showered and dressed in record time. They had a quick coffee and muffin in the lobby café, where each shared what they had learned during their respective conversations. "What do you think Mr. Chu is going to tell us?" Molly asked her husband, not really expecting an answer.

"Not a Clue," Patrick replied, but I must say he sounded adamant that we meet in person and as soon as possible.

"All right then. There is no point in putting this off. Let's do it" Molly was already collecting her purse and sweater and heading for the door.

The trip across the Huangpu River to Tommy Chu's office was beginning to feel very familiar. However, the moment they saw Mr. Chu, they both realised this particular meeting was going to be anything but ordinary. The look in the man's eyes as they took their seats at the boardroom table, was the look of a person about to deliver very bad news.

This time there was no offer of refreshments or small talk. Mr. Chu got right to the reason for the meeting. "Mr. and Mrs. O'Neil let me begin by telling you that the information I am about to share is not about the child you are searching for. However, what I have found out is directly related to the case. I believe it is important that you have this information as you move forward."

Not knowing what Mr. Chu was about to tell them Patrick and Molly waited for him to proceed. "As part of my investigation I followed up on many leads, including the various locations your late husband lectured from the time when the child was born until the time of his death." He addressed this comment to Molly and apologised for bringing up what he was sure were painful memories for her.

Molly nodded her thanks and asked him to continue. "Mrs. O'Neil, you told me Mark Connor was killed by a young anti-government insurgent." Molly nodded again, looking and feeling more uncomfortable by the moment. "Because of the circumstances and timing of Dr. Connor's death, I decided to delve into the accused man's background. In doing so I discovered that he and several members of his family belonged to a well-known drug cartel."

Still confused, Patrick asked Mr. Chu to explain the connection between Mark's murderer and these terrible people.

"Yes, of course," he said moving directly to the point. "According to the police, Ai Syun, the child's biological mother, owed the cartel a great deal of money. The police believe Ms. Syun was trafficking drugs and then using the proceeds to feed her own habit." Mr. Chu further explained that the authorities had been following the family for some time and while they were not particularly interested in Ai Syun per say, they did keep close tabs on her in hopes of having her lead them closer the head of the cartel.

"For a period of time Ms. Syun was held hostage and made to do unspeakable things to pay off her debt. In order to escape, she was able to convince her captors that a rich doctor from Canada had fathered her child. She told them she had recent contact with Dr. Connor and that she threatened to tell his wife about the baby unless he agreed to pay off her debt to the cartel.

Ms. Syun was eventually released under the condition that she would collect the money from your late husband and give it to her captors. The man who murdered Dr. Connor had been sent to follow Ai Syun to ensure the money was returned. When it became evident that Ai Syun had evaded his custody, the young man was afraid to admit that he failed in his task. According to the report I received it would appear that he took it upon himself to find Dr. Connor. Mr. Chu took a sip of water from the cup on his desk. He looked directly at Molly as he finished delivering his findings. "Mrs. O'Neil. I am sorry to report that your husband was murdered by a man he never knew, for an offense he did not commit."

Patrick helped his wife from the chair. He shook Mr. Chu's hand and thanked him for the work he had done. "We will be meeting with Mei Hui's adoptive parents tomorrow and we will no longer be needing your services, but we thank you very much for all you have shared with us." Molly did not speak as they left Mr. Chu's office for the final time.

Both were silent during the return trip. Once at their hotel Molly told Patrick she loved him more than life itself before asking him to allow her some time on her own. Without a question he kissed his wife tenderly and left the room.

Tears that were never shed at Mark's funeral now poured from her eyes like a waterfall. Molly cried for a brilliant life taken needlessly and far too soon. She cried for the two daughters who never met their father and for the troubled life Mark must have endured as he tried to hide his secret from his wife and family.

Browsing through the family pictures she brought to help in her search for the truth about Mei Hui, Molly stopped at a photo of Mark taken at his graduation from medical school. Holding it with both hands, she spoke directly to his young, handsome face. "I wish you had trusted me enough to let me help you. I really did love you. Rest in Peace, dear Mark."

And with that admission, Molly replaced the picture, dried her tears and waited for her husband to return.

Chapter 46

Patrick was pretty sure that waiting to meet with Mei Hui's parents the following day would seem like an eternity for Molly. While he was out giving Molly the alone time she asked for, he decided to check out some of the local restaurants they hadn't yet tried. One of the many great things about The Bund is that you were literally in the midst of gastronomic heaven. Patrick used his eyes and nose to guide him and within minutes he found an upscale bistro that boasted fine dining and excellent entertainment. He booked a table for eight o'clock that evening.

Like Molly, Patrick was also grateful to have this time to himself. Strolling along the waterfront proved to be the perfect setting as he tried to process all that was happening to his family. From the time they began planning for the trip to China, Patrick had vowed to do whatever he could to support his wife while she searched for answers. He knew that his love for Molly was unconditional. But try as he might not to dwell on it, somewhere, just under the surface he felt the constant presence of a third person in their marriage. Now with confirmation that Mei Hui *was* Mark's daughter Patrick couldn't help but wonder if there would ever be a time in his marriage when Mark Connor wouldn't be present in some way or another.

When he felt himself getting tired from walking, Patrick found a bench across from the same playground where Molly sang to the children from *Xiao Hua* orphanage. Watching the families in the park brought back memories of Cole and Ava when they were young children. He remembered when Cole had asked Santa to make Molly his real mother and how willingly she had stepped into that role.

"Damn!" he said, chiding himself aloud for doubting Molly's love for him and their family. "Of course we're going to get through this… just like we did everything else." Two little boys from the playground pointed at him and giggled as they watched the silly man talking to himself.

Molly seemed much better by the time Patrick returned to the hotel and he was delighted when she said she would love to go on a dinner date with him. He was concerned that she might feel too upset to go out for the evening. Instead, Molly embraced the idea. She even made an appointment for a facial, manicure and hairdo.

As she sat in the magnificent Sap and Salon being pampered in every imaginable way, she gave herself a good talking to. Patrick had been an absolute saint through all of this. He was kind, patient and understanding. Never once complaining about the humps and bumps they already experienced on this journey and never asking more from her than she was able to give. *Well, that ends today*! she told herself. *Tonight my husband will be having a date with the girl he married.* And with that as her motivation, Molly sat back and let the experts do their work.

For two-and-a-half hours, Molly was massaged, scrubbed, buffed and polished. She moaned with delight as the tiny Chinese masseur kneaded out all of the kinks and aches in her back and neck. *How the hell can someone that small exert such a wonderful, powerful force with those tiny little hands*, she pondered?

All too soon her massage came to an end and it was time for her to move to the next station. Wrapped in a fluffy white robe and slippers, Molly was escorted to the hair salon, which smelled of orchids and lavender. The hairdresser unwrapped the towel that had been placed on Molly's head before her massage and then shrieked with glee. As she ran fingers though Molly's long, thick russet hair, she beckoned to the other stylists to join her. Molly felt like a model as half a dozen women in white smocks oohed and aahed at the colour and texture of her hair.

When Molly gave her permission to do whatever she wanted to with her hair, she thought the young stylist would cry with delight.

As if by magic, a glass of chilled campaign appeared, and Molly shut her eyes, sipped the delicious bubbly liquid as she let the stylist do her thing.

"Miss Molly, miss Molly!" Molly heard the sound but assumed she was dreaming. Only when she felt the light tug on the apron that covered her did she realise that she had dozed off while getting her hair done.

Slowly opening one eye and then the other, Molly stared into the mirror that reflected an image she barely recognised as her own. "Oh my!" Molly whispered, bringing her hands to her face. "You are amazing!" Standing to face her stylist, Molly threw her arms around her in a bear hug and kissed her cheek. The other girls in the salon laughed at their colleague's obvious embarrassment. Paying her bill and leaving a large, well-deserved tip, Molly strolled back to her hotel feeling and looking like a new woman.

"Holy shit!" was Patrick's response as his wife walked in the door. "Wanna stay home tonight and order room service?"

"Not a chance, Molly announced spinning around to give her husband the full effect of her transformation. "I may never be able to pull this look off again and I sure as hell don't want to waste it."

Molly took extra care with her make-up and selecting her outfit for the evening. When she emerged from their bedroom, Patrick's breath caught. "You look stunning darling," his eyes confirming everything he was thinking and feeling. "How did I get so lucky?" he asked as he walked toward his wife.

The jade green vintage cheongsam dress she wore covered one shoulder leaving the other exposed and exotic looking. Not one to wear much in the way of make-up, Molly applied a light coat of eyeliner and mascara, just enough to accentuate her green eyes. A tinted lip-gloss was the only other cosmetic she used. With one last look in the mirror, Molly slipped on her black stiletto sandals and joined her handsome husband who was patiently waiting for her.

From the moment they entered the elevator in the hotel, until they returned to their room at midnight, Molly felt like a princess from a fairy tale. The restaurant Patrick chose lived up to its five-star reputation and the entertainment was spectacular.

Patrick held her close as they danced to one of their favourite songs and he whispered into her ear, "Everyone is looking our way and wondering who this beautiful woman in my arms could be."

Molly smiled and blushed at the compliment. "I love you Pat and this has been a wonderful evening… but let's go back to our room." Not needing any further encouragement, Patrick accompanied his wife to the hotel where they made love until they fell asleep in each other's arms.

Shocked at how late they'd slept but enjoying how good she felt, Molly thanked Patrick again for the wonderful evening he'd planned and told him she was ready to face whatever the day brought. Silently, she prayed that she would feel the same way at the end of the day.

The café was quite busy when the O'Neil's arrived, and Molly wished she had thought to describe herself to Brenda. As they stood in the doorway scanning the room, Patrick smiled and led his wife toward a table by the window. "How do you know this is them?" Molly asked while trying to slow down her husband who was now walking even faster.

"Lucky guess," he replied, "or perhaps it was because there is a balloon on the table with a Canadian flag attached."

Before Molly had a chance to comment, the couple rose to greet them. "Good morning," the man called cheerfully. "We are William and Brenda Luo. I assume you are the O'Neil's?"

"Yes" they answered together, reaching out to shake hands with the Luo's.

By the time they finished their first cup of coffee, Molly and Patrick learned that Brenda was a fellow Canadian, born and raised in Ontario. Twenty-six years ago, as a young public health nurse, she'd moved to Shanghai as part of an exchange program. Near the end of her placement she met and immediately fell in love with William Luo. The look in her eyes told Molly the couple still felt as strongly about each other.

Picking up the conversation, William told the O'Neil's, "I was practicing law in my father's firm, as was expected. Brenda and I met in court where she was the advocate for a young woman who had been brutally raped. My father's firm was representing the accused and it made me sick to think I was bound by law to defend this monster. Our firm lost the case and the man was sentenced to jail for a very long time. For months afterward, all I could think of was the beautiful woman who stood beside the terrified young victim throughout the ordeal of the trial. I thought how strong and brave she was." William stopped and winked in Patrick's direction. "But mostly I thought how much I wanted to see her again."

"What a wonderful story." Molly's eyes were brimming with tears as she listened.

"Thank you," Brenda replied. "You were so gracious to tell us your own story. I am pleased we could share ours."

Before Molly or Patrick could respond, William cleared his throat. "There is one more thing we would like to share with you." He beckoned toward the entrance of the café where a young woman stood looking in their direction. "May I introduce our lovely daughter, Mei Hui Luo?"

Mei Hui joined her parents, kissing them both on the cheek before turning around to greet Molly and Patrick. With a slight bow she addressed her parents' guests. "I am so pleased to meet you and thank you for coming to find me. Although I always believed that someday you would."

Unable to speak for the lump in her throat, Molly reached for Mei Hui's small hand and held it in her own. Patrick did the same as he greeted the girl for both of them.

Back at their table, Mei Hui took the seat next to Molly who was still desperately trying to speak over all the emotion she was feeling. Seeing that she was overcome, Brenda continued with the story.

"Mei Hui was almost two years old when we adopted her and smart enough to know her name. So many things had changed for the child in such a short time, we decided immediately that she should keep her name." William also told the O'Neil's that in English her name means beautiful wisdom and he assured Molly that their child more than lived up to her moniker.

Finally, Mei Hui spoke and to Molly it was like hearing her own child's first words. She spoke perfect English as well as her native Chinese dialect. "I have always known that I was Mother and Father's special, chosen child," she began. "Although they did not have a lot of information to share about my biological parents, they told me whatever they knew. I grew up wrapped in love and I could never imagine any other parents than those I have been blessed with." She smiled at her mother and father as she continued speaking.

"I know who my birth mother was, and I am aware of the troubled life she led. I also know that Dr. Mark Connor was my biological father and although I don't actually remember meeting him, I have been told that he spent one afternoon with me just prior to my adoption being finalised."

It was obvious to Molly that Mei Hui was a happy and well-grounded young woman who harboured no regrets about her early life. Rising from her own chair Molly crouched down beside Mei Hui and thanked her for being so open with them and asked. "Now, do you have any questions for us?"

"Only about a million!" Mei Hui replied, causing the two sets of parents to laugh at her candour.

"That's our girl," Brenda told the O'Neil's. "You never have to guess what's on her mind," she announced lovingly. "I assume you and our daughter will be seeing more of each other in order to answer her 'million' questions. But I wondered if there was anything else William and I could add?" Brenda directed this query to Patrick and Molly.

Without a pause Molly asked if either of them knew Mark or Kent Granton. Shaking her head, Brenda told the couple neither she nor her husband had ever met them. "However," she continued, we are all familiar with their work. Mei Hui was especially taken with

Dr. Connor's research. But that is a story I am sure she will tell you later."

Molly hesitated for a moment before she asked her next question. "Brenda, may I ask you how you came to adopt Mei Hui. I know that it was private adoption, which is why I wondered if there was some connection between your family and Mark?"

"I would be pleased to answer that question," William replied. "Brenda and I were not able to have children of our own, although we both very much wanted to start a family. I mentioned earlier that I was not happy working for my father. After the rape case that I told you about, my father and I had a terrible argument. He felt I was not committed to the firm and I told him that I was simply not committed to *his* firm. I think you can imagine how well that went over." Molly and Patrick could hear the sarcasm that was in his voice at the mention of his father's name.

"When this wonderful woman agreed to go out with me, I knew that I would not be returning to the Luo & Luo Law Firm. I took a job at what would be the equivalent of your Legal Aid division and dedicated my practice to helping women and children." With great pride he told the O'Neil's, "I now have fifteen lawyers working with me and I believe our work is making a difference."

As part of my *pro bono* work, I sat of the Board of Directors of the *Xiao Hua* orphanage. The director of the orphanage at the time was a colleague of mine. He was aware that Brenda and I were considering adoption and he told me about this very special little girl who had come to them under the most inauspicious circumstances. After hearing her story, we arranged to meet the child in private, at the administrator's office. Once we did… well as they say, the rest is history. There was absolutely no way were leaving there without our daughter."

This time Molly didn't even pretend to hide her tears and while Patrick put his arm around her to offer comfort. Molly was sure his eyes were as red and wet as her own.

"OK. I think we've all cried enough for one day," Brenda choked out as she and her daughter sniffled in each other's arms.

"Agreed!" the men said in unison. When everyone hugged their goodbyes, Molly, Brenda and Mei Hui all exchanged phone numbers and email addresses. "I will call you soon." Molly promised as she gave Mei Hui one last hug.

Chapter 47

This time Molly didn't give a second thought to the time difference or anything else for that matter. The minute they returned to their hotel, she had the phone in her hand. Her first call was a message she left on Sam's answering machine asking him to contact her when he got home from work. The next was to Ava.

"Mom? Is that you? Oh my God, are you all right?" Before she could respond to her daughter, Patrick motioned to Molly that it was four o'clock in the morning in Nova Scotia. "Yes, we're fine, I'm so sorry… I just realised the time. Do you want to go back to sleep and I'll call you later?

"I wasn't actually asleep," Ava yawned as she replied, "I'm home. I mean I'm at *your* home in Cape Breton. In fact, right at this moment I'm sitting on my old bed catching up on some reading." Molly didn't have to ask to know that Ava was going through Mark's academic papers and his other publications. "I guess I lost track of the time. So, what's up with you guys?"

"Hi sweetie. It's Dad," Patrick said as he picked up the extension in the other room. "Can you handle any more drama today?"

"Bring it on Dad. But this one must be a doozie if you are calling me at this time of the day!"

Talking in turns Patrick and Molly told Ava about their meeting with the Luo family. "Holy crap, you met the mystery kid? Is she really my half-sister? Does she know about me? What does she do?"

Molly interrupted her daughter while she could still remember all the questions in order. "Yes, she is your half-sister. She didn't know about you until today and in all the excitement and tension we didn't even get around to asking about her occupation. But I can tell you this," her mother continued, "we are going to be seeing her again. Mei Hui said she would like to ask us some questions and hopefully fill in some of the blank pieces in her own puzzle. Ava, are you OK with this? Please tell me how you are feeling."

"Wow Mom, I'm not sure if I can even begin to articulate how I'm feeling. I mean I'm really excited that you found her and talked with her. I think I'm even sort of pumped about having an older sister. It's just a lot of stuff to digest all at once!"

Patrick's heart was aching as he listened to the conversation. Hard as he tried, he could not come close to imagining what this must be like for Ava. "Sweetie, what about if we say good night for now and give you some time to think about all of this? We'll call you in a couple of days after you've had a chance to process the latest developments."

"Good plan, Dad. And anyway I think my marathon reading session is finally catching up with me. So I will sign off for now." Her parents said goodbye and told her to call if she had any questions in the meantime. "OK guys, I will," was her sleepy reply. "And don't worry about me flipping out. Again. I promise you I'm fine!"

"I hope she is," Molly told Patrick when the line went dead.

Sam didn't bother to return their call. Instead he showed up at their hotel early that evening, touting a large bag of Chinese food and two bottles of excellent wine. "I thought this sounded like a dinner and drink kind of event," he announced as he stepped into their suite. "And by the way, I booked a room here for tonight." He complimented Pat on his choice of lodging saying that he could get used to living like this pretty easily.

The meal was the best Chinese cuisine they had ever tasted, and the wine was exceptional. As Sam listened to the news, he commented that maybe two bottles of wine weren't going to suffice. Laughing at his newly found brother-in-law Patrick assured Sam that after everything that happened, including the talk with their daughter, two bottles of wine was probably more than enough for them to share.

"So, when are you planning to meet with the girl again?" Sam asked, causing Molly and Patrick to stare blankly at each other. "Not a clue," they answered.

Sam nodded his head. "I'm not surprised. I guess Ava isn't the only one who needs time to sort through all of this."

The trio finished their meal and had a nice visit before saying good night. They planned to get together for breakfast in the morning before Sam returned to Chongming Island. As he made ready to depart for his own room, Sam turned to Molly and Patrick. "Thank you so much for letting me part of this. I can't tell you how much I missed having you in my life."

Molly had no plans for the next day, nor did she want any. She picked up a book she was looking forward to reading; however, by the time she completed one chapter she was fast asleep. Covering his wife with a throw, Patrick took the opportunity to give Cole a call.

He wasn't surprised in the least to learn that Ava had already filled Cole in on all the recent news. "She really *is* OK with this," Cole told his father. From the background Laurie confirmed what Cole said and added that Ava was so excited she could barely get the words out fast enough.

"Thanks guys. I'll be sure to pass that message on to Mom. I know she has been worried."

Molly's even breathing told Patrick his wife was still asleep, so he took the opportunity to place a call to Ryan to say hello and to see how things were back home. He really missed his buddy and was looking forward to nice chat. The two friends talked amicably about the weather, the terrible condition of the roads in Cape Breton now that the frost had lifted and of course the upcoming Stanley Cup finals that neither of their teams was likely to be playing in.

"It's all because of that damn league expansion!" Ryan complained, referring to the fact that there were now thirty teams in the NHL. "If they had kept it at the original six the sport would be a hell of a lot better *and* my Leafs would be kicking the shit out of your Habs." Patrick had heard this tirade a hundred times before, but he smiled realising just how much he missed spending time with his friend.

Other than asking how their trip was going, in the most general of terms, Ryan did not grill Patrick on the particulars. He knew his friend well enough to know if Patrick wanted to talk, he would. It was only when Marie finally grabbed the phone from her husband's hand that the proverbial elephant stepped out of the corner.

"Hi Pat," Marie sang in the receiver. "If you two are finished talking, can I please speak with Molly? We had Ava over for dinner last night. She told us what was going on and I just want to make sure Molly is OK."

"I'm OK, said Molly from the phone in the hotel bedroom. I miss you Marie." Once it became clear that the two women were on the line together, Ryan tried to be heard over the din telling Patrick they might as well sign off.

"Travel safe and come home soon Pat. It's not the same in the neighbourhood without you." And with that the two men hung up allowing their wives to talk without interruption.

And talk they did. Marie listened as Molly described her meeting with the Luo family. "God Mol was it difficult to see the girl knowing…" her words trailed off. "If you mean did it bother me to know that Mark had fathered this child, honestly Marie, it really didn't. Do I hate that he never told me about it? You betcha! But I guess the one good think that came from all the time and effort we've spent trying to solve this puzzle is that I'm finally able to put aside the anger that I carried all these years."

Back in her kitchen in Cape Breton, Marie shook her head. Who else but Molly would find something positive in what was clearly a painful situation? "Mol, you are one of a kind," Marie told her friend. "So what happens next?"

Molly said that she was going to spend some more time with Mei Hui over the next few days. Although Marie was surprised to learn that the two women would be meeting again, this time she didn't express an opinion, choosing instead to act as her friend's sounding board. Happy for the opportunity to think out loud, Molly chattered on while Marie patiently listened. When she realised that she hadn't even given Marie a chance to get a word in edgewise, Molly apologised and thanked her for listening and for at least *trying* to understand.

"You know I'd do anything for you honey. Tell me how I can help? I'll get on a plane today if you need me." Marie offered.

"I know, my friend" Molly answered, drying a tear from her eye. "And I love you for it!"

Patrick came back into the room when he heard Molly say goodbye to Marie. Standing behind her chair, he put his arms around his wife and kissed the top of her head. "So kiddo, what's next?"

"Honey, you are the second person in the past two minutes to ask me that question. And I really don't have any idea, Pat. Any suggestions?"

Without saying another word, he handed Molly the phone. "Call her. Set up a time to meet and let's see what comes of it." Relieved, Molly took the paper from her purse and dialled the number before she had a chance to change her mind.

"*Ni Hao*, hello," her voice was as lyrical and sweet as Molly remembered from the previous afternoon.

"Hello Mei Hui. This is Molly O'Neil. How are you?"

Breathing an obvious sigh of relief, Mei Hui admitted to Molly that she had been staring at her phone number for the last hour trying to find the courage to initiate the call. The admission made both women laugh. Apparently, their mutual bond of nervousness served to make them both feel more comfortable. They decided to meet for lunch the next day and this time Mei Hui selected the restaurant. Molly scribbled down the address telling Mei Hui she was looking forward to seeing her again.

"Thank you, thank you, Pat! I am so glad you suggested I do that. I feel better already and I'm actually looking forward to our meeting." Patrick told Molly he was happy she made the call too. "Remember my love, I'm happy to come with you if you want me there."

Molly leaned over and kissed her husband on the cheek. "I know you would, baby, and I appreciate the offer, but I really think I would like to do this on my own."

Sleeping better that night than she expected to, Molly awoke refreshed and ready for whatever the day had in store. Admittedly, she did fuss a bit over what to wear. Not excessively so, she just wanted to look nice when she met with Mei Hui.

Back in her own apartment in Suzhou, Mei Hui was going through a similar preening ritual. Her bed was beginning to look like the dressing room after Macy's Thanksgiving Day sale. Finally, she decided on a chic pencil skirt and short jacket made of white linen with a soft-beige embroidered cherry blossom pattern. She knew the colour and style suited her and she liked the idea that it combined elements of both the Western and Asian culture.

As she picked out shoes and accessories, Mei Hui made a mental list of all the things she would ask Molly. When she spoke with her parents the night before, Mei Hui's mother offered to accompany her to the meeting but as with Molly, Mei Hui declined, opting to go on her own.

Molly arrived at least half an hour before the appointed time. She didn't want to be late but even more so, Molly was happy to spend a few minutes checking out Mei Hui's neighbourhood. At this point she was anxious to learn everything she could about Ava's newly found half-sister.

Making her way to the restaurant Molly frowned as she read the name, Tangwaiwai's Spicy Hot Pot Shop. *OK, she thought, this will be another new experience. I hope my stomach agrees.*

As Molly strolled around the area, she noticed her lunch guest walking toward her. The two women smiled as they spotted each other and as soon as they were close enough, they reached out and embraced. By the time they were seated in a delightfully decorated booth, they were already chatting like old friends.

When their waiter arrived, Molly quickly learned two important lessons. The first being that a Hot Pot meal consisted of a variety of raw meat, fish and veggies that you cooked yourself by swirling the food in a pot of boiling water and then dipping each piece in a series of mouth-watering sauces. The second thing Molly learned was that this could well be her new favourite food.

Mei Hui insisted on ordering for both of them, which turned out to be an excellent idea. Every morsel Molly popped into her mouth, she claimed was the most delicious. Mei Hui was happy that her guest was enjoying herself so much, and she told her so.

As they ate, Molly timidly asked the first question. "Mei Hui, it occurred to me that when we first met, I neglected to ask you if you worked."

"I do... or at least I will be starting very soon" Mei Hui replied. "I am in my final year of medical school and I graduate this June."

Surprise registered on Molly's face as she congratulated the beautiful, intelligent young woman seated across from her. "That is wonderful. In what field of medicine will you work?"

Now it was Mei Hui's turn to be tentative. Not looking directly at Molly, she began speaking. "Remember when I told you I knew Dr. Mark Connor was my biological father?" Mei Hui asked rhetorically, to which Molly nodded. "Well, I should also tell you that over the years, I searched for everything I could find about him during his brief life." Mei Hui now raised her eyes to see if what she said had she had offended Molly.

"Of course, you would." Molly said, taking Mei Hui's hand. The gesture was so tender and sincere Mei Hui feared she would begin to cry. "Honey, Mark was your birth father and he was a brilliant physician. It is natural that you would be curious about him." Seeing that Mei Hui was not yet able to talk, Molly continued. "My daughter, your half-sister, was born after Mark was killed. She never knew her father either. I am sorry to say that our marriage wasn't the strongest, but that never stopped me from telling Ava about her father and the wonderful work he accomplished. Mei Hui, Ava is a nurse practitioner and her research deals with the impact of social and cultural factors on infectious disease."

From across the table in a voice barely above a whisper, Mei Hui announced,

"Mine is, too."

"Excuse me!" Molly called out, raising her hand for attention as their server passed the table. "Do you think we could see your wine menu over here?"

Chapter 48

It was four hours before Molly returned to her hotel. Patrick kept himself busy by pacing the floor and staring at his watch. Jumping out of his seat when he heard the door open, he went to greet his smiling, albeit somewhat tipsy, wife.

"I'm fine and everything went well. I just need a little nap before I can talk about it." Molly air kissed Patrick as she passed him in the foyer, leaving a train of clothes between the door and their bedroom. More than a little surprised by her behaviour, Patrick peeked into the room moments later to find Molly sprawled on top of the bed, snoring to beat the band.

As it turned out, the little nap lasted for nearly three hours. Awakening in a dark room with a large headache, Molly slowly sat up and rubbed her eyes. "Anybody home?" she called out into the darkness.

"Yep," came the reply from the doorway. "How's the head?" Molly assured him it was nothing she couldn't handle and then begged Patrick for a cup of tea and some toast. "Coming right up, my little lush!" Patrick answered, laughing as he returned to the kitchen to prepare the cure.

Realising that she had already kept him waiting far too long, Molly threw some cold water on her face, slipped into comfy clothes and joined her husband in the dining room. As she ate the lunch Patrick prepared for her, she began her story.

Molly began by telling Patrick that in addition to sharing DNA, Ava and Meu Hui were both involved in exactly the same area of research. "I guess I shouldn't have been so shocked given that both girls were aware of their birth father's work. Still, it does add another element of intrigue to the story."

"It sure as hell does!" Patrick blurted. "What else did you find out?"

"Well, she knows a lot about her birth mother's unfortunate life and she actually went to visit her in hospital a few years ago." Seeing Patrick's surprised look, Molly continued. "Her mother died of complications from excessive drug use shortly after the visit. Mei Hui said she was quite certain Ai Syun didn't realise she was there, but she was still glad she went. If nothing else, Mei Hui said the visit provided some level of closure for her. She also told me she was aware of the trust fund that Mark had established for her. Apparently, her adoptive parents allowed Kent to contribute to the fund as Mark had requested, but they had no intention or need to use it for Mei Hui's upbringing. The fund has grown substantially, and Mei Hui is still not certain what, if anything, she will do with the money."

Molly stopped talking as she ate more of the snack Patrick prepared. With the nap and some food in her stomach, she was feeling much better. "Did Mei Hui have any questions for you?" Patrick asked as his wife reached for another piece of toast.

"She certainly did! Pat, it was so sweet and kind of sad. Almost all of her questions were about Ava. What she was like as a child. If she had a boyfriend... and of course, countless questions about her current research. I showed her all the pictures I brought with me and promised I would make copies. And before I left then she gave me something."

Patrick could tell by the change in Molly's voice that this next piece of information was going to be a big one. "Pat," Molly said, taking a tissue out of her pocket, "she gave me this." Slowly undoing the crude wrapping paper, Patrick found himself holding a gold locket. Without asking the obvious question, he fumbled his large fingers around the tiny clasp until it popped opening revealing a small picture of a much younger and very pregnant Molly. "Whoa... didn't expect that. How in the hell did she get this?"

Molly replied that the locket was given to Mei Hui on her thirteenth birthday. Her mother told her it had been sent to the bank

266

where her trust fund was set up. Not knowing who the woman in the picture was, Brenda Luo held onto it for many years and then decided to give it to her daughter the day she became a teenager.

"Mei Hui told me she used to pretend I was her real birth mother and that I had put her up for adoption for honourable reasons."

"Poor kid," Pat said holding Molly's hand as she gently cried. "What did you say to her?"

Wiping her tears away, Molly said, "I told her I believed this was probably Mark's way of letting her know she was not alone in the world. I was pregnant with Ava when that picture was taken. The picture also coincided with the time Mark delayed my trip to visit June and Sam in Dongtan. Pat, I believe that once Mark knew we were having a child, he tried to make things right for everyone. I think the reason he didn't want me to go to China was because he was trying to finalise Mei Hui's adoption. I am also willing to bet, that was when June thought she saw Mark and a small child in Shanghai.

"Wowzers!" Patrick exclaimed. "No wonder you got pounded this afternoon!"

When Molly finished sharing the details of her conversation with Mei Hui, she crossed the room and joined Patrick on the sofa. Sitting on his lap, she nestled into Patrick's warm neck. "Honey," she whispered, "I promise this is nearly over and soon our life will be our own again. But right now, I have to call Ava." Patrick, who hadn't yet had dinner made his way to the hotel restaurant knowing that Molly would most likely want to be alone when she spoke to their daughter.

"Oh, for the love of God, just do it," she admonished herself as she once again found herself staring at the telephone. Ava answered on the first ring by saying, "What took you so long, Mom? I've been waiting for your call."

"Well, I hope you still feel that way when I finish, honey," Molly cautioned her daughter as she retold the story of her afternoon with Mei Hui.

Ava listened without saying a word, which was something of a miracle according to Molly's experience with her daughter. When she finished, Ava immediately inquired as to how Molly was feeling. She thanked her mother for being honest with her and then closed by telling Molly she was coming to China.

"What? *When?*" This was totally not what Molly expected to hear.

"Be there in two weeks. Less if I can swing it. I love you Mom. Tell Dad I'll see him soon." And with that Ava disconnected the call and Molly stared at the phone one more time before gingerly replacing it on the charger.

Chapter 49

For the first time since they left Cape Breton, Molly and Patrick found themselves with absolutely nothing more to do other than wait for the arrival of their daughter. Patrick had been every bit as shocked as his wife when she'd told him Ava was coming to China. Not certain of exactly when she would be arriving, Molly and Patrick spent their time doing whatever they pleased, and both agreed it felt wonderful. After an evening with Sam, catching him on the events of the last few days, the couple enjoyed the luxury of seeing, eating and drinking in the sights, sounds and tastes of Shanghai.

Molly called Mei Hui and after sharing the news of Ava's pending trip, she made a second call to Brenda and William Luo. "I know our daughters are both adults." Molly said to Brenda. "But please let me know if you or William have any hesitation about Ava contacting Mei Hui."

"Hesitation!" Brenda exclaimed. "This is a blessing to our family. I can't even imagine Mei Hui's excitement when you told her that she was going to meet her half-sister."

There was no question that Mei Hui was overjoyed at the idea of meeting Ava and now Molly could rest comfortably knowing that her parents felt the same way. Two days later the O'Neil's received a dinner invitation from the Luo's and the evening turned out to be an absolute pleasure. As hostess gifts, Patrick brought a bottle of Cape Breton's finest Glen Breton Whisky for William while Molly gave Brenda and Mei Hui customised earrings from Sea & Sand Jewellery and Moore.

The only awkward moment of the evening was when Molly attempted to return the locket Mei Hui had given to her. "Thank you, Molly, but that piece of jewellery never really belonged to me. It was important for me to have it when I was younger. Now I have you and Patrick in my life and very soon, I will have Ava." Mei Hui blushed a little, hoping she didn't sound overly forward by pushing herself on the O'Neil family. Without hesitation, Molly put her arms around Mei Hui and assured her that, like it or not, she was officially connected to the O'Neil's for life!

Both clans laughed putting an end to any further awkwardness before William Luo announced. "Let's crack open that Glen Breton and see if it's worth making a trip to Cape Breton Island."

True to form, Ava tied up all the loose ends at home and within ten days of her call, Molly, Patrick and a very anxious Mei Hui stood waiting in Pudong International Airport. The airport was huge, and Molly was glad to have Mei Hui with them to help navigate the tangle of isles and corridors. In an effort to keep the ladies calm as they waited for Ava's flight to arrive, Patrick made as much small talk as he could manage. But truth be told, he had to admit that he was pretty nervous himself.

It seemed like an eternity after the plane touched down before the first passengers finally began to make their way into the arrivals lounge. Amidst the ensuing hustle and bustle, it was difficult to pick out anyone in the throng of people. Even with Patrick's height, he wasn't able to see over the crowd. And then, like the sound of booming thunder after lightning strikes, they heard, rather than saw their long-awaited guest of honour.

From the far corner of the baggage claim area came a voice that could only belong to one person. "OK parental units. Are you just going to leave me here juggling all this luggage by myself or is someone going to help me?" Molly broke away first and ran toward the sweet, loveable, albeit overbearing woman that was her daughter. From the opposite direction, Ava ran just as quickly into her mother's waiting arms, laughing and crying all at the same time. When she untangled herself from Molly, she turned toward Patrick. "God, I missed you, Dad!" she exclaimed, hugging her father with all her might.

"I missed you too, sweetheart. Welcome to China!" And given the number of pieces of luggage that surrounded his daughter, it looked like her stay was not going to be a short one.

"I'll explain the ton and a half of luggage later." Ava told her parents as she peered over her father's broad shoulders. Standing off to one side but closely observing everything that was going stood an attractive young woman. When their gazes met, Ava immediately sensed a feeling of familiarity. Giving her father one last kiss, she stepped away from her parents and walked purposefully toward the beautiful stranger with the exotic dark eyes.

Patrick and Molly held their breath, not sure what would happen next. Without preamble, Ava enveloped the startled woman in a giant bear hug, "Well, hello there, I'm Ava Connor O'Neil. I'm guessing you must be Mei Hui.

"Yes, I am," she answered breathlessly but with no intention of breaking the embrace, "and I am so excited and pleased to meet you."

"Awesome, because I'll be doing a work placement at Sacred Heart Hospital starting one week from today. And if you'll have me, I would like to rent a room in your apartment?" Mei Hui nodded rather than attempting to find words to express just how great she thought that idea was. "Good," Ava continued "Then let's get a move on, Sis. We've got a lot of catching up to do!"

From the side line, Molly snapped a picture of the girls as they walked away. Their arms linked, and their heads pressed together, just like perfectly interlocking pieces of a puzzle.

Epilogue

So many wonderful things happened in the year since Molly and Patrick returned from China.

Laurie gave birth to a beautiful baby boy and, as predicted, he was indeed a bruiser. Iain Cole O'Neil was born on October 12th. Weighing in at a whopping eleven pounds eleven ounces, baby Iain quickly became the crown prince of the O'Neil clan. Except for Kelly Ann, who was still feeling somewhat ambivalent about her baby brother, everyone else was thrilled with the new addition to their family.

During one of Patrick and Molly's frequent visits to see the children, Laurie expressed her concern about Kelly Ann's reaction to the baby. The admission caused Cole and his parents to burst into gales of laughter. "Don't worry, dear," Molly tried to sound serious as she attempted to mitigate her daughter-in-law's apprehension. "Compared to Ava and Cole, these two are like love birds."

Although Ava couldn't go home for the birth of her nephew, she and Mei Hui kept in close contact with the family through FaceTime. Watching the two of them goo and gawk over the baby warmed Molly's heart. The girls had become so close, Molly constantly had to remind herself that only one year ago neither even knew the other existed. I guess blood really is thicker than water, she thought.

In June, Mei Hui graduated from medical school and two months later, Ava completed her placement and was registered as a nurse practitioner. Brenda and William Luo planned a graduation party to recognise both achievements, only this time the O'Neil's were not able to be there for the big event.

Sam Friedman, however, was more than happy to attend on their behalf.

Knowing her family could not be there in person, Brenda suggested to Ava that she invite her uncle for dinner. Sam who was always happy for the opportunity to spend time with delightful niece and his new step-niece eagerly accepted the Luo's' kind invitation.

Of course, Molly and Patrick were not entirely left out of the festivities. From their kitchen table, they joined in the celebration via FaceTime. Molly even planned to have a meal at the same time as the Luo's were having theirs, although for the O'Neil's the meal was actually breakfast, given that it was only eight a.m. in Cape Breton. So, as the Luo's ate a traditional Chinese dinner and the O'Neil's their bacon and eggs, the computer was passed up and down the table, so each person could see and talk with each other.

For Molly, the experience was bittersweet. While it was such a blessing to see Ava looking so happy and content, she missed not being able to jump in the car and visit her daughter whenever she wanted to. Molly was thankful for the love that Brenda and William showered on Ava. It just didn't erase the reality that they were currently living half a world apart.

It was those memories and the constant calls and messages from both girls that sustained Molly until, after nearly a year, the time had come for her to return to China.

In the already cramped back seat of their rented van, Laurie juggled baby Iain on one shoulder while Cole attempted to keep Kelly Ann from climbing over the seat to join Nanna and Papa up front. Despite their best packing efforts, the cargo space was filled to the brim with luggage, plastic baby and toddler essentials and enough gifts to make a good Christmas for a small country.

From the driver's seat Patrick smiled broadly as he, once again, navigated the chaotic streets of Shanghai while Molly held on tight and tried to enjoy the ride.

As they sped along the busy highway, it was all Molly could do to contain her excitement. She was back in Shanghai, a city she had come to love. This time their son, daughter-in-law and two beautiful grandchildren accompanied her and Patrick. But it was the reason for the trip that made this day so special.

In less than one hour they would be at William and Brenda Luo's home where Ava, Mei Hui and Sam anxiously awaited their arrival. For dinner that evening Brenda was preparing the same meal she served at the girls' graduation party… only this time the whole family would be at one table.

The following day, the family would once again sit together, front row and centre at the ribbon-cutting ceremony of the LOC Centre for Infectious Disease Control at Sacred Heart Hospital.

From the moment Ava and Mei Hui moved in together, they knew they were destined to open this clinic. The two girls chose to study in the field of infectious disease, just as their biological father had. Further, they both managed to use his research as part of their own studies. The seed money for the project came from the fund that Mark Connor had established for Mei Hui as well as from the inheritance Ava received from the father she never knew. With the support of Sacred Heart Hospital and an anonymous sponsor, the Luo, O'Neil, Connor (LOC) Centre would officially open tomorrow with the entire family in attendance.

A combination of good navigation skills and extremely good luck had the O'Neil's pulling up in front of the Luo's' home within minutes of their anticipated arrival time. As if by design, the door of the van and the Luo's' front door opened at the same moment.

As the passengers, along with most of the luggage from the rear of the van, spilled out onto Brenda and Williams front lawn, the usually quiet neighbourhood was transformed into a noisy extravaganza.

Introductions were made, friendships renewed, and babies were hugged and kissed as they made their way from open arms to other open arms. Molly made a beeline for Ava whom she held until she thought she would break her in two. It was only as she loosened the grip on her daughter that she noticed the man standing well off to the side behind the unruly crowd.

Still holding Ava's hand, they walked together to where he stood… hand in his pockets and a look of uncertainty on his face. "Let me guess," Molly said as she used her free arm to hug the last guest. "Dr. Kent Granton, anonymous sponsor…am I right?"

"Oh Mol, as if I would ever be brave enough to say you were wrong about anything."

Kent put his arms around Molly and they held each other in silence. Words were not necessary to convey the private yet poignant message they shared.

"OK, old man, that's my wife you're making out with!" Always knowing exactly what to do at moments like this, Patrick smiled as Kent dropped his arms to his side. Reclaiming the hand that only moments before embraced Molly, Patrick gave it a hearty shake as he warmly welcomed yet another new member to their rapidly growing clan.

Dinner was unbelievably delicious, and the Luo's were perfect hosts. When the children were asleep in a cot and a crib that Brenda had been thoughtful enough to prepare, the rest of the family moved into the living room for cocktails. Touching both girls lightly on the arm, Molly, who remained in the kitchen, asked Ava and Mei Hui to stay back for a moment before they joined the rest of the guests.

The two young women sat together, wondering what Molly wanted to tell them. Without hesitation, she reached into her purse and removed two small boxes, which she handed to the girls. "I am so proud of both of you and this is something to commemorate your special day." Kissing Ava first and then Mei Hui, Molly finished by saying, "You know, your father would be very proud too."

Together they opened their beautifully wrapped gifts and then looked up at Molly. Each girl held half of the locket Mark had left for Mei Hui so many years ago. A clever jeweller in Cape Breton had carefully separated the gold heart and fashioned a new top for each piece. On one side was a picture of each girl as a baby. Before leaving China a year earlier, Molly had asked Brenda to send her an early photo of Mei Hui while Molly selected one of Ava at about the same age. On the other side of both lockets Molly had placed a tiny, interlocking piece of a jigsaw puzzle.

Touched beyond words, Mei Hui and Ava rose from their chair and hugged Molly. Before these two amazing young women returned to their guests, and to the rest of their lives, Molly watched as her girls wordlessly unhooked their own locket and secured it around the other's neck.

CPSIA information can be obtained
at www.ICGtesting.com
Printed in the USA
LVHW090449081221
705595LV00015B/164

9 781784 655921